The odyssey begins . . .

I HAD ARRANGED FOR MUSICIANS to play soothing music, but my father was clearly agitated.

"This is all very pleasant, Hermione," he said. "But I'm eager to be home again, next to my dear wife."

I sighed, my heart heavy with the news that I couldn't delay much longer. Father drained the last drops of wine from his goblet, and when I motioned for a servant to refill it, he shook his head. "Finish your meal, and let's be on our way."

My hands had begun to tremble, but at that moment a brilliant rainbow arched across the sky and a young woman with golden wings appeared, startling us both. "It's Iris, Hera's messenger," Father said to me.

"King Menelaus," Iris addressed him, "I bring you a message from Hera, wife of Zeus. Your wife, Helen of Sparta, has sailed away with Prince Paris of Troy, taking your son Pleisthenes and much of your treasure with her."

"Helen, gone?" My father reeled, looking as though he had been struck. "Where is she—?" He corrected himself. "Where are they now?"

"They intended to sail for Troy," Iris reported.

Beauty's Daughter

Other Books by Carolyn Meyer

Jubilee Journey

Loving Will Shakespeare

Marie, Dancing

Miss Patch's Learn-to-Sew Book

Rio Grande Stories

The True Adventures of Charley Darwin

Where the Broken Heart Still Beats

White Lilacs

Young Royals series

Mary, Bloody Mary

Beware, Princess Elizabeth

Doomed Queen Anne

Patience, Princess Catherine

Duchessina: A Novel of Catherine de' Medici

The Bad Queen: Rules and Instructions for Marie-Antoinette

The Wild Queen: The Days and Nights of Mary, Queen of Scots

Beauty's Daughter

THE STORY OF HERMIONE AND HELEN OF TROY

CAROLYN MEYER

Houghton Mifflin Harcourt
Boston   New York

www.hmhco.com

Text set in Dante MT.

The Library of Congress has cataloged the hardcover edition as follows:
Meyer, Carolyn.
Beauty's daughter : the story of Hermione and Helen of Troy / by Carolyn Meyer.
p. cm.
Summary: When renowned beauty Helen runs off to Troy with Prince Paris, her enraged husband, King Menelaus, starts the Trojan War, leaving their plain daughter, Hermione, alone to witness the deaths of heroes on both sides and longing to find her own love and place in the world. Includes historical notes.
Includes bibliographical references: page.
1. Hermione (Greek mythology)—Juvenile fiction. [1. Hermione (Greek mythology)—Fiction. 2. Interpersonal relations—Fiction. 3. Helen of Troy (Greek mythology)—Fiction. 4. Beauty, Personal—Fiction. 5. Kings, queens, rulers, etc.—Fiction. 6. Love—Fiction. 7. Trojan War—Fiction. 8. Mythology, Greek—Fiction.] I. Title.
PZ7.M5685Bdm 2013
[Fic]—dc23
2013003923

ISBN: 978-0-544-10862-2 hardcover
ISBN: 978-0-544-43915-3 paperback

Manufactured in the United States of America
DOC 10 9 8 7 6 5 4 3 2 1
4500525923

For Abigail Elena Mares

Ancient Greece

ILLYRICUM

MACEDONIA

Amphipolis

CHALCIDICE

EPIRUS

Mt. Olympus

Corcyra

•Dodona

THESSALY

Iolkos

Ambracia

Larissa

AETOLIA

Delphi

EUBOEA

Ithaca

Aulis

Thebes

PELOPONNESE

Athens

Mycenae

Argos

Tiryns

IONIAN SEA

Sparta

Pylos

0   50 miles
0   80 km

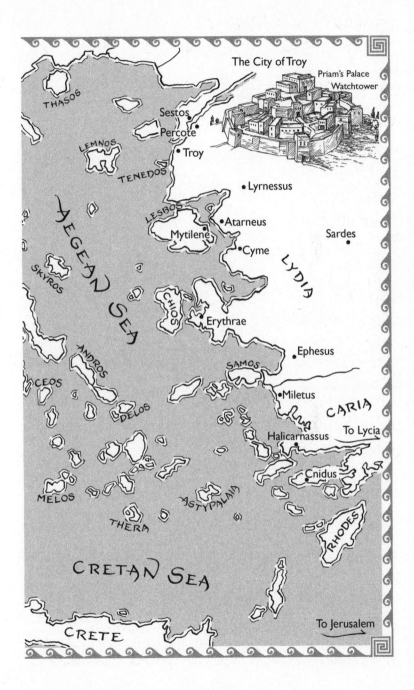

The City of Troy

Priam's Palace
Watchtower

THASOS

Sestos
Percote
• Troy

LEMNOS

TENEDOS

LESBOS

Mytilene

• Atarneus

• Cyme

• Lyrnessus

Sardes

LYDIA

AEGEAN SEA

SKYROS

CHIOS

Erythrae

• Ephesus

SAMOS

• Miletus

CARIA

To Lycia

ANDROS

CEOS

DELOS

Halicarnassus

• Cnidus

RHODES

MELOS

ASTYPALAIA

THERA

CRETAN SEA

To Jerusalem

CRETE

Prologue

I LOOK LIKE MY FATHER. Everyone agrees about that. "Hermione, you're the very likeness of King Menelaus!" they used to tell me when I was a child. "Red hair and all!"

This was not a compliment. I knew what they meant: *You don't look the least bit like your mother.*

My mother is the most beautiful woman in the world. Everyone is in agreement on that, too. Her name is Helen — Helen of Sparta at one time, but later Helen of Troy, after she went away with the Trojan prince and left me behind. There was some disagreement about whether she went willingly or if the prince abducted her. Knowing my mother, I would not be surprised if it was her idea — she and the prince sailing off while my father was away, and taking most of my father's treasure with them. It's something she would do.

My father went to war against Troy, vowing to get Helen back and his treasure as well. I'm not sure which was more important to him—his wife or his gold. Most likely it was his honor that was at stake, sending him and his brother—Agamemnon, king of Mycenae—and a vast array of armies from all around Greece to fight and to die, all because of my mother.

Helen's story has been told many times, by many men. But this story is *mine*.

Book I
Hermione

The Magnificent Helen

WHEN I WAS YOUNG, my mother used to tell me tales about her early life. Even her birth was unusual. Her mother—my grandmother, Leda—was married to Tyndareus, king of Sparta. One evening as Leda walked in the palace garden by the River Eurotas, a huge swan with gleaming white feathers stepped out of the water and approached her. When Leda leaned down to pet the gorgeous bird, she lost her balance and fell in love. I don't know precisely what happened in the garden that night—my mother was vague about it—but in due time Leda gave birth to an egg the color of blue hyacinths. Her seducer was actually the great god Zeus, ruler of all immortal gods and mortal beings, who had disguised himself as a swan. The egg hatched, and a beautiful baby girl emerged. Whether he suspected the truth of the situation or not, Tyndareus accepted the baby as his own daughter and named her Helen.

"I doubt that Leda told my father about the swan, but the

midwife surely mentioned the egg," my mother told me. Helen joined a family of twin brothers, Castor and Pollux, and a sister, Clytemnestra. "It was an uneventful childhood," she said. "Until I was kidnapped."

Even as a young girl, Helen was irresistibly beautiful. Men could not keep their eyes off her. Theseus was one of them. The son of Poseidon, god of the sea and of earthquakes, Theseus had made up his mind to marry a daughter of Zeus, and Helen was certainly the most desirable. He had a terrible reputation for abducting women—whatever Theseus wanted, Theseus took.

"I remember it all very well," said my mother. As she told me this, we were bathing in a large pool in the palace, heated with rocks from a fire, while our maids scrubbed us with sponges and rinsed us with warm water poured from silver pitchers. "I was about your age, barely eleven. My breasts had not yet budded. I knelt at a temple, making an offering to the goddess Artemis, when suddenly this brute galloped up on his horse, seized me, and carried me off." Helen smiled dreamily, looking almost pleased as she described the scene.

"Weren't you scared?" I asked. "I would have been."

"Oh, I was frightened of course, but Theseus kept telling me not to be afraid, that he wouldn't hurt me. He promised to take me to a place where I would be very safe and feel quite contented. 'My brothers will be furious,' I warned him. 'Castor and Pollux will come for you, and they will kill you!' This was not a lie. The Dioscuri—that's what my twin brothers were called—would never have allowed me to be harmed without seeking revenge."

Our maids stood waiting nearby with drying cloths and perfumed oil to rub on us. As I climbed out of the pool, my mother's eyes flicked over my naked body, still flat as a young boy's. She pursed her lips and shook her head. "Will you never get any curves, Hermione?" she asked, sighing. "You have no more shape than a door post."

I blushed, embarrassed, and reached for a drying cloth to cover myself.

The maids pretended not to hear. My mother rose and stepped from the pool, confident of her own beauty, her shapely body and graceful limbs, smooth and white and perfect as marble.

"Theseus told me tales as we rode through the night," my mother continued, her eyes half-closed as the maids went about their tasks. I could see the admiration in their glances. "Always about how wonderful he was. He claimed he had founded the city of Athens and had a great palace there. Such a braggart! Men are like that, you know."

I *didn't* know, but I nodded sagely, because like the maids I wanted to hear the rest of the story.

According to Helen, she and her abductor arrived toward dawn at a small village, where Theseus handed her over to his mother, Queen Aethra. "The old queen told a few stories of her own!" Helen said, laughing. "On her wedding night she slept first with her husband, King Aegeus, and then later with Poseidon, so that her son had some of both fathers and was both human and divine. A demigod."

Like your own parents, I thought. I was thinking of Zeus, the magnificent swan who'd made love to my grandmother. I understood that my mother, too, was a demigod.

Theseus planned to keep young Helen hidden away until she was old enough to marry, and she stayed for several years in Queen Aethra's care. "It was very pleasant there," my mother said. "Theseus kept his word and didn't bother me. He went off on another wild adventure, this time to visit Hades, god of the underworld. Hades offered him a seat, pretending to be hospitable, but when Theseus sat down, his buttocks stuck fast to the bench! Hissing serpents surrounded him, the Furies with snakes in their hair lashed at him, and a fierce three-headed dog, Cerberus, sank his teeth into his arms and legs. Eventually he managed to get away, but he left a part of his buttocks there." My mother stifled a laugh. "When Theseus married someone else, his children all had flat behinds. A proper punishment for a man who made a habit of abducting young girls!"

My mother's maids draped her in a finely woven peplos that reached to her ankles, fastened it on her shoulders with jeweled brooches, and cinched her narrow waist with a belt of golden links.

"How did you ever get away?" I asked.

"After several years my brothers found me," Helen said. "Assured that I was still a virgin, they brought me back to Sparta. Queen Aethra came with me, for I'd grown fond of her."

Aethra, now very old, was still with my mother. She had taken charge of my little brother, Pleisthenes, who adored her.

"And then," I prompted, "you married Father."

"Yes," she sighed. "But it was very complicated."

I knew that. With Helen, it was *always* complicated.

EVERYONE KNEW THE STORY of how Helen, once she had been safely returned to Sparta, came to marry Menelaus. I, too, had heard her tell it many times; I never tired of hearing it. Her sister, Clytemnestra, had married a man named Tantalus. But after Agamemnon, king of Mycenae, killed Tantalus in battle, he forced Clytemnestra to marry *him*.

"Castor and Pollux were furious," my mother told me. "But Agamemnon can be very persuasive when he wants something, and he convinced our father to let him have my sister as his wife. She was not at all happy about it, and our brothers had no choice but to defer to Father. Clytemnestra and Agamemnon were married. I met Menelaus at their wedding."

Menelaus was the brother of the king-killer widow-snatcher.

"I don't wish to sound boastful, Hermione, but at that time everyone—every *man*, I should say—considered me the most beautiful woman in the world. And they still do!" She laughed in pleasure at this notion. I couldn't disagree with her. I took her word that there was no one as beautiful anywhere in the world of Greece or beyond it. Her hips were rounded, her breasts perfect, her skin flawless, her brow high and clear. Helen's long golden hair shimmered in sunlight as well as in torchlight, like the finest silk carried from the faraway Orient. And her eyes—those eyes of hyacinth blue!

As I've said, I didn't resemble my mother in any of the important ways. I was my father's daughter, from copper red hair to skin darkened and freckled by the sun and eyes as black as olives. Like Menelaus, I was thin, and as my mother had pointed out, entirely lacking in shapeliness. On the plus side, my memory was excellent, like my father's. Sometimes a little forgetting can be a good thing. But I am unable to forget. Only my voice is like my mother's, clear and melodious. I was grateful at least for that.

It was no wonder that every man who looked at Helen, from the ridiculous flat-bottomed Theseus to the handsomest Greek prince, desired her and was willing to go to any length to have her.

"Suitors came to Sparta from every part of Greece," my mother liked to tell me, knowing there would be no such lineup waiting impatiently at the palace door when I was old enough to wed. She never gave a moment's thought to what it was like being the unspectacular daughter of a spectacularly great beauty.

"All these men came with the most delightful gifts for me and my father," she said, describing the treasures brought to Tyndareus's palace. "But my father refused to accept any. From gilded chariots and handsome horses to the most magnificent jewels and embroidered robes, the treasures filled the megaron—the great hall—of our palace. And I wanted all of it!"

"But why didn't Grandfather accept the gifts?"

Helen shrugged her splendid shoulders. "He was afraid of starting a quarrel among my suitors. Those who had been refused would turn against the one who had been chosen. With such men a quarrel could quickly become bloody. But one man knew he had not a chance of being chosen. Odysseus was short legged and far from handsome. He didn't even bother to bring a gift, because he had a fair idea of which man Father actually wanted as a new son-in-law: Menelaus, the brother of Agamemnon, my sister's husband. But Odysseus was a clever fellow. He quietly promised to help Father avoid a quarrel if Father agreed to help him marry the girl he wanted, a rather plain creature named Penelope. Father leaped at this solution to his dilemma."

My mother paused to sip watered wine from a two-handled cup of hammered silver. A cool breeze had sprung up, and our maids hurried to bring us our woolen cloaks.

"Odysseus told Father to make the suitors swear to defend whichever man among them was chosen to marry me. Tyndareus agreed, and that very day he sacrificed a horse and cut it into pieces, then ordered the suitors to stand on those pieces and swear an oath to come to the defense of the winner, no matter what happened. I watched all this from behind a screen—it was a bloody mess, I can tell you!"

"And of course you chose Menelaus," I said—always my contribution to her story.

Helen frowned. Even frowning, my mother lost none of her beauty. "Do you think I had any choice in the matter?" she asked. "It was my father's decision to make, not mine. It could have been Great Ajax or Little Ajax or Menestheus or Philoctetes or Patroclus, or any one of many others—it made not the slightest difference. I was to marry, and that was the end of the discussion. So Father called out, 'Helen, my dear, come crown your husband with a laurel wreath.' I did as I was told and set the wreath on Menelaus's head. Everyone cheered, though of course the cheers were not sincere, for every man except the winner was disappointed that he hadn't seized the prize. Menelaus smiled triumphantly and took my hand. Three days later we were wed. And now here we are," she added with a shrug.

I was born like any ordinary baby—there was no nighttime visit from Zeus in disguise, no improbable blue egg. In the years that followed, two baby boys were born and died. Then came little Pleisthenes, who looked more like Helen than I did, blessed with our mother's hyacinth eyes and golden ringlets. My dear grandparents, Leda and Tyndareus, died, as did Helen's twin brothers. Menelaus became king of Sparta.

Beginning when I was very young, my father took me for long walks into the countryside, just the two of us, and he told me stories of the twelve gods who live on Mount Olympus. There was Zeus, the mighty king of the gods, and Hera, his wife and sister, the queen; Zeus's son, Apollo, is the god of light and prophecy. I particularly liked the story of Apollo's twin sister, Artemis, goddess of the hunt and of childbirth—she was born first and assisted in the delivery of her twin. That was not the only strange birth: according to Father, Athena, the virgin goddess of wisdom and warfare, sprang fully grown from Zeus's brow.

"Zeus has had many lovers and many children by them. Hera is a jealous wife and often tries to take revenge on her rivals. This causes all kinds of problems. Aphrodite, goddess of love, beauty, and desire, is married to Hephaestus, god of fire, but she's had many affairs. Fidelity in marriage doesn't mean a thing to her." My father chuckled. "The gods are magnificent: they hold our lives in their hands and control our destiny, but in some ways they're not much different from ordinary mortals."

We grew close on these walks as my father explained to me the ways of gods and men—closer than my mother and I would ever be.

Visitors from Mycenae

THE YEAR I TURNED eleven was the most important of my young life. The sheep, relieved of their thick winter coats, leaped about friskily, and the women of our household had taken up their spindles. We worked our way through heaps of fleece that had been washed and carded by the slaves. Spinning went on everywhere. Whether we were out walking or sitting by the hearth, talking or staying silent, our hands were always busy. I could spin a fine, even thread, and I was proud of that.

As the days passed and the bright moon waxed and waned and waxed again, I could sense my mother's growing discontent. Helen was restless and moody. She often sighed deeply, and when I asked if something troubled her, she shook her head and, smiling wistfully, said, "No, no, nothing." But I didn't believe her.

Toward the end of summer we received a welcome visit

from Agamemnon and Clytemnestra and my cousins, Orestes and his sisters Iphigenia, Electra, and Chrysothemis, all older than I. Leaving their great ship anchored at the port of Gythion at the mouth of the River Eurotas, they were rowed upriver to Sparta in small boats, accompanied by scores of servants and attendants. Agamemnon was a big man, taller and heavier than my father, broad chested and strong, with long hair and a full, dark beard. During the day, the two men rode off together to hunt while my mother and my aunt sat in the palace garden, drinking wine and complaining about their husbands. I passed the time with my cousins. Orestes liked to show off his skill with a bow, dropping birds unlucky enough to be flying within range. While his sisters and I dutifully applauded Orestes' marksmanship, the girls rattled on and on about whom they might marry someday.

"I wonder who they'll find for you," Iphigenia mused, coolly appraising me. She was nearly thirteen, closest to my age, and I knew what she was thinking: *You're not a beauty like your mother, Hermione.*

"I'm only eleven," I reminded her. "I don't care a fig about a husband." I was thinking: *You're nothing to brag about either, Iphigenia.* But that wasn't entirely true. She had beautiful hair, ebony black and thick, and she spent a great deal of time fussing with it, asking me which way she should wear it. She also had breasts, and I envied them.

Orestes brought down another unfortunate bird. Then he glanced at me and smiled, and I smiled back. He seemed a nice boy, Orestes, with merry brown eyes flecked with gold, like tiny pinpoints of light. His smile charmed me. It wasn't perfect—his two front teeth overlapped—and I liked that.

AT THE BEGINNING OF the grape harvest, Agamemnon and his family prepared to go home to Mycenae. A farewell banquet was laid out—platters of roasted lamb and venison, baskets of bread, bowls of olives and pomegranate seeds—and noble families from nearby towns were invited to join the feast. Our guests lounged on couches, enjoying the food and drink and passing around a myrtle branch. It was the custom for the one holding the branch to sing a song, recite a poem, or tell a story. The shadows were growing long, and many of the banquet guests had already left for their homes when heralds announced the arrival of a courier from Troy, a city that lay across the Chief Sea, far from Sparta. The courier, having no small boat to bring him from the port, was dusty and weary from his journey by foot over the mountains when he stumbled into the hall to deliver his message: King Menelaus would soon receive a visitor, Paris, son of Priam, king of Troy.

"When may we expect this prince?" asked my father.

"His fleet is being prepared. With the blessing of the gods, Prince Paris will arrive at the end of the harvest, before the new moon."

This news created plenty of excitement. A royal traveler

from such a great distance was a rare thing, and a Trojan prince was assured an elaborate reception. The food and drink at our table nearly forgotten, my father and my uncle Agamemnon immediately got into an intense discussion of King Priam and the enormous wealth of Troy, its importance in trade for silks and spices from the Orient, and its military capability and political situation. This was the kind of discussion that made the women at the table yawn in boredom.

When the last guests had gone, my mother proposed a walk in the orchard. Clytemnestra and her daughters were already strapping on their sandals. I wanted to stay behind to listen to the men, as Orestes was doing, but I wouldn't have been welcome. Little Pleisthenes tugged on our mother's peplos, but I was the one who scooped him up and set him on my hip.

"Aren't you the lucky one!" Clytemnestra said, linking her arm with Helen's. "Prince Paris coming to visit! I hear he's divinely handsome and captivating as well."

"Really?" my mother said, seeming only mildly interested. "I know nothing about him."

But Clytemnestra appeared to know a lot about Paris, the youngest of King Priam's nineteen legitimate sons by his second wife, Queen Hecabe; there were another thirty sons by various concubines and an uncountable number by lowly servants. Paris was gifted with good looks and a winning personality, she said, but he lacked ambition. "The eldest brother, Hector, is the ambitious one."

"So Paris is indolent, then?" my mother asked, idly plucking flowers from bushes and then dropping them, leaving a fragrant trail.

"Not exactly indolent," Clytemnestra explained, "just the badly spoiled favorite. It's an interesting story—I'm surprised you haven't heard it. A seer warned Priam that a baby soon to be born would be responsible for bringing about the fall of Troy. Soon after, Queen Hecabe gave birth to a boy, and the seer tried to persuade Priam to have the infant killed. King Priam couldn't bring himself to do it. He called in his chief herdsman, Agelaus, and ordered *him* to kill the baby. Agelaus carried the baby away, but he couldn't kill him either. Instead, he took the newborn up into the mountains and left him there to die. Five days later, the story goes, the herdsman went back, expecting to bury the body. Instead, he found the baby alive and healthy, suckled by a she bear."

A she bear nursed the baby! I tried to imagine that.

We reached the riverbank, our servants spread blankets, and we sat down. "And then what happened?" I asked. Iphigenia and I waited eagerly to hear Clytemnestra's story. The servants, too, edged nearer. The myrtle branch was never passed to a woman at our banquets; it was only among ourselves that we told stories.

"Agelaus took the baby home with him to raise as his own son. He killed a newborn goat and presented its tongue to King Priam as proof that his orders had been carried out and the

baby was dead. But little Paris—the name given him by Agelaus—was no ordinary child. He was so beautiful, so intelligent, and so strong! He was just six when he chased down
a band of cattle thieves and retrieved the cows they had stolen. Still, no one knew that Paris was of royal blood. He was
only a common slave, in charge of Agelaus's cattle. When he
got older, Paris arranged to have the best bulls of the herd
fight one another. Eventually his prize bull was defeated, but
not by any ordinary bull. As a joke, Ares, the god of war and
manly courage, had turned himself into a bull. The other gods,
watching the contest from their home on Mount Olympus,
were much amused. They all loved Paris. It seems that Paris
has always lived a charmed life."

"Is that the end of the story?" Helen asked. "Surely not!
He's no longer a slave but a prince!"

Clytemnestra was enjoying her role as storyteller. "There
is more. King Priam sent servants to Agelaus, ordering him
to bring his best bull to be awarded as a prize at the funeral
games held each year in honor of King Priam's son who had
been lost at birth. Paris heard about it and made up his mind
to compete in the games. He still had no idea that he was the
king's son. No one knew. First he won the boxing match, and
next the foot race. That so angered Priam's other sons that
they challenged Paris to a second race. He won that as well!
The princes were so furious that they swore to kill this inter-
loper."

Clytemnestra paused and called for a cup of watered wine. "And then?" Helen cried when a servant had filled their goblets. "What happened then?"

Clytemnestra sipped a little and continued, "As they drew their swords and prepared to attack Paris, Agelaus rushed up shouting, 'King Priam, you must not kill him! This is your long-lost son!' To prove it, the old herdsman produced the tiny bracelet that was on the baby's ankle when he was abandoned and left to die. Paris's mother, Hecabe, saw the bracelet and burst into tears. The king was overjoyed. The jealous brothers were unhappy, and the priests and seers tore their garments and warned King Priam that the young man must be killed at once, or Troy would be brought to utter ruin. But Priam could not be persuaded. He had lost his son once, and he was not going to lose him again. 'Better that Troy be destroyed than my beloved son be taken from me.'"

For a moment we were silent, spellbound by the story.

My mother scrambled to her feet, her face flushed, a few damp curls clinging to her forehead. "This glorious Paris whom you have described so winningly—has he chosen a wife? And if he has, who is she?"

Clytemnestra rose, gesturing to her maids to adjust the folds of her peplos. "He hasn't married yet," she replied. "Though many women are drawn to such a man—how could they not be? A girl named Oenone, the daughter of a fountain nymph, was always seen with him. They say that the two used to hunt and tend their flocks together."

"More of a sister than a lover, then?" Helen asked, sounding relieved.

"I can't say for sure," Clytemnestra replied, giving my mother a sharp look.

We started back to the palace as darkness gathered around us like a soft blanket. Pleisthenes sagged in my arms, and I set him down, whispering that he must walk a little. He pouted, just like his mother. When a slave girl tried to pick him up, he began to wail, and I ended up carrying him anyway, while he clung to my neck.

Torches had been lighted, and in the megaron a troupe of traveling musicians was entertaining the men with songs of ancient heroes. We sat down to listen, though nothing sounded as enthralling as the story Clytemnestra had just told us. Pleisthenes crawled into my lap and fell asleep. Our mother seemed not to notice, and after a time his nurse lifted the drowsy boy from my arms and carried him away. Not long afterward my eyes, too, felt heavy. I wandered off to the sleeping quarters, curled up on the thick fleeces piled on my low bed, and was soon sleeping soundly.

As Dawn stretched her rosy fingers into the vault of the sky the next day, our two families boarded several flat-bottomed royal barges and small papyrus boats tied up along the muddy banks of the River Eurotas. We floated downriver to Gythion, where the river meets the sea and Agamemnon's great ship lay at anchor. The weather was fine. A steady breeze promised smooth sailing to Mycenae.

Clytemnestra embraced my mother. "You must tell me all about the visit from the Trojan prince," she said. "Promise you'll leave nothing out!"

My mother laughed and gave her word. Orestes flashed his winning smile at me, and Iphigenia said she hoped I'd come to visit her soon, though I didn't feel she really meant it. Her older sisters ignored me, as usual. After making sacrifices at a local shrine to Aeolus, god of the four winds, Agamemnon's family boarded their ship. We watched from the beach as the anchor stones were hauled up and oarsmen rowed the ship away from the shore. The square sail billowed with a steady breeze, carrying the ship toward the horizon. When it had shrunk to a speck in the distance, we returned to our boats, and our slaves rowed us up the river to Sparta.

"The harvest will soon be over," my mother observed that evening. She was sitting beside my father and twisting a lock of her shining golden hair around her finger. I thought she looked almost happy. "And then we'll have another visitor! How splendid, Menelaus! We must show our guest a good time."

My father smiled indulgently. He'd give Helen anything she wanted. After all, he was the fortunate husband of the most beautiful woman in the world.

The Arrival of Paris

HELEN, WHO HAD BEEN drifting through the long, dull summer days as though half-asleep, now suddenly awoke from her trance and threw herself into planning for the visit of the Trojan prince. We must have new furniture, she told my father: a larger table for banquets, and more couches. The fleeces for the beds should be replaced. She needed a new peplos, maybe several. My mother thought my clothes were shabby—Clytemnestra had said so, reminding her that even a young princess should not be dressing in a short chiton. It wasn't something that Helen would notice otherwise. Animals must be slaughtered, my mother continued, feasts prepared, entertainments arranged. So much still to be done, and the harvest was almost over!

As the moon neared the end of its fourth quarter, Menelaus sent a number of servants downriver to the small island of Kranai, near Gythion. They were instructed to set up a camp on the lovely stretch of beach, ready to greet Prince Paris when his fleet reached the shallows. A messenger would bring word to Sparta of the Trojan prince's arrival at Kranai.

Everything went as planned. The harvest had been completed; grain and olive oil and wine filled row upon row of clay amphoras standing in the royal storehouse. The fattest sheep and cattle were slaughtered, loaves of bread baked, figs soaked in honey and spices. Extra musicians were hired. My mother arranged the new furniture and tried on her new gowns. A luxurious bedroom was prepared for the prince, and female servants were assigned to bathe him and rub his skin with scented oil. I noticed that my mother gave this task only to older, homelier women. Now we waited eagerly for the prince we'd heard so much about.

"Did you see Paris's ship with your own eyes?" Menelaus asked the messenger who came at last, and the messenger described a carving of Aphrodite, the goddess of love, holding her son, the little winged Eros, on the prow of the prince's ship. Menelaus listened to the report and nodded, satisfied. The royal barge was dispatched to fetch Paris.

I was nearly as excited as my mother. We were both by the river's edge when the barge arrived and Paris stepped off. I was not disappointed. I thought I had never seen such a handsome man. I could not help but admire the prince's dazzling smile, his thick dark hair curling over his neck, his long legs and strong shoulders, and, most striking of all, his golden eyes, gleaming like a cat's.

The moment my mother saw him, their eyes locked. Neither seemed able to look away. I wondered, *What does Father think?*

But Menelaus was oblivious. He didn't seem to notice a thing. While Paris stared at Helen with open admiration—I would even say adoration—my father launched into his usual speech about the honor of receiving such a distinguished guest. Helen and Paris continued to devour each other with hungry looks.

I held my breath to see what would happen next. But nothing did—at least, not then.

My brother and I were introduced to Paris, who flicked a glance and a brief smile in our direction before turning his attention back to Helen. Musicians with wooden flutes, lyres, and drums made of animal skins escorted us up the broad stone path to the palace. Little boys scattered herbs to be crushed under our feet. When we reached the gates, Menelaus ordered them flung open, crying out, "Enter here, great friend! My house is your house!"

Paris took Menelaus at his word.

For nine days my father and his honored guest hunted together, often with my mother joining them, for Helen was a keen shot. Each evening there was a banquet with the finest roasted meats and delicious wines, rich cheeses and delicate cakes dripping with honey. Paris described to us the palace in Troy, where he and his brothers lived in quarters hung with colorful silks from the Orient, ate and drank from plates and goblets of hammered gold, lounged on benches inlaid with ebony and ivory brought from distant places. I was entranced by what he told us.

But I was also distracted. You would have had to be blind not to see that Paris had fallen madly in love with my mother. He gazed at her, sighing, as she plucked the strings of her golden lyre. If she set down her wine goblet, Paris reached for it and deliberately drank from the very spot where her lips had touched the rim, his eyes on her to make sure she saw what he was doing. He could scarcely bear to leave her side. Once, when we had gone walking along the riverbank, I saw him pick up a stick and scratch a message in the sand. I stepped close enough to read it and gasped.

Helen, I love you.

My mother hurriedly scuffed the letters with her sandal. "You will cause me no end of trouble!" she hissed at Paris, who merely flashed his most seductive smile and reached for her hand, right under my father's nose. Helen jerked her hand away.

How could my father not see what was happening right in front of him? In fact, his mind was somewhere else. Menelaus was busy preparing to leave for Crete, to take part in funeral rites for his grandfather. The obligation had come up suddenly, and he couldn't refuse.

"My deepest apologies, dear friend," he said to Paris. "But it's my responsibility to attend the obsequies. I'm sure you understand."

Paris assured Menelaus that he understood completely: one's duty to one's family, and so on.

"Until I'm able to return, my esteemed wife will see that you receive the greatest hospitality our kingdom has to offer." He turned to my mother. "Won't you, dearest Helen?"

"With pleasure, my lord," replied my mother, her gaze modestly lowered. Or maybe she just didn't want my father to look into her eyes and read the truth.

With the sun high overhead, Menelaus boarded a small, fast boat for his journey downriver to the gulf, where his ship lay provisioned and ready to sail. I begged to go with him as far as the mouth of the river, thinking that I might be able to say something, to whisper a word or two of caution about what I saw plainly and he plainly did not.

"Stay with your mother and our guest, Hermione," he said, fondly running his hand over my shock of red curls that so closely matched his own. "I'll be back before the next full moon, and you can tell me all about it."

Menelaus kissed Helen and my little brother and me, promising to order a signal fire to be lighted on Mount Koumaros when he entered the gulf. And then he was gone.

THE BANQUET THAT NIGHT was smaller and quieter without the presence of the king. No reciting, no singing, though my mother did play a little on her golden lyre. Everyone wanted to retire early. Maybe after nine nights of feasting and drinking and music and storytelling, they were all tired. My eyes were also heavy, but I was determined not to go to bed before the others. My mother began to yawn. She wished us all a good night. "Don't stay up too late, Hermione," she said, and I promised I would not. She scarcely glanced at her honored guest, which I thought was odd.

Not long after Helen had gone off to the bedroom she always shared with my father, Paris, too, made a show of yawning and stretching. When he left the megaron, on impulse I followed him, silently slipping along the corridors leading to the guest quarters. I hid myself behind a stout pillar until his door was closed and the bolt shot into place. Crouching on the cold stone floor, I waited. The servants, left to clean up after the banquet, finished their work and went off to their quarters. The palace fell silent. Not a sound. I pinched myself to stay awake and as the night grew cool wished I had brought a woolen shawl with me.

I'm being stupid, I told myself. *Nothing is going to happen.* But still I didn't move.

My head had drooped down on my knees by the time I heard the bolt on Paris's door slide back. The hinges squeaked as the door opened and closed again, followed by the sound of soft footsteps. I breathed lightly and wished my heart did not pound so loudly. Paris hurried past my hiding place without seeing me. Suspecting that he was making his way to my mother's bedroom, I decided to go there by another way, making it less likely that he would sense my presence.

I ran along the open passageway. As I was about to pass

my little brother's room, I noticed that his door stood ajar and peeked inside, expecting to see his nurse asleep on her pallet and Pleisthenes' golden curls spilling across his pillow.

No one was there. No child, no nurse. No longer caring if anyone heard me, I rushed to my mother's bedroom.

Empty. I stared in confusion. *Where are they?*

I flew across the columned portico and through the great hall and the anteroom. Guards standing rigidly by the entrance seemed not to notice me as I raced by, bound for the riverbank. The queen's barge was not tied up at its usual place, the boatman gone.

I tried to call out to my mother, even though I suspected she was nowhere near. What could I do? If I found another boatman, I'd insist that he take me down to the gulf, where Paris had left his fleet, his ship with the carving of Aphrodite and Eros. I felt sure that Helen must have gone there with him. But even if I found them, how could I, just a child, coax her to come back? Would she even listen to me? I didn't think so.

I started back up the stone path to the palace, passing on the way the enormous storehouse where the wine, oil, and grain were kept. Behind it was the smaller treasury where my father locked up his gold—plates, vases and cups, diadems, bracelets, necklaces and rings—and also his weapons and shields. Something felt strange. The usual treasury guards were on duty, but they stood by as though in a trance. I marched up to one of them and put my face close to his.

"Guard!" I shouted. He didn't even blink. I slapped him,

hard. Still nothing. What was wrong with him? I spun around and looked carefully at the others. It was as if someone had put them under a spell.

Seeing that the treasury door, armored in bronze, stood ajar, I pushed it open and stepped inside. A narrow blade of moonlight cut across the bare floor. Except for a few dusty trunks bound with leather, the vault was empty, my father's treasure gone.

Not only my mother and the treasure were missing, but Pleisthenes was missing too. That hurt me deeply, maybe more than anything. My brother loved me, and I loved him. Helen never paid as much attention to him as I did, yet it seemed she had taken him with her. But why hadn't she taken *me*? Didn't she love me? Or would I simply have been in the way? A nuisance to her and Paris, reminding her that what she was doing was wrong! I didn't want to leave my father. But I didn't want Helen to go without me, to leave me here.

My mother had abandoned me for handsome, charming Paris.

My anger grew—not only at Helen and Paris, but also at my father for being so blind, for leaving the two of them here together, alone. How could he not have seen what was going on? Or hadn't he *wanted* to see?

I hated them all. And I had no idea what would happen now.

Aphrodite's Spell

THE GREAT HALL, WHERE we had enjoyed so many banquets, was deserted. I took one of the flickering torches down from the wall and carried it with me while I searched the palace. First I returned to my mother's bedroom. Her gowns, her jewels—nearly everything—was gone, except for her loom, which stood empty against the wall, and her silver spindle, which was lying on her bed. I didn't know if she'd forgotten the spindle or left it for me, but I took it to my room and hid it there.

In the anteroom, Pentheus, Father's vizier, sat slumped at the table where he kept the king's accounts, staring at nothing. *Drunk again,* I thought, hurrying past him unnoticed. Servants sleeping in their quarters could not be roused, and the guards at their posts all seemed to be under the same kind of spell. Only the horses in the stables were alert.

In one of the stalls I stumbled accidentally over a man who

huddled in a corner, staring up at me. "You," I said, shoving him roughly with my foot. "I am Princess Hermione, daughter of King Menelaus and Queen Helen. Get up and tell me who you are."

He wobbled to his feet. "Mistress, my name is Zethus, servant of Prince Paris," he said with a shaky bow. "A son of King Priam by a servant girl of such low station that I am not recognized as one of his thirty sons by his concubines."

I held the torch closer for a better look. The man was a filthy mess. "Your master is gone. Paris and Helen and my little brother, and much of my father's treasure—all have gone, as I suspect you know. Tell me why you're still here, Zethus," I ordered.

Zethus shuffled his feet. "I drank too much wine. Very delicious wine, from King Menelaus's private stock! I came out here to relieve myself, and that's when Aphrodite arrived and put all the king's servants and guards into a trance."

"Aphrodite?" I gasped, remembering my father's stories about her. "The goddess of love was here?"

"Yes, mistress. Paris is her great favorite. She will give him whatever he wants, and he wants Helen."

"And you say that Aphrodite put my father's guards and servants under a spell?"

Zethus nodded. "I watched it happen. The spell will be broken with the first appearance of Dawn," he explained. "The guards will come to themselves, but they'll have no memory of the previous night."

The stars in the blackness of the heavens had begun to fade. The spell wouldn't last much longer. What would happen when the palace servants and guards awoke and realized that I was the only member of my family still here?

"My father will come back from Crete and discover that everything of value to him is gone. He doesn't anger easily, but when he does, beware!" I warned Paris's disheveled servant.

Abruptly, Zethus dropped to his knees. "Princess Hermione, please let me help you."

I studied this Trojan. The king was far away, and until he came home again, I did not know what to do. To begin, maybe the best course was to question this stranger and find out more about the Trojan prince who had taken my mother.

"All right," I said. "I'll call for a servant to see that you have a bath and clean garments. And then we'll talk."

THE SKY HAD PALED to the color of pearls, and the night guards had shaken off their spell. I stopped a pair of them as they headed back to their quarters. I had known these two, as I had most of our servants, for nearly all my life.

"How did you pass the night?" I asked. "Did you notice anything unusual?"

They smiled at me. "No, Princess Hermione, not a thing," said the older of the pair. "A night like any other," added the younger.

"You didn't hear any odd sounds? Didn't notice that the treasure house is empty? That all the boats and boatmen are gone? That Queen Helen and our guest, Prince Paris, left while you were on duty, and took Pleisthenes with them?"

The guards stared at me, stunned. "Has an alarm been raised?" asked the older one.

"No. No alarm was raised. But tell me—did you have a visit from a goddess?"

They looked at each other in confusion.

"Aphrodite?" I prompted. "Perhaps you saw her."

"The mist . . ." mumbled the younger. "Do you remember the mist?" he asked the older guard. "We spoke of it, how strange it was."

"I do remember, yes! But nothing after that. Nothing until the last star had been extinguished and Dawn came."

Later, when Zethus reappeared, bathed and dressed in clean clothes and looking quite respectable, I told him what the guards had reported.

"That was certainly Aphrodite," he said. "She spreads a fine mist that makes men forget everything. You must not punish them. It was the work of the goddess. The guards aren't to be blamed."

"Tell that to Father when he comes home!" I exclaimed. "He'll need some convincing not to order the death of every man who failed him. Starting with his vizier." I wondered what had become of Pentheus.

We sat in the anteroom brightened by sunlight flooding through openings in the walls. Servants brought us a meal of cheese and fruit. I saw now that Zethus was not much more than a boy, only a few years older than I. I watched him devour his food. It was obvious that he'd been brought up simply but well. I asked about his family, and he smiled, showing strong, even teeth.

"My father is King Priam, as I've told you. My mother is a servant to Priam's daughter, Cassandra. I admire Princess Cassandra—she doesn't have an easy life."

"Why is her life hard? She's the king's daughter."

"She has the gift of prophecy. She can foretell the future."

"A useful gift, surely?"

"It might be, but the problem is that no one believes her. It was the god Apollo's doing, my mother told me. Cassandra received the gift of prophecy from Apollo, but when she resisted his advances, he spit into her mouth so that no one would ever believe her. At any rate, Priam is convinced that Cassandra is mad, and he keeps her locked up in a tower with only my mother for company. I've seen her—she's very beautiful. They say that Cassandra is the second most beautiful woman in the world."

"The only one more beautiful is Helen?"

"Yes," Zethus admitted. "And since I've seen them both, I know it's true."

"Now you must tell me about Paris," I said. "Why has he won Aphrodite's favor?"

"I'll tell you the story," Zethus said. He pushed away his empty bowl, and I leaned forward to listen.

"The gods and goddesses had gathered on Mount Olympus

to celebrate the marriage of Thetis, a beautiful sea nymph, to Peleus, king of Phthia, a grandson of Zeus. The only one not invited to the wedding was Eris, the goddess of discord, whom nobody likes because she is always causing trouble. Furious at being excluded, Eris hovered above the gathering on a cloud and tossed a golden apple down onto the banquet table. The apple was marked 'For the fairest,' and three of the goddesses tried to claim it: Hera, Zeus's wife; his daughter Athena, the goddess of wisdom and warfare; and Aphrodite, the goddess of love. They asked Zeus to choose the fairest, but he wasn't willing to anger the two not chosen. Instead, he suggested that the decision be made by Paris. Foolishly, Paris accepted Zeus's challenge, and the competition began.

"Each goddess tried to bribe him. Hera promised to make him lord of Europe and Asia if he'd award her the apple, but Paris wasn't interested in power. Athena offered to make him a great warrior; that didn't tempt him either, because he dislikes fighting. But Aphrodite knew his weakness: he loves women. She promised him the most beautiful woman on earth as his bride.

"And so," Zethus continued, "Paris picked Aphrodite, and Hera and Athena vowed to get even. It complicated matters that the most beautiful woman on earth—Helen—was already married. But Aphrodite didn't care. She arranged to bring Paris here to Sparta, where he met your mother. It was love at first sight. He was determined to have her. You see what happened next. Aphrodite cast her spell and allowed Paris and Helen to escape."

I listened to Zethus's story with growing alarm. "All of my mother's former suitors have sworn to join with King Menelaus against anyone who tries to take her away," I told him.

"I know," he said. "I've heard the story."

"When Father comes home and discovers that his wife, his son, and his treasure have been stolen, he'll call for those men who pledged to support him. I'm sure they'll bring her back," I said, hoping I was right.

"They will sail to Troy, and there will be much bloodshed," Zethus predicted. He drummed on the table. "One thing more — Thetis and Peleus, at whose wedding the problem began, now have a son, Achilles. He's known to be a mighty warrior. Menelaus will certainly want him to fight to get Helen back. As for the goddesses, Hera and Athena will be on the side of the Greeks, but Aphrodite will help Paris as much as she can. The war is likely to last for a long time."

I wanted to ask more questions, but activity along the riverbank drew our attention. Boats were arriving from downriver. I ran toward the boatmen, who were leaving the slaves to tie up the craft.

"Where is Queen Helen? Where is my brother?" I shouted.

The boatmen stared uneasily at their feet. "They're with the Trojan prince. At Kranai they boarded the ship with the figure of Aphrodite and Eros on the prow. They sailed eastward."

"And the king's treasure?" I demanded. "Where is that?"

One of the boatmen stammered, "We were ordered to load it into the holds of the ships."

I glared at him. "Why didn't you refuse to do it?"

"I beg your pardon, my princess, but it was not possible to refuse. A mist came upon us, and we were powerless to resist what Prince Paris and Queen Helen ordered. It was Aphrodite's doing."

I stamped my foot in frustration. "You!" I shouted at Zethus. "You're a Trojan! You're one of them! Why didn't you stop it? You must have known what was happening." I began to pummel him, pounding his chest hard.

Zethus looked startled at my outburst. "I take it you've not had much to do with the gods and goddesses of Mount Olympus!" he exclaimed, seizing my wrists. "Or you'd know that you can't oppose them. They always have their way. Always!"

Zethus let go of my wrists, and I sat down on the beach and cried. When I was finished weeping I stood up, brushed off my chiton, and stalked up the stone path to the palace. "I have a lot to do before Father returns," I said to Zethus, who was still hovering. "You can stay here, but you may not find a warm welcome from him when he learns what your countryman has done."

"If it is your will, Princess Hermione, I shall stay to help you however I can."

"All right, then," I said, suddenly overcome with exhaustion. I left him and lay down to rest and didn't awaken until Helios, the sun, had nearly completed his blazing journey across the heavens in his fiery four-horse chariot.

The King's Return

WE WAITED, HARDLY DARING to breathe, for the return of King Menelaus. I wanted to get it over with, and at the same time I dreaded his anger and his disappointment. I knew the servants must have been gossiping among themselves, whispering about the handsome Trojan prince who had come as a guest and left as a thief, taking his host's wife away with him. What an insult!

Once, when I heard laughter coming from the cook house at the rear of the palace, I crept close to the door where I could gather snatches of conversation: about how the queen had not found her husband to be a real man, and how she had run off with the first man who dared to ask her.

"Maybe it was her idea in the first place," one of the servants suggested.

"Maybe she bribed the Trojan prince with the king's treasure," another said.

I stood fuming, hands balled into fists, until I could bear it no longer and burst through the door, bringing about a shocked silence among the meat roasters, cheese makers, and bread bakers. "I know what you're talking about," I shouted. "If you want to gossip about my mother, you should know the truth. Queen Helen did not leave willingly. Paris forced her to go with him. She would never have left King Menelaus!" I insisted passionately. "Aphrodite cast a spell on Helen so that she could not put up a fight. I saw it with my own eyes as he dragged her away!"

That last part was not true. I had no idea what had really happened. I had seen the looks Helen and Paris exchanged, his message of love scratched in the sand. I hated the thought that it may have even been her idea to leave. I liked the explanation I was inventing so much better, and the more I spoke, the more it seemed like the truth. My mother was abducted! Kidnapped! She had not wanted to go. Paris was holding her against her will. She would come back as soon as she could get away from her captors. I believed the lie I was inventing, because I had to. It was better than admitting to myself that my mother had chosen to abandon me.

"King Menelaus will rescue Queen Helen!" I cried while everyone gaped at me, open-mouthed. "He will bring her back to us!"

I turned and fled, back to my sleeping room, where I flung myself on my bed of fleeces and sobbed.

⟨ornament⟩

THEN I HAD TO deal with Pentheus. As Father's vizier, he oversaw the overseers—those who made sure the fields were planted, tended, and harvested, the grapes turned into wine and the olives pressed of their oil, the horses groomed, goats and cows milked and their milk turned into cheese, meals prepared, and sheep sheared and their wool woven into cloth. Pentheus was even in charge of our personal servants, the women who bathed and dressed us, the man who trimmed Father's beard.

The vizier was also the king's confidant. He had been with him since boyhood. Father loved him like a brother, but my mother didn't trust him. I'd heard my parents argue about him.

"Pentheus sticks his nose where it has no business," Helen had complained. "He has spies among my slaves who listen to my conversations with my women and report to him every word that's said."

Father always defended Pentheus. "*Everything* is his business," Menelaus answered mildly.

"I don't like it," Helen insisted. "I'm entitled to some privacy, surely."

"I think you're exaggerating, my dear," said Menelaus. "But I'll speak to him. The slaves need to be more discreet."

I agreed with Helen. But I thought I knew why Pentheus paid so much attention to my mother: he was in love with her. This was to be expected. There wasn't a man who didn't adore her. What she didn't admit to Father was that she encouraged Pentheus's affection. My mother loved to be loved. I supposed she couldn't help herself.

Pentheus seemed dazed when I confronted him. "Queen Helen is gone?" he asked incredulously.

"The Trojan prince abducted her," I said, now completely believing that myself. "Pleisthenes is with them. I have no doubt that Paris intends to carry them back to Troy."

"But how could I not have known?" he asked, his voice thin and cracking. "Why was the alarm not raised?"

I explained about Aphrodite and the spell she had cast on everyone—including him. I added nastily, "But of course he will blame *you* when he learns what happened."

Pentheus buried his head in his hands. For a moment I felt a little sorry for him, though I had never liked him. Finally he raised his head and looked at me with watery eyes. "I am aware of that," he said, his voice unsteady.

"In any case, we must prepare for the king's return," I reminded him.

"Yes, yes, of course," he said. "No need to concern yourself, Princess Hermione. I'll attend to everything."

But he did not. The next day I learned that Pentheus was nowhere to be found. No one seemed to know where he was. The stable master revealed that the king's vizier had galloped off before dawn, saying only that he had urgent business to which he must attend.

"The coward," I muttered to Zethus. "I don't believe Pentheus had urgent business. He just urgently needed to run away."

"I can't say that I blame him," Zethus said. "That means when your father comes back and learns what happened, he'll turn his fury on me. I'll be the target—the Trojan stand-in for the Trojan prince—and he will have me killed. It will be much better if I leave now."

"No, Zethus, you must stay!" I begged. "You promised! Please. I need your help."

I wanted him to move into the palace, maybe even to occupy the beautiful room that had been prepared for Prince Paris, but Zethus dismissed that idea immediately. He was stubborn, but I was even more stubborn. I stopped begging and *ordered* him to stay—after all, I was a princess, though a very young one, and I could command that, couldn't I?

Finally we reached a sort of compromise. Zethus would continue to sleep in the stable with the horses, and I would take him some bread and cheese every day and let him know when I had word that my father would soon arrive. When we were sure that Menelaus was on his way home and I would be all right, Zethus would make his way down the river to the gulf and look for a trader's ship to take him back to Troy.

I sent a staff of servants to set up a camp on the beach at Kranai to greet King Menelaus, just as he and my mother had done for the arrival of Paris. A fine meal would be prepared for him, and barges would be waiting to bring him home. I gave orders for signal flares to be lighted if my father arrived at night, and runners to be sent if he came during daylight hours.

Day after day we waited for word that my father was home from Crete. Though I slept only fitfully, I was indeed asleep when a serving maid came to awaken me.

"The signal fire has been sighted," the maid told me. "I'm to tell you that King Menelaus's ship has entered the gulf. He will no doubt reach Gythion by morning."

I leaped from my bed. I'd been arguing with myself about the right way to break the news of what had happened, and though no way was perfect, I thought it might be better not to let my father reach Sparta before he'd learned the truth.

I sent the servant for Zethus and ran down to the river. The boatmen were all asleep, but I had the guard awaken the one I knew best. "Tell him that King Menelaus is entering the gulf and that I want to be taken down to greet him."

Zethus arrived, pulling on his tunic. We climbed into my small boat and, traveling rapidly with the current, reached the mouth of the river. My father's large-prowed ship was already swinging at anchor farther out in the harbor. I ordered the boatman to stop near the beach where merchant ships from many places were loading and unloading their cargo. Before Zethus stepped ashore, he pressed into my hands a little wooden carving of a ship. It was executed in fine detail, from the arching prow to the rows of tiny oars.

"I made it for you, Princess Hermione, with gratitude for your many kindnesses."

I thanked Zethus, and we took our leave. I watched as he began to make his way from ship to ship along the beach, in search of one that would help him get home. Then I instructed my boatman to take me to the king.

The sailor on watch recognized my boat. A rope ladder was let down and a sailor helped me to scramble up, though I was in no need of any help. Father, looking surprised and pleased, greeted me heartily.

"Welcome, daughter!" he boomed as I boarded the great ship and was folded into his embrace. Then he asked, peering into my boat, "And your mother? Is Helen with you?"

"She was unable to come," I answered carefully. "And so I came instead."

I had been onboard the royal ship only a few times when I was much younger, and Father now proudly led me from the great carved prow to the rear, explaining the ropes that controlled the billowing sail and pointing out the benches where slaves sat and rowed, twenty-five on each side. He showed me where he slept and where he ate, and then I suggested that we go ashore on Kranai. "We've prepared a welcoming meal for you on the beach," I said. "I'm glad to have you home again, Father."

"I'm glad to be here," he said fondly. "And I look forward to seeing your lovely mother and that lively little brother of yours."

"I'm sure you do," I said. "The barges will soon be here to take us to the palace." I hoped to have the chance now to tell

him what had happened, to prepare him, maybe even to
his anger.

On the beach, the smell of roasting meat filled the air. Servants hurried to lay out the meal. I had arranged for musicians to play soothing music, but my father was clearly agitated.

"This is all very pleasant, Hermione," he said. "But I'm eager to be home again, in my own bed, next to my dear wife."

I sighed, my heart heavy with the news that I couldn't delay much longer. Father drained the last drops of wine from his goblet, and when I motioned for a servant to refill it, he shook his head. "Finish your meal, and let's be on our way."

My hands had begun to tremble, but at that moment a brilliant rainbow arched across the sky and a young woman with golden wings appeared, startling us both. "It's Iris, Hera's messenger," Father said to me. "You see the herald's rod she carries in her hand?" I gazed at her in awe.

"King Menelaus," Iris addressed him, "I bring you a message from Hera, wife of Zeus. Your wife, Helen of Sparta, has sailed away with Prince Paris of Troy, taking your son, Pleisthenes, and much of your treasure with her."

"Helen, gone?" My father reeled, looking as though he had been struck. A good-size man and broad shouldered, he appeared small, shrunken. "Where is she—" He corrected himself. "Where are they now?"

"They intended to sail for Troy," Iris reported, "but as they did so, Hera sent a fierce storm that blew the Trojan fleet off course. They have reached Cyprus. Hera believes that the lovers will spend several months enjoying themselves in Phoenicia and Egypt before Paris orders the bows of his ships turned at last toward Troy."

When the first stars of evening appeared in the sky, the rainbow and the goddess vanished as quickly as they had come. I braced for the full strength of Father's fury, but nothing happened. Instead, he looked deeply saddened and weary beyond words. I reached out and took his hand. "Father," I whispered.

He shook his head. "Where are the barges, Hermione?" he asked tiredly. "I want to go home."

Homecoming

THE MOON SENT SILVERY beams skittering across the black surface of the River Eurotas as our slaves heaved against the oars and drove the royal barge toward Sparta. Father paced agitatedly across the deck, sometimes pausing and leaning against a rail, staring down into the dark water.

By the time the boatmen had steered the barge toward the pylons where the royal boats were tied up, something had changed in him. The shock had worn off, pushed aside by a seething anger. He stalked silently into the palace. Guards shook off their drowsiness and anxiously watched the king. Servants, warned of his return, stumbled from their beds. King Menelaus strode through the palace, saying nothing.

He peered into my brother's room and found it empty. "Pleisthenes?" he called softly, and leaned down to touch the fleeces where his son had slept. "Pleisthenes?"

He checked the room adjoining it Aethra, the former queen and now the boy's nurse.

Empty.

I followed behind him, stepping softly, trying to make no noise. I had to know how he would react, had to see it with my own eyes. Finally he reached the marital chamber that he had shared for more than a dozen years with my mother. He stared at the empty bed. "Helen," he said, as softly as he had called out to his little son. Then, louder, "Helen!" Of course there was no reply. "Helen!" he shouted. "Helen!" He was answered by silence. *"Helen! Helen!"* Now he was roaring, so loudly that I put my fingers in my ears. "HELEN! HELEN!"

Menelaus burst out of the bedchamber and rushed down the hall, still shouting my mother's name. The guards stood stiffly, wincing as he bellowed, frightened by his terrible anger. Still I hurried after him, staying out of his sight, though he saw nothing but his own red rage.

Finally he charged out of the palace courtyard like an enraged bull and bolted toward the treasure house. I didn't try to follow him there. It would be just as awful, I knew. I heard him shouting for Pentheus, his vizier. But Pentheus was long gone, surely never to return to shoulder the blame that would be heaped on him.

The night wore on and morning came. At some point I slept a little, though I'm not sure Father did. When the servants set out a meal at midday, he came to the table, stared at the food with haggard eyes, ate little, but drank a quantity of wine. Still he said nothing. Sometimes he wept. Sometimes he actually laughed, though I didn't know at what—there was no merriment in it. I wondered if my father had gone mad.

I continued to tiptoe around him, not knowing what to do. Then the madness left him as suddenly as it had come. He called for a servant and ordered him to have his ship prepared for a voyage.

Finally he called for me.

"We're going to Mycenae, to King Agamemnon and Queen Clytemnestra," he said. "You will stay with your aunt and cousins, and your uncle and I will go to all of Helen's rejected suitors and demand that they make good on their oath. Then we will go to Troy and bring your mother home."

I collected a few things to take with me, expecting a rather short journey, though Zethus had warned me that it might not be. I decided to take my mother's silver spindle, and then added the tiny carved ship Zethus had given me. None of my other possessions held any deep meaning.

I was glad to be leaving our palace at Sparta, with its vast, echoing chambers, suddenly filled only with sadness, misery, and deep anger. I began to look forward to the journey. For a long time I had wished to travel on my father's great ship. I would see my aunt and cousins again. I had few friends my own age in Sparta. Electra and Chrysothemis paid no attention to me, but I got along well enough with Iphigenia, though she *was* awfully vain. The only cousin I truly liked was Orestes.

With a company of guards and servants, we traveled down the river to Gythion and boarded Father's royal ship. Seamen swarmed the deck, preparing for the journey. Slaves hauled up the great anchor stones that dragged on the sea floor. The rowers on their benches bent to their oars, and the ship moved slowly away from shore. When we reached open water, the great white sail was hoisted and caught the wind. The ship gathered speed, skimming the whitecaps, throwing out sparkling necklaces of foam. We sailed southward first, crossed the gulf, and then turned northward and followed the coast of the Peloponnese.

Father's broad brow was dark and his manner brooding. We spoke little. At sunset the sail was lowered and the rowers took us toward the beach. The anchor stones were let down, and we went ashore. Slaves put up sleeping shelters, built fires to keep wild animals at bay, and prepared a meal. A few musicians and the storyteller who traveled with us tried to entertain us, but their songs and stories brought Father no pleasure. I watched him pace the dark beach restlessly, until at last sleep overtook us. The next morning we continued our journey.

After two more days the ship arrived at a rocky shore below the walled city of Tiryns, built high up on a hill.

Father ordered runners to make their way overland from Tiryns to Mycenae with a message for King Agamemnon. "Tell him that King Menelaus has come with his daughter, Princess Hermione, but without his wife, Queen Helen of Sparta."

A BLAST OF TRUMPETS announced the arrival of King Agamemnon at Tiryns. My father and my uncle greeted each other first as kings and then as brothers. I could easily read their expressions, even if I couldn't hear the actual words they exchanged, as my father explained what had happened: wife, son, and treasure—all gone, stolen by the Trojan prince. Father was gesturing wildly. Agamemnon's brow furrowed deeply. He asked questions, and Father replied, his voice rising to a shout. Shaking of heads, nods, and finally the two brothers embraced and walked together to where I was waiting.

"Come, Hermione," Agamemnon said in a gruff voice, so much deeper than my father's. "We will go to the citadel to meet Clytemnestra and your cousins."

"I'm ready," I said.

A carrying chair was brought from the ship by slaves who bore the poles on their shoulders. Most of the time I preferred to walk rather than to be jolted in a chair, but when my feet were sore from the rough path, I willingly climbed in and let myself be carried. The great citadel loomed over the city of Mycenae. We entered through the Lion Gate, where two standing lionesses were carved into the rock. Clytemnestra and her children came out to greet us, bringing us figs recently picked and still warm from the sun. Iphigenia held my hand, and Orestes smiled at me sympathetically. Baths had been prepared for us, and after sleeping quarters had been arranged and I'd eaten and rested, Clytemnestra sent my cousins away and sat down by me.

"All right, Hermione, tell me what happened. Spare no detail."

And so I did, starting with the arrival of Prince Paris, how my parents extended to him every hospitality, how it soon became apparent to everyone that Paris had fallen in love with my mother.

"And King Menelaus?" Clytemnestra demanded. "Your father noticed none of this?"

I shook my head and stared at my feet in the new sandals my aunt had given me. "None of it," I admitted. "He was blind to it all."

"Fool!" Clytemnestra muttered. "I could have predicted this," she said darkly. "It might have been prevented if Menelaus had simply paid attention." She sighed. "And now he wants help to get Helen back. In my opinion, she made her choice and she should stay in Troy, if they'll keep her."

"Oh, no," I protested. "It wasn't my mother's choice. Paris abducted her. I'm sure of it."

Clytemnestra looked at me with a small smile and shook

her head. "It pains me to tell you this, Hermione, but you're wrong. I know my sister. Helen went willingly."

Her reply upset me deeply, and I burst into tears. If what my aunt said was true, my mother had truly abandoned me. I could not forgive her.

MENELAUS AND AGAMEMNON MADE their plans. First they would send an embassy to King Priam and demand the return of Queen Helen and of the treasure stolen from Sparta.

"And if Priam refuses?" Menelaus asked.

"He's a proud and stubborn old man," Agamemnon said. "It's likely he *will* refuse. And when he does, then we will go to every man who took the oath on the bloody pieces of the horse that Tyndareus sacrificed. I'll remind them that by stealing Helen, Prince Paris has insulted every man in Greece. Who can be confident that his wife will be safe?"

Agamemnon and Menelaus had no doubt that the Greek princes would honor their oath with pledges of ships and warriors. "But first," my father said, "we must consult the oracle at Delphi and ask if she means for us to proceed." Agamemnon agreed.

The two men left soon after, and before the quarter moon had turned full, they had returned, firm in their resolve. "We will begin preparations now," Agamemnon said.

Three days later, my father went off to find Nestor, king of Pylos, to ask for his help. Nestor had seen more than a hundred winters, but even at his great age he was much admired for his bravery and his speaking abilities. Menelaus trusted him to persuade the Greek leaders and soon brought him to Mycenae. How ancient Nestor looked, with a long white beard that nearly covered his chest! Agamemnon would join Nestor and Menelaus in their next journey, to Ithaca to convince Odysseus that he, too, must be a part of this.

"You watch, Hermione," Clytemnestra muttered when the men left for Ithaca. "I know Odysseus, and he's a shrewd one. He and his wife, Penelope, have a little son, Telemachus. Odysseus will not want to leave his comfortable home to make war on Troy, and he's sure to figure out some way to avoid his responsibility."

Clytemnestra was right. Menelaus, Agamemnon, and old Nestor came back from Ithaca with an extraordinary story. Odysseus had heard the three kings were coming, and he had guessed what they wanted. He pretended to be mad, putting on quite a performance, according to my father.

"He dressed as a peasant," Menelaus told us, "and as soon as he heard that we had arrived he began plowing a field with an ox and an ass yoked together, which everyone knows will not work. He sowed handfuls of salt in the furrows instead of seed, and he chattered away in nonsense, pretending not to recognize us. We knew it was an act, but we had to prove it. Penelope was standing nearby with little Telemachus in her arms. I whispered to one of our attendants to seize the infant and set him in the furrow in front of the plow. No sane man would allow his only son to be killed, and as expected, wily Odysseus reined in his mismatched team, giving himself away. Telemachus was spared, and Odysseus has to join in our mission, whether he wants to or not."

The days passed; the moon waxed and waned. King Priam sent his answer: Queen Helen would remain in Troy. Paris would not let her go.

While my father and my uncle traveled through the countryside, assembling their supporters, I stayed in Mycenae with Clytemnestra and my cousins. Iphigenia and I spent our time with our tutors, learning to write and do sums, which I enjoyed much more than my cousin did. Instructed by Agamemnon's round-faced, big-bellied court minstrel, I practiced on the lyre, the instrument my mother had played so skillfully.

When our fathers returned from amassing still more ships and soldiers for their mission to Troy, we welcomed them with feasts and entertainment—I played the lyre, not nearly as well as my mother; Iphigenia sang sweetly with her two sisters, and Orestes recited poetry in a rich, melodious voice that had not yet begun to change from a boy's to a man's.

Odysseus was with them, unhappy to be there, already missing his wife and son. I could guess how he felt: just as Father must have felt. All of us ached for those who should have been with us. I missed my mother. Even more, I missed little Pleisthenes.

"What do you suppose he's doing?" I wondered aloud.

"Probably learning to play knucklebones," Iphigenia said. "Or whatever games Trojan children play."

I didn't want to know what my mother was doing, what her life was like in Troy, if she was happy with Paris, if she thought about me. I tried not to dwell on it, and yet it was almost always on my mind.

Iphigenia's maidservant was fixing my cousin's hair in a new style, arranging little curls across her forehead. "What do you think, Hermione? Do you like it this way? Or is it better the old way, pulled back with combs?"

"Either one is nice," I said, trying hard to hide my envy of her beautiful hair. No one even attempted to do anything clever with my wild red locks.

All day and into the night the men discussed plans for their mission to Troy. I preferred to sit and listen to their talk when I could no longer bear to be around Iphigenia and her hairstyles and carnation-scented perfumes and cosmetics and clothes. Or her questions about whether or not I had become a woman yet. I had not. That bothered me enough without being asked about it continually.

I usually felt more at ease with her brother, Orestes. And since Orestes liked to sit with the men in their planning sessions, I often sat nearby — quietly, and out of the way, of course. Greek women were not usually included in such discussions, but since I was not yet "a woman," as Iphigenia constantly reminded me, no one objected. They might not have even noticed that I was there. Menelaus, as I have pointed out, was not the most observant person. And now he was especially distracted. It had been months since we'd walked together into the countryside and we'd talked about the lives of the gods and goddesses of Mount Olympus.

The two kings pored over maps of Greece and had scribes keep an accounting of which princes had pledged to join the mission and who had yet to be persuaded, calculating how many ships and soldiers each would provide. Menestheus, who'd replaced Theseus, my mother's childhood abductor, as king of Athens, pledged fifty ships. The king of Cyprus sent a handsome breastplate for Agamemnon and a promise of fifty ships. One by one the pledges came from all around Greece.

I happened to be present when they talked about Achilles.

"Calchas has already foretold that we can't defeat Troy without the help of brave Achilles," Agamemnon reminded Menelaus. Calchas was a seer for whom the men had great respect. And they had even more profound respect for Achilles, son of Peleus, the king of Phthia, home of the Myrmidons, the fiercest warriors in all of Greece. There was a rumor that Achilles' mother, Thetis, the sea goddess, didn't want her son to join the mission to Troy, knowing that he would not return alive, and she was ready to go to unusual lengths to stop him.

"I'll talk to him," old Nestor told Menelaus. "You know how

persuasive I am." He turned to Odysseus. "And you'll come with me, my friend. We'll have Achilles' agreement in no time, I assure you."

White-bearded Nestor and short-legged Odysseus set off together and a number of days later returned with Achilles' promise to lead his army of Myrmidons to Troy. His cousin and closest companion, Patroclus, would be with him.

The plans were ready. Ships would gather at Aulis, a wide beach in a large bay between two rocky peninsulas and sheltered by steep cliffs. Father showed me the crude map he'd drawn. With his finger he traced the route they'd follow from Aulis, sailing across the Chief Sea to Troy.

"We must pray that Aeolus sends us strong winds," Father said. "We can be there in three days."

THE LEAVE-TAKING WAS VERY hard. Iphigenia and her older sisters, Electra and Chrysothemis, were weeping. Orestes strutted around, proud to count himself among the men leaving home to go to war, though he was barely thirteen. I asked to go too and was laughed at by everyone. Orestes laughed even harder than the rest. "Girls don't go to war! They do not fight!"

"You're wrong about that," I said. "The slave women are going! Men can't be away from home without women servants. No one is asking them to put on armor and carry a spear."

But Menelaus didn't laugh at me. He patted my red curls and

smiled fondly. "I need you to stay here and wait for me, daughter," he said. "And I promise that I will bring your mother home again."

"You swear it?" I asked tearfully.

"I swear it, Hermione."

I believed him.

Gathering at Aulis

MY AUNT, MY GIRL cousins, and I accompanied the men from Mycenae as far as the walled city of Tiryns and watched them descend the rocky path from the cliff to the beach. I stood alone, apart from the others, hoping that Father would turn and see me. He did not, but Orestes paused and looked back. I raised my hand in farewell, and he waved. I watched until he was lost in the crowd, wondering when I would see him again.

A dozen ships were being loaded with leather shields, bronze helmets, tin greaves to protect their legs, and piles of spears and swords and javelins. When I spotted Father on the deck of one of the ships, I kept my eyes on his flame red hair until the conch shells sounded and the fleet moved away from the beach and started down the coast.

The only one who did not seem in the least distraught at

the departure was my aunt, Clytemnestra. Before the ships were out of sight she called for the porters to bring her chair and carry her back to the palace.

Agamemnon's messengers arrived to report to Queen Clytemnestra that the first of the promised ships had arrived at Aulis, with more gathering there daily from all around Greece. But the king of Cyprus, who had agreed to send fifty ships, instead sent just one real ship and forty-nine miniature ships with little clay figures representing their crews. Agamemnon, we learned, called upon the god Apollo to avenge the insult. Apollo did so, killing the king, whose fifty shamed daughters then threw themselves into the sea.

But others made up for the deceit. King Idomeneus of Crete pledged a hundred ships if Agamemnon agreed to share the command with him, which he did. Great Ajax, said to rival Achilles in courage, strength, and good looks, joined them. Teucer, considered the best archer in Greece, was there. Also present was Little Ajax, small in stature but the best spear thrower and the second-best runner—Achilles was first in that as well. Diomedes brought several great fighters with him, and a man from Rhodes came with nine ships.

Eventually a thousand ships crowded into the bay at Aulis. Provisioning these ships and men was assured by one of Apollo's priests, whose three daughters possessed the power to turn whatever they touched into oil, wine, or grain.

≈≈≈≈

TWO FULL MOONS HAD passed since King Priam of Troy had refused Agamemnon's demand for the return of Queen Helen. Everything was ready. We waited at Mycenae for word that the fleet had left Aulis, bound for Troy. Calchas, the seer, promised to help them steer a steady course by his second sight. But the winds were not favorable for sailing, days passed, and the ships were unable to leave. The men grew impatient, then angry. Something had to be done.

Odysseus brought a message from Agamemnon. I was surprised to see him, and eager to hear what he had to say.

"I bring you great news!" short-legged Odysseus announced. "Achilles has decided to marry before he undertakes this great expedition, and he has asked Agamemnon to offer him the most beautiful of his three daughters as a bride. Someone, I can't say just who, has offended Apollo's sister, Artemis, the archer with golden arrows. A wedding will please the goddess, and she'll call upon the winds to shift."

Clytemnestra's three daughters were astonished and delighted and immediately jealous of one another. "I am surely the one, am I not, Mother?" Chrysothemis asked in her shrill voice. Electra shot her a nasty look. "Don't be stupid, Chrysothemis. You know that Father has sent for me. I'm plainly the choice."

Iphigenia didn't even bother discussing it. She simply began packing her finest necklaces and bracelets, her loveliest gowns, and a shimmering veil. While Iphigenia prepared for a wedding she was certain would happen, the other two argued and insisted that they would all go to Aulis and let Achilles make his own choice. I packed too, not much concerned with gowns and jewels but taking my mother's silver spindle, the only thing I had to remember her by.

In fact, I was very unhappy in Mycenae and was glad to be leaving. I had heard Clytemnestra speaking to Odysseus, calling my mother a slut and a whore who had caused all of this misery. My aunt had made it clear to me in a hundred little ways that she would not have to put up with me if Helen hadn't done what she did. I did not much like either Electra or Chrysothemis, and they had shown no great fondness for me. Iphigenia and I got along tolerably well, but if she was right, she would marry Achilles, and who knew where she would go then.

The next day our procession left Mycenae for Tiryns and the royal ship waiting for us there. I hoped I would not return.

IPHIGENIA, THRILLED AT THE prospect of what she believed was her coming marriage to brave Achilles, chattered endlessly about his strength, his courage, his superb good looks. Her sisters argued with each other, not ready to concede anything. Clytemnestra seemed proud that one of her daughters had been chosen for such an honor; I did wonder, though, how much—if at all—she looked forward to seeing Agamemnon. My mother had told me of how Agamemnon had murdered

Clytemnestra's former husband, King Tantalus. Had she forgiven him after all these years? I wasn't sure I could ever forgive a man who had done such a cruel thing.

After three days we arrived at Aulis. Who could have imagined such a scene! A thousand ships lay at anchor, long wooden vessels coated with black pitch to protect them from salt water and painted with huge, glaring eyes on the bows. Cheers greeted our ship as it maneuvered through the dense crowd, right up to the beach. All three of Agamemnon's daughters stood ready, dressed in their wedding garb, smiling anxiously. Achilles came forward, carrying a garland of flowers for the bride. I knew it must be the great warrior, for he was the tallest and handsomest, and everyone stepped aside in awe of him.

Achilles placed the garland around Iphigenia's neck and led her toward a huge stone altar where a sacrificial animal would be slaughtered. Her beaming mother and two pouting sisters followed. Agamemnon waited at the altar, wearing a robe of deep purple. On his brow a golden diadem gleamed in the afternoon sun.

Odysseus, who'd traveled with us from Mycenae, had melted into the crowd on the beach. Iphigenia and her family were taking part in an elaborate welcoming ceremony. I glanced around, searching for Father, always recognizable by his red hair and beard. I found him standing a short distance away and ran to him.

"I'm glad you're here, Hermione," he said, embracing me,

and steered me away from the crowd. We made our way up the scree at the base of the cliff.

"When will the wedding be held?" I asked. "I want to have a good view of it."

"Soon," he said, but I felt that he was avoiding looking at me.

He chose a flat rock, but I wasn't pleased with it. "I can't see well," I said, and insisted on finding a better spot. Why was he hesitating? Finally I found a satisfactory seat and pulled him down beside me.

"We've been here for many days," Menelaus said, "because the winds haven't been favorable."

"I know. Odysseus told us."

"We've made all the proper sacrifices to Apollo, but his sister, Artemis, is angry with Agamemnon. My foolish brother once bragged that he's as good a shot as she is. You don't say something like that about the goddess of the hunt and not expect her to be angry! To punish him, she's keeping the winds at bay until he does what she demands."

"Odysseus says a wedding will please her. And Achilles has chosen Iphigenia for his bride."

My father was silent—for much too long, I thought. Down on the beach a howl rose from the women, and I jumped up. Father grabbed my hand and pulled me back down beside him. "Artemis has demanded the sacrifice of Iphigenia."

"What?" I cried. "They're going to kill her?"

Father nodded, saying nothing.

I convulsed with horror. "She's not here to marry Achilles? It was all a lie? And her father is letting it happen?"

Father shook his head. "Agamemnon knew Clytemnestra would never allow it. But the other Greek leaders were threatening to abandon the mission and return home. I couldn't let that happen, Hermione! In the end, Agamemnon agreed."

I glared at him furiously. "So you persuaded him to lie!"

"It's more complicated than that, daughter. My brother only pretended to go along with my plan. He sent Odysseus to fetch Iphigenia and her sisters with the promise that one of them would marry Achilles, but at the same time, he sent a coded message to their mother, warning her that it was all a ruse. I learned about the coded message and had the messenger intercepted and killed."

"You made sure the warning never reached Clytemnestra?" I asked incredulously.

"I did." He didn't even sound remorseful.

"I don't understand, Father—how could you do this?"

"Because I want to get your mother back, and this is the only way to do it."

My poor cousin was going to die. My heart filled with loathing of everyone, including my father, who was involved in this terrible deception. Down on the beach the crowd had begun to chant. I shook off my father's hand. "I'm going to be with her," I told him, not bothering to hide my anger. "Don't try to stop me."

I scrambled down off the rocks and raced along the beach toward the excited crowd. I wondered where Orestes was— surely he would try to save his sister! All eyes were focused on the stone altar. Breathing hard, I pushed my way through until I reached the front. Iphigenia lay on the altar, dressed in the lovely gown in which she had planned to be married. Her wrists were bound with a silken cord, and her ankles, too, were tied. I expected her eyes to be rolling in terror—as mine surely would have been—but she looked very calm and at peace.

Agamemnon finished the ritual washing of his hands. Clytemnestra was hysterical, wailing and sobbing, her arms pinned to her sides by two strong guards. "I will put out your eyes, husband!" my aunt cried shrilly. "You will never draw another peaceful breath if you raise your sword by so much as the breadth of a finger! I will kill you, I swear by the gods!" She struggled futilely to free herself, and I was sure she would make good on her threat if she got away from them.

"It is the will of the gods!" Agamemnon shouted, and drew the silver-handled knife that hung beside his sword. "I sacrifice my own daughter because it has been demanded by Artemis. The goddess cannot be denied!"

"Murderer!" Clytemnestra screamed. "I curse you, Agamemnon!"

I rushed forward and seized Iphigenia's bound hands. "I'm with you, dear cousin," I whispered. She turned toward the sound of my voice, but her eyes were glazed as if she'd been drugged, and she seemed not to recognize me. "It's Herm-ione," I told her. "I won't leave you."

The murmuring of the crowd began to grow louder. Voices called out, some shouting that the sacrifice must be made to appease the gods, others shouting that the princess must be allowed to live. Where was Orestes? Surely he would come! But he did not.

As the cacophony grew, strong, handsome Achilles raised his arms and called out, "King Agamemnon!" His command-ing voice brought instant quiet. My uncle, who was holding the knife against his daughter's throat, hesitated. "By what authority have you used my name to deceive this beautiful virgin, your own daughter?" Achilles demanded.

"Artemis requires it," Agamemnon grunted, looking some-what shamefaced. "Otherwise the northeasterly gale will con-tinue, and we will not sail."

"Find some other way to appease her," Achilles said sharply. He turned his attention to Iphigenia and with his own knife cut the silken cords that bound her hands and feet. "You're free, Iphigenia," he said. But the crowd turned against him and roared its disapproval, threatening to stone Achilles if he saved her. A goddess had demanded a sacrifice, and she must be satisfied.

But my cousin didn't move. "I am willing to die for the glory of Greece," she said, gazing up at Achilles with her soft brown eyes. "And for love of you, Achilles." She wasn't going to flee! I thought she was unbelievably brave. I knew that I could never do what she was doing. She closed her eyes and murmured, so softly that I nearly missed her words, "Do what you must do, Father."

Eyes bulging, teeth bared, Agamemnon drew back and swiftly brought the bronze blade to Iphigenia's throat as Clytemnestra unleashed a terrible scream and fainted. A deafening clap of thunder split the air, and the bright sky went blacker than the blackest night. It was as if we had all been struck blind. There was a rush of wind, and when the darkness vanished as suddenly as it had come and the sun again blazed on Agamemnon's killing knife blade, Iphigenia was gone. In her place on the altar lay a hind, a female deer, with an enormous rack of antlers. The sacrificial knife fell on the beast's throat, blood spurted in a red fountain, and the crowd gasped.

One of Artemis's priests stepped forward and in a high, reedy voice addressed the astonished crowd. "Princess Iphigenia has been spared," he told them. "She has been wrapped in a cloud and taken away by the great goddess to serve as her priestess in the land of the Taurians."

Immediately the northeasterly gale shifted. The black ships would sail.

A Thousand Ships

THE BEACH AT AULIS thrummed with excitement, and I was swept into the activity swirling all around me. Many men came to the altar where the dead hind lay, touched her great rack, and dipped their fingers in the animal's still-warm blood. Clytemnestra swayed, clutching the arms of Electra and Chrysothemis, the two daughters still left to her, both wearing stunned expressions. Agamemnon, too, looked stunned, but also relieved. I could no longer locate my father.

I turned my attention to Achilles, handsomer by far than Paris, in my opinion, with a hard-muscled chest and the long, sinewy legs of a fleet-footed runner, masses of pale locks falling over a wide brow, and finely chiseled features. He moved with confidence and authority. He had acted nobly, trying to save my cousin's life. I had already decided what I was going to do. I would not return to Mycenae with my aunt and her two daughters. Iphigenia was gone to Tauris, a land that lay far to the north. Orestes, who had been restrained while his sister lay on the altar, would sail with Agamemnon. There was nothing at all for me in Mycenae.

I would go to Troy.

I intended to smuggle myself onboard Father's ship. I was angry with my father for betraying Iphigenia, but still I wanted to be with him. When it was too late to turn back, I would reveal myself to him. He would be happy to see me, I was sure of that. Perhaps a little angered at what I had done, but proud of me too. We would forgive each other.

But I had no idea where my father was in that noisy, churning crowd, or how to find his ship among the thousand.

Achilles glanced at me briefly. There was no reason for the great warrior to notice me, but I reached out my hand, and his gaze returned and rested on me.

"Who are you?" he asked, frowning.

"Princess Hermione, daughter of Queen Helen and King Menelaus. I'm looking for my father's ship," I said.

I knew at once I'd made a mistake. I should not have given myself away. I should have made up a lie, told Achilles that I was a servant. Now it was too late. He would no doubt offer to take me to my father, who would then turn me over to my aunt and insist that I return to Mycenae as planned. A boy trailing behind Achilles stared at me sullenly. He bore a strong resemblance to the great warrior—the same pale locks, the same chiseled features. I wondered if he was Achilles' son.

Achilles was laughing. "I should have known—those bright

red curls!" At that moment I cursed my red curls. What man could ever love a girl with such hair! "Come along, then, and we'll find your father," he said, and continued striding along the beach, assuming I suppose that I would follow him. And I did. The boy ignored me.

Up ahead I glimpsed my father. I ran to catch up with Achilles and tugged at his tunic, thanked him, and assured him I knew my way and no longer needed his help. He nodded then, smiling his beautiful smile, and he and the boy turned away.

Enterprising people from nearby villages had set up a marketplace on the beach and were selling all manner of things: baskets of bread, piles of vegetables, sandals, clay pots, scarves dyed bright colors . . . *scarves!* Exactly what I needed! I slipped into the market, trying to be inconspicuous. But I had nothing with which to pay, except my mother's silver spindle, and that was not a fair trade.

And so I stole a scarf so dull and ugly that I was probably doing the merchant a favor, getting rid of one that no woman could possibly want to buy—or so I told myself. I ducked out of sight, threw the dun-colored scarf over my hair, and sidled away from the market and onto the crowded beach. I hurried toward the ships. Men were clambering aboard, and I spotted Father at the stern of his vessel, deep in conversation. I studied those belonging to my father's fleet, trying to decide if it was better for me to be on his gleaming new lead ship, where he would soon find me, or to smuggle myself aboard one of the smaller ones, where he would not realize I was there until it was too late to send me back.

My decision was made for me. A group of women were carrying bundles, their last-minute purchases at the market, onto one of the small ships. An aged crone grabbed my elbow. "Why are you standing there gawking, girl?" she demanded. "Best you come along with the rest of the lot, if you expect to find a decent place to sleep."

I let her shove me up a rope ladder and into the hold of an old ship, battered and bad smelling. Then I realized that all of those onboard, except for a crew of rough-looking sailors, were women and girls. Slowly it dawned on me that they were concubines.

I needed to get off this ship.

It was too late. The crone had already taken charge of me. She yanked off my dun-colored scarf and grinned when she saw my red hair. I sighed. I'd been discovered.

"Ha!" she cackled. "I'll wager you're the daughter of King Menelaus himself, aren't you?"

I nodded, miserably.

"And who's your mother? Eh? Afraid to tell us?"

The other women had dropped their bundles and were staring at me. I opened my mouth to answer. Was it not obvious that I was Helen's daughter? Who else could I be? "Why, I'm the daughter of Queen Helen!" I said, and was greeted with roars of laughter.

One of the women stepped forward and flounced around me, snapping her fingers and swinging her hips. "We all know who your father is, but we're not so sure about your mother! It could be almost any one of us, couldn't it?" she asked, grinning at the others, who responded with raucous laughter, "Oh, yes! Any one of us!"

Hot with embarrassment, I realized many of these concubines had lain with my father. My red hair gave me away as the daughter of Menelaus, but nothing about me hinted that I was the daughter of Helen, the most beautiful woman in the world. They assumed that I was the king's bastard child. Why else would I be there among them?

The crone stepped back and looked me up and down, pinching me here and there. "Ay!" she cried. "You're not even a woman yet, are you, my girl?"

I shook my head.

"Well, I have no idea who sent you to travel with us, for you aren't old enough for this." The other women and girls stood around, smirking, watching to see how this would play out. "I should have you put ashore," she said thoughtfully. "Let somebody else worry about you."

"I beg you not to put me ashore!" I implored. "I must go to Troy!"

The old woman's expression softened. "All right," she said. "But don't be a bother, do you hear? You'll have to look after yourself. I don't have time to put up with whining children."

"I won't whine," I promised.

"You'll be expected to help however you're needed."

"I will," I said, though I had no idea what sort of help would be expected of me. I had no knowledge of any kind of duties. I'd always had my own servants to help me dress, fasten my sandals, empty my slop jar, wash my chitons in the river, carry my sleeping fleeces out to air in the sunshine. Now I could be required to perform these chores for others.

While we talked, there was shouting out on deck, and I felt the movement of the ship beneath my feet. We were on our way to Troy.

EVERYONE WAS IN A fine mood. Aeolus, the god of wind, puffed his cheeks and blew steadily, filling the great square sails of ships on all sides of us. The rowers kept a steady rhythm and the ship moved rapidly over the dark waters, navigating the narrow strait between the mainland and the island of Euboea. At the close of the first day our old ship pulled into a cove near the town of Styra, and the townspeople paddled out to greet the ships, bringing us food and drink. As darkness fell, the crone—her name was Marpessa—led me into a cramped, rank-smelling space behind racks of amphoras, two-handled clay jars holding supplies of oil, wine, and grain and bound together with rope.

"We'll sleep here," Marpessa told me. "The men don't bother me—it's been many years since they have—and they won't bother you as long as you're here with me."

I understood, and I was grateful. I slept curled in a rough

woolen robe with no soft fleece beneath me, my head on my lumpy leather sack. It was not at all comfortable, and the old crone snored loudly, but I was too tired, too drained from the excitement of the day, to care.

We sailed around the southern tip of Euboea the next day and started up the eastern coast of Greece. Soon, we were told, we would turn away from the safety of the shoreline and begin the long voyage across the Chief Sea. Many had lost their way here, wandering aimlessly from one small island to the next, until they reached their destination or were lost forever. I thought of Zethus and wondered if he'd found his way home.

While we were camped on a beach at sunset, a strange ship was sighted, heading directly toward our fleet. No one recognized it. The anchor stone was let down, and a small boat brought a single passenger to shore. It didn't take long for the rumors to reach us: the beautiful young man who leaped gracefully from the boat and walked confidently toward Father's ship had been identified. He was Corythus, son of Oenone and Paris, born before Paris abandoned Oenone for my mother. Insanely jealous of Queen Helen, Oenone had decided to betray the Trojans and had sent her son to guide the Greek ships to Troy. Menelaus accepted the offer. Oenone would have her revenge.

The long journey began, with Corythus's ship leading the way. When the winds dropped, the rowers took up their oars, and the swift black ships flew on. There were stops on the

islands of Skyros and Lemnos and Imbros to replenish supplies of fresh water. We were now very close to Troy, but we
would make one more island stop, this one on Tenedos. A
lookout at the top of the mast shouted that he could see the
great city of Troy in the distance.

The ships were beached, the women's ship at a discreet distance from Father's and those belonging to the leaders of the
mission. When darkness fell, the old crone marked the location of our battered vessel with a torch, and the men found
their way to the concubines who had come on this voyage to
serve their pleasure. At night I heard their thumps and cries,
but Marpessa threw her cloak over me, and they didn't know I
was there.

From these men we learned what to expect. Our destination was close, they said, but we would lay by on Tenedos for
a time and wait. Meanwhile, King Menelaus, accompanied by
Odysseus, would enter through the gates of Troy, meet with
King Priam, and make one last demand for the peaceful return
of Queen Helen.

"May it go well with them," the women said, gossiping
about it among themselves.

"May it go well with them," I murmured, always at the edge
of their conversations.

The women passed the days with singing and arranging one
another's hair and sleeping, for the nights were busy with their
duties of pleasing the men.

Toward sunset at the end of five anxious days we sighted my father's royal boat returning from Troy. We strained to see if Queen Helen was aboard and guessed that she was not, for there were no sounds of celebration. That night our women heard from the men who'd accompanied Menelaus what had happened.

"At first we were treated respectfully," the men reported. "We were given food and lodging at the house of one of King Priam's chief councilors. But the meeting with King Priam came to nothing. He refused to return our queen. Not just Paris but Priam and all of the Trojans have fallen in love with Helen, and they're determined to keep her. They adore the beautiful Greek queen! A great crowd gathered outside the councilor's house, threatening to murder us all. But our host is a good man, and he refused to turn us over to them. Most of the Trojans drew back, grumbling, but the angriest refused to leave and threatened us. We didn't feel safe until we'd put a distance between ourselves and Troy."

I wondered what fate would come to Corythus, the son of Paris, who had guided us there. His ship had disappeared. Certainly he would not be able to show his face in Troy again.

Our women were kept busy that night, for the men had taken too much wine, and they sang and shouted and boasted loudly of their valor. Marpessa feared that they would find me.

"What will happen now?" I asked Marpessa from my hiding place among the clay jars.

"War," she said. "The men want war. Listen to them! They haven't come all this distance to turn around and sail back to Greece without Queen Helen."

On the Beach

IN THE EARLY MORNING darkness our ships moved silently away from the island of Tenedos and were rowed the short distance to Troy. From the deck of the women's ship I gazed up at the great citadel silhouetted against the brightening sky. The enormous fortress stood surrounded by stone and earthen walls and guarded by watchtowers and massive wooden gates. Below it sprawled the rest of the city, so much larger than Sparta, larger even than Mycenae. Somewhere up there, in a magnificent palace with walls hung with silk and tables laid with golden plates, slept my mother and my little brother.

Soon they'll be back with us, I told myself. *Soon we'll all go home to Sparta.*

The ships drew up within sight of the city walls. I planned to slip away and run along the beach until I found Father's ship. I was grateful to Marpessa for protecting me from the drunken, lecherous men who visited the concubines on our ship, but now I wanted Menelaus to know that I was there.

But things didn't go as I planned. The war had begun.

When the conch shells were blown, the first of our courageous warriors jumped from his ship onto the beach and rushed toward the city walls. Trojan guards in the watchtowers saw this. A rock struck the warrior squarely on the temple. Blood gushing, he fell, but even before his body hit the ground, a second figure made a tremendous leap—it could only have been brave Achilles—seized the rock, and flung it back with such deadly aim and force that the Trojan it struck was lifted from his feet and thrown against the wall. Hundreds of Trojans swarmed down from the walls, throwing rocks at the invaders. Achilles hurled rock after rock, and one Trojan after another fell dead.

The fierce Myrmidons followed close behind Achilles. All day the battle raged. At sunset the fighting stopped, and men from both sides came out to carry their dead from the beach. That evening our men ate and drank, then came to visit our women for the comfort they needed.

The next day was the same, and the day after. So this was war. I was thrilled by the bravery of our men, sickened by the suffering and death.

Then I heard that a prediction had been made by Calchas, the seer. He prophesied that the war would continue for nine years. In the tenth year, he said, Troy would fall.

Ten years!

I was still only a child. If Calchas was right, I would be a grown woman when the fighting ended. What would this mean? Ten years spent here on this beach, my mother with Paris on the other side of the great stone wall, the men of Troy sworn to keep her there, the Greeks just as determined to get her back, both sides fighting and dying, day after day, year after year?

It was Fate, Calchas said. One could not argue with Fate. Nothing would change it.

When the rope ladder was lowered for the men to climb up that evening, I slipped away from Marpessa, crept down the ladder, and felt my way along the beach. Slaves had hauled up the pitch-blackened ships and wedged timbers along the sides to steady them. The ships loomed fierce in the pale moonlight. I paused near each one and listened for the sound of my father's voice.

But it was Achilles' voice I heard. "Hector's is the death I desire most," Achilles was saying. "He's a brave man, they say, and a good fighter. But I will have him, Pyrrhus. You watch!"

"Hector is brave, but you're braver, Father," I heard a young boy reply. "He's strong, but you're stronger!"

Quite a pair of braggarts, I thought, and decided this Pyrrhus must be the boy I'd seen with Achilles at Aulis.

Farther on up the beach Odysseus could be heard telling someone about his wife, Penelope, and his little son, Telemachus. "I miss them so much!" he said. "But I worry. If one is to believe the prophecy of Calchas, by the time I reach home again, my boy will not even recognize me."

At another ship an officer was playing at dice with his friends. "I invented them, you know," he boasted. "Entertainment for a game of chance, but also useful for predicting the future." The men laughed, and I was so close I could hear the rattle of the bones as the men shook them and threw them on a flat stone.

I was stumbling with weariness when at last I recognized the voice I most wanted to hear: my father's. Menelaus and Agamemnon were discussing how they would mount their attack on the citadel, which was defended by so many fighters and fortified with such thick walls, while our own ships lay exposed on the beach.

"We must build our own defenses at once," Menelaus said.

I huddled in the darkness, careful not to attract the attention of the watchman on deck, while I listened to the two kings outlining their plan. Our men would build a wall of timber, stones, and mud, with gates just wide enough to let our chariots pass through. Others would dig a wide, deep trench beyond the palisade and sink sharp stakes in it.

"No Trojan can pass those defenses," they agreed, and clapped each other on the shoulder.

I waited until Agamemnon strode off toward his own ship. Father yawned and turned to climb up to the deck. "Father," I said.

He stopped, grasping the rope ladder, squinting into the darkness. "Who speaks?"

I stepped out of the shadows. "It is I, Hermione." I expected him to rush toward me, to fold me into his arms. But he didn't. He merely stared at me.

"What god has taken the form of my daughter?" he asked.

"Neither god nor goddess, Father," I said, laughing, and stepped close enough to touch. "See? It's truly your own Hermione."

He pulled me close to his chest, and I felt his bushy beard against my cheek. His tears dropped on my face as he held me at arm's length to study me before pulling me close again. "But how . . . ?" he stammered. "Who . . . ?"

"I couldn't bear to go back to Mycenae. And I wanted to be with you, and to help you get my mother back." I explained then how I had boarded the women's ship at Aulis.

"And you've been on the women's ship all this time?" he asked incredulously.

"I stay with the old crone, Marpessa. She's been very kind to me. She makes sure the men who visit the women don't bother me."

"And you have not been defiled?" he asked.

"I'm not yet a woman," I said, embarrassed to have to confess it to my father.

"I thought not. But they didn't find out who you are?"

"I told them I was the daughter of Queen Helen, but they only laughed at me. They think I'm your bastard."

Father grunted but made no comment.

"You will not return to that ship," he said firmly. "You will stay with me. I have servants who will see that you're properly cared for."

"Will I have a sleeping fleece?" I asked. That was the one hardship I'd found difficult to endure. At home I'd always had clean fleeces for my bed, but on the women's ship I'd had to share Marpessa's ragged and smelly pile of empty grain sacks.

"You will have as many fleeces as you wish, my dear Hermione," Father assured me. "Now come with me."

He climbed the rope ladder to the deck of his ship, and I followed wearily. The watchman glanced at me curiously as Father led me through the narrow passage between the rowers' benches to his barren quarters. "You will stay here for the present," he told me. "I'll sleep among the men. You have nothing to fear."

"I'm not afraid," I told my father, smiling up at him. I had forgiven him for sacrificing Iphigenia, and I was happy to be there with him and gave no thought to the danger.

The next morning the men gathered on the beach and made offerings to the gods. Then they strapped the metal greaves to their legs, donned their bronze helmets, picked up their leather shields made of layers of bulls' hides, gathered their sharpened spears, and prepared to fight.

Book II
The War

The Tenth Year

CALCHAS WAS CORRECT. THE war dragged on and on, year after year, with heavy losses on both sides, no clear winners, and countless souls hurled down to the House of Death. During these long years I witnessed the behavior of the gods—some favoring the Greeks, others the Trojans, sometimes switching sides unexpectedly. Every winter the fighting was suspended, as is customary, and our men spent their time improving our fortifications. Each commander lived in a well-made tent or a hut built of hewn fir with a thatched roof, surrounded by a cluster of the soldiers' rude shelters. The Greek encampment on the beach had taken on an air of permanence.

With the arrival of spring in the tenth year of the war, the fighting was about to begin again. I was so weary of it! Surely the men must have been weary of it too. Didn't they long for their homeland, yearn for their wives and children? Yet it had been going on for so long that war had become the only life they knew.

I was twenty now, no longer a child, and I lived comfortably in my own tent with several women servants, but sometimes I missed the company of the concubines. Without them, it was much harder to find out what was going on in other parts of the camp. From time to time I sent one or two of my servants to Marpessa, now old and bent and nearly toothless, and in exchange Marpessa sent a couple of her women to stay with me for a few nights and to pass on whatever rumors they'd heard from the men. Father, consumed by the war, had no knowledge of this.

Achilles, I was told, had grown increasingly restless. He regularly led his Myrmidons on raiding parties, attacking cities allied with Troy, taking prisoners and seizing whatever loot was at hand. The list of his conquests was long: Lesbos, Phocaea, Colophon, Smyrna, and many more. It was the custom to enslave the women who were taken captive. One of his captives was a beautiful girl named Astynome, the daughter of Chryses, a priest of Apollo on the island of Sminthos. Astynome's father had sent her to the city of Lyrnessus to attend the feast of Artemis, assuming she would be safe there. But Lyrnessus was one of the cities attacked by Achilles, and Astynome was anything but safe. Another of his captives was Hippodameia, bride of King Mynes. On the very day of the wedding, Achilles killed the bridegroom and the bride's father, mother, and three brothers, and seized Hippodameia. Achilles returned to the Greek encampment with the two captives. Astynome was awarded to Agamemnon. Achilles took Hippodameia for himself.

Both girls were about my age. Astynome was dark haired with sparkling eyes and skin the color of honey. Hippodameia was blond and blue eyed, nearly as tall as Achilles, and willowy. Both were intelligent and good tempered, but their eyes were filled with terror, and my heart went out to them. I understood well that if the Greeks were defeated, the Trojans would take *me* captive, and my fate would surely be as dire as theirs.

While the men were caught up in their ugly business of war, I became friends with the captives. Sometimes we went to bathe in the springs near the River Scamander. The river flowed down from Mount Ida, across the Trojan plain, and into the Hellespont, the narrow passage between two seas. One spring bubbled with hot water, the other with cold, no matter the season. In pools scooped out in the hollow rocks the Trojan women also came to bathe. Our washerwomen brought our clothes here; theirs did too. Each side secretly watched the other.

Every few days I walked to Achilles' tents at the southern end of the beach to visit Hippodameia. I was struck by the complete lack of real comfort there. Achilles' were the tents of warriors. His son, Pyrrhus, was now a man; his mother was the daughter of the king of Skyros, in whose court Achilles had been sent to live as a child. Now Pyrrhus was one of Achilles' lieutenants. He was nearly as handsome as his father, but spoiled and arrogant, his lip curled in a permanent sneer. Hippodameia and I avoided him.

Agamemnon's luxurious shelters on the north end were entirely different. One day I went there to visit Astynome and found her in tears. I assumed that Agamemnon was the cause of her unhappiness, but I was wrong.

"My father wants to take me home," Astynome said, weeping. "He came for me and offered to pay a huge ransom. But Agamemnon refused and drove him away with cruel words! He told Chryses not to be seen anywhere near the Greek ships."

I nodded sympathetically. "It's the way of war."

"I don't want to go home," Astynome sobbed. "I want to stay here. Agamemnon treats me very well. He tells me that I'm much finer than his wife."

That did not surprise me. I never thought he cared much for Clytemnestra, or she for him.

"My father is praying to Apollo for help," she said. "There will be trouble, I'm sure of it. I'm afraid I'll be sent back, no matter what I say."

As Astynome predicted, magnificent Apollo came storming down from Mount Olympus, shooting his deadly arrows among the Greeks. Apollo's aim was unerring, and hundreds of our soldiers fell dead. The corpses were gathered and burned in fires that blazed night and day. It had become too dangerous to leave the shelters. I no longer visited the springs to bathe in the pools with the captives. We lived in fear of the lethal arrows whipping through the vast encampment.

I was taking refuge with my father when Calchas made his way cautiously to Menelaus's shelter. The seer had been a sturdy white-haired man when we'd left Greece ten years earlier, but now he was an ancient with a straggly white beard and knobby legs as thin as sticks.

Father was deeply agitated. "Nine days of this! It has got to stop," he complained to Calchas. "Apollo is relentless, and he's on the side of that priest, Chryses."

"There is only one solution," Calchas said in a raspy voice. "Agamemnon must send the girl back to her father."

"He won't do it. He says he's entitled to Astynome as the spoils of victory. Besides that, he's grown quite fond of her. She *is* a lovely girl—better looking than Clytemnestra," Menelaus added. "Nicer disposition, too."

"Then you must find him another, someone just as lovely," Calchas advised. "I promise you, Apollo's deadly aim will continue to cost Greek lives until Chryses gets his daughter back."

Father groaned. "All right, then. Let's go talk to Agamemnon. But I'm not confident he can be convinced."

I stepped forward. "I'll come with you," I said. "I know Astynome. We've become friends. Maybe I can help make it easier for both of them."

"Much too dangerous, daughter," said my father, shaking his head. "Stay here."

But Calchas said we could reach Agamemnon's shelters safely if we left at once, and I went with them.

We found Agamemnon and Astynome cozily sharing a goblet of wine. It was plain that Agamemnon did not want guests to intrude on their intimate moment, but he managed a polite welcome, offering us wine. Father brushed aside Agamemnon's hospitable gesture and went straight to the point. "You must return Astynome to her father and stop the killing."

Astynome burst into tears, and I went to comfort her. She pushed me away—rudely, I thought, but I couldn't blame her. None of this was her doing. Agamemnon flatly refused, as we expected.

But then Calchas began to speak in his high, old man's voice. "There's no hope of a Greek victory against Troy if Apollo continues to cut down our soldiers with his lethal arrows."

Slowly, Agamemnon's stubbornness ebbed away, until he was forced to admit that there really was no other choice.

"Send her to her father without delay," Calchas piped, "with the most generous gifts you can find for Chryses, and animals to sacrifice to win Apollo's favor."

Agamemnon threw up his hands. "All right," he said grudgingly. "I value this girl more than I do my wife, but I'll give her back if that's the best thing for my people." He turned to Astynome, who clung to his arm, weeping. "Go, then, dear love," he said, more tenderly than I'd ever heard him speak, and patted her hand. He glanced at me pleadingly, and I took her elbow and coaxed her away.

Astynome was sobbing hysterically while I did what I could to calm her. Unfortunately, Agamemnon failed to wait until we were out of earshot before exclaiming loudly, "This is a disgrace to me! An insult! I must have compensation for the loss of Astynome. Bring me another prize, Menelaus. I want Hippodameia."

Astynome heard and howled even louder.

"He's saying that because he's angry," I whispered, trying to console her. "He just wants to put proud Achilles in his place."

I led Astynome to my hut. She was to stay with me while arrangements were made for a ship to return her to the island of Sminthos. For three days she never stopped weeping. Apollo, seeing that efforts were being made in good faith to send her home, ceased shooting arrows at our men. But that was not the end of our troubles. It was only the beginning.

The Warrior's Prize

ON THE FOURTH MORNING after Agamemnon agreed to send Astynome home, he dispatched two heralds to inform Achilles that he must now surrender Hippodameia to him. With the heralds went Agamemnon's son, my cousin Orestes. And Orestes, having observed the close friendship I'd developed with the two captive girls, asked me to accompany him to Achilles' tents. I leaped at the chance.

Once a shy boy with a sweet smile and a love of poetry, Orestes had grown into a handsome young man with broad shoulders, strong arms, and well-muscled calves. He served as a lieutenant under his father's command and was known among the men as a skillful archer. His smile was as winning as ever, and when he recited poetry or sang the songs of our faraway country, my heart sang too. Though often in each other's company, we were seldom alone. Nevertheless, I knew that I loved him.

I probably fell in love with Orestes when we were children. While we were mere infants, our grandfather, Tyndareus, king of Sparta, had promised me to Orestes. After Tyndareus died, my mother told me about the promise he'd made. She said she'd speak of it again when I was older and ready for marriage, but she left with Paris before we had that conversation. It was something I had always known and taken for granted but hadn't thought about much. Until now.

Many nights I dreamed of becoming Orestes' wife. But we were at war. Death lay all around us. This was not the time to speak of marriage, or even to think of a life together. Yet I *did* think of it, imagining Orestes' lips on mine, my fingers tracing his smooth brow. I wanted to believe that he loved me, too, though we had never said the words. Our grandfather's pledge had not been mentioned. I wasn't sure he even knew of it.

Instead of the future, we talked about the past, things we remembered from our childhood. Pleisthenes was always on my mind, and I confided to Orestes how deeply I yearned to see my little brother again. Orestes spoke often about his best friend, Pylades, son of his father's friend, King Strophius, and fondly recalled the months they'd spent together as children in Krisa at the foot of Mount Parnassus. He'd give anything, he'd told me, to have Pylades fighting by his side at Troy.

"Pylades was ready to come," Orestes said now, as we walked along the beach toward Achilles' tents. The dark sea was like a wild beast that day, the surf hammering the shore. "His father was willing. But his mother made offerings to

Artemis, and the goddess of the hunt saw to it that Pylades was gored in the thigh while hunting wild boar. Now he must walk with a stick."

We'd reached the camp of the Myrmidons and paused to consider our next step. "I'll talk to Achilles," Orestes said. "You see to Hippodameia. I have no idea how she'll feel about making this change."

"I'll do as you ask," I said, "but I *do* have an idea of how she'll feel. I've spent enough time with her to know that she's fallen in love with Achilles. She won't want to leave him."

"Astynome fell in love with Agamemnon too. I would not have expected the captives to fall in love with their captors," Orestes said. "Would you?"

"Who can predict such things?" I had first met Achilles when I went with Iphigenia to what she thought was to be her wedding and nearly turned out to be her death. He was rugged, powerful, fearless—and beautiful. Nine years later, he hadn't changed. He was still all the things that Iphigenia had loved and now Hippodameia loved too. "What I can predict, though, is that Achilles is going to be angry."

"'Furious' is probably more accurate." Orestes sighed. "All right, let's do what we were sent to do." He signaled for the heralds to announce our presence.

Achilles burst from his tent. "Why have you come here?" he demanded, his face close to Orestes'. "What do you want?"

Orestes held his ground and didn't allow Achilles to force

him to step back. "I've been sent by my father, King Agamemnon, to speak to you on a personal matter."

Achilles turned his burning glare on me. "And you, Hermione? Why are *you* here?"

I managed a weak smile. "To visit with Hippodameia."

He gestured with his thumb. "Go in, then," he ordered.

Hippodameia seemed glad to see me. I suggested that we go out walking. I wanted to get her away from the rage that was sure to erupt at any moment. She was agreeable, and we were preparing to leave—but first she wanted to show me the veil she'd almost finished weaving. I had acted too slowly, and now it was too late.

"I refuse!" we heard Achilles roar. "She is mine, and I will not give her up!" Every word was clear.

Hippodameia's eyes widened, and she looked at me for an explanation. Orestes' words were muffled, but his tone sounded calm and reasonable. "What are they talking about?" she whispered.

Before I could answer, there was another roar from outside the warrior's tent. "I will keep her, and I will take that message to Agamemnon myself!"

"It's me they're talking about, isn't it?" Hippodameia said, her voice unsteady.

I nodded. "Agamemnon has agreed to send Astynome back to her father, Chryses, to stop Apollo from killing our men. Now Agamemnon wants you in Astynome's place."

"I won't go," Hippodameia said, suddenly stubborn.

"King Agamemnon demands it."

"He can demand whatever he wishes." She spoke calmly, her voice strong with resolve. "I won't go. I'll kill myself."

I gaped at her, stunned. There were no tears in her lovely blue eyes, no hysterics in her voice. I believed she would do as she threatened. Afraid that she might do something terrible right then—were there any knives around, a sword that she might plunge into her own breast?—I seized Hippodameia's soft white hands.

"No! No!" I cried. "Please listen to me, dear friend, and come with me now. Agamemnon will be kind to you, I'm certain of that. Astynome doesn't want to leave either, and I'm sure something can be arranged. If you want to stay with Achilles, you'll be returned to him, just as soon as Chryses agrees to allow his daughter to come back. Then everything will be right again."

I continued coaxing and pleading, having no idea if the peaceful solution I promised her was possible.

Achilles stormed into Hippodameia's quarters, followed by Orestes. "Go! Take her, then!" Achilles growled, his face dark with murderous fury. "But pay the price for it as you lose your greatest warrior!" He rushed out again without even a word to poor Hippodameia.

Orestes and I exchanged worried glances. His lips were pressed in a tight line. "We must go, then," he said. "I'm sorry, Hippodameia."

"I told her that a solution could be found," I put in.

Orestes hesitated. "Maybe so."

We began the long walk up the beach to Agamemnon's tent, Hippodameia between us, her head down and her footsteps lagging. "This must be very painful for you," I ventured, wondering if she was still thinking of killing herself and what could be done to keep her from it.

"It's in the hands of the gods," she said, staring at the ground. "And one can't defy the gods. I was captured on my wedding day, still a virgin. I expected the worst when Achilles brought me here, the spoils of war who meant no more to him than anything else he had seized. But he has treated me with great kindness. I know that he cares for me, even if he doesn't love me yet."

"But you believe that someday he will?"

"It's my greatest hope! The person he loves more than anyone, more even than his son, Pyrrhus, is his cousin, Patroclus," Hippodameia said. "Achilles eats with Patroclus, drinks with him, fights beside him, stays up talking with him throughout the night. Patroclus, too, is kindhearted—he visited me daily and consoled me when I found myself alone and a prisoner of the man who murdered everyone in my family. He says that Achilles is sure to fall in love with me and will someday want to make me his wife. Patroclus promised to provide our wedding feast with days of singing and dancing and roasted meats and fine wine and honey cakes, after the war ends."

Hippodameia smiled, thinking of the glorious future that

would one day be hers. She described such a lovely scene that for her sake I wanted it to be true. "I'm sure Agamemnon won't harm you in any way." Even as I spoke the words, I hoped I was right. I was never quite sure *how* my uncle would behave.

Before we reached the king's tents, Achilles, swift runner that he was, raced past us, shouting for Agamemnon. A crowd gathered quickly; I spotted Pyrrhus on the edge of it, sneering as usual. Orestes and I with Hippodameia between us made our way through the crowd toward the king's tent, the largest and most luxurious in the Greek encampment. Agamemnon emerged with brow furrowed, fists on hips, hard jaw jutting. "You called for me, Achilles?"

The argument quickly reached white heat. Agamemnon demanded his prize *now,* and Achilles shouted that Agamemnon—"the greediest man alive, armored in shamelessness"—must wait, because all the plunder seized from the conquered had already been divided among the warriors and could not be reclaimed.

Agamemnon's eyes blazed with anger. "Do not dare to cheat me, Achilles! You, the most violent man alive!"

Achilles shot back, "I have no reason to be here on this miserable beach! The Trojans never did me any harm! No, I followed you, to please you, to fight for you and win your honor back." Achilles turned abruptly to my father, who stood helplessly to one side. "And you, Menelaus, you dog face! What do *you* care? You look neither right nor left but seize everything you want, and now you're threatening to take away my lovely girl, the prize I deserve!"

Achilles wheeled again on Agamemnon. "Whenever my men sack some rich Trojan city, they are the ones who take the brunt of the savage fighting. But when it's time to divide the plunder, you step forward and seize the lion's share, and I return to my ships clutching some pitiable scrap, some pittance you've allowed me. Well, I've had enough! I'm taking my men and my ships and returning to Phthia."

"Go, then!" Agamemnon bellowed. "I won't beg you to stay! You are less than nothing to me."

Achilles reached for his sword and whipped it from its sheath. Orestes leaped forward to stop the flashing blade. Pyrrhus smiled, a nasty look in his eyes. I gasped and cried out, "No!"

In that instant Zeus's daughter Athena in her helmet and breastplate swept down from the heavens. The goddess of wisdom and war seized Achilles by his hair and ordered him to put up his sword. "Stop fighting, both of you," I heard her say. In the same instant she was gone, soaring back to Mount Olympus. Everyone looked puzzled. It all happened in less than a heartbeat. Had I really seen her?

Achilles sheathed his sword, but his anger still boiled. He roared insults, calling Agamemnon "a coward with dog's eyes" and "a fawn's heart who spends his time in his tents instead of on the field of battle." Nestor emerged from the crowd and tried to talk sense to the two wrathful men, but neither wanted to listen to the old sage's words.

Achilles stalked off. Agamemnon ordered a fast ship to be hauled down to the sea with gifts for Chryses and ten sacred bulls for a sacrifice to the gods. Odysseus took the helm, and beautiful Astynome, face streaked with tears, stepped aboard. Twenty of the strongest oarsmen sped the priest's daughter on her way.

Agamemnon turned to Hippodameia, who waited nervously nearby, and greeted his new mistress. "Welcome, my lovely girl," he said in a tone as sweet as honey. Hippodameia smiled up at him with a quivering lip, her head held high, and followed a servant to her new quarters.

And Achilles, the mightiest of warriors, striding back to his tents in the thickening darkness, vowed to fight no more. Pyrrhus turned and looked back, his burning eyes fixed on me.

The Battle for Queen Helen

AGAMEMNON AND MENELAUS sacrificed a fat ox, praying to the gods and tossing out handfuls of barley as an offering. Up and down the beach in every part of the Greek encampment animals were slain and butchered, the meat stripped from the bones, wrapped in fat and pierced with spits, and roasted over blazing fires. A feast was laid out.

"Take food and wine now," their commanders ordered, "then take your rest. When Dawn first spreads her golden cloak over the fields, ready your chariots and your battalions. Agamemnon will lead the fight."

I watched them pour a few drops of wine on the ground as an offering to Zeus before they drank, and I saw them eat and drink and then go off to sleep. I hoped that Orestes would come to me, that we could share a few moments, have a few words together before the first great battle of the new season. We had not seen much of each other since the preparations began. But he didn't come, and though I longed to see him, I understood why. He would be with the other men.

The next day the earth thundered beneath the pounding feet of thousands of men armored in bronze, ready to fight and die on the great open plain outside the walls of Troy. I watched them go. Our duty as women was to prepare for the return of the victorious, care for the wounded, and mourn the dead. I was proud of our courageous warriors but nearly sick with worry. I worried for the safety of my father and Agamemnon. I worried even more for Orestes, an expert archer, still young but in command of men much older than himself. And I thought of the Trojan women, my mother surely among them, who must also be watching anxiously as their men got ready for battle. How did Helen feel, I wondered, knowing that she was the cause of so much misery and death? Did she take some responsibility? Or was it all just a game to her?

I didn't want to be alone, and I was pleased when Hippodameia came to find me, bringing a basket of clean wool. I took out my mother's silver spindle, and we spun, our spindle stones whirling, twisting the fibers into strong thread. Spinning calmed us, a distraction from the brutal sounds of battle.

"I didn't know who you were at first," Hippodameia said, "until Agamemnon explained that you're the daughter of Queen Helen and King Menelaus."

"It's because of my mother that all these men are fighting." It grieved me to speak of it. "I haven't seen her in ten years, since Paris came to Sparta and took her away."

Hippodameia reached into the basket for more wool. "I met Queen Helen several times, when I was still a child."

"You *did?* You've spoken to my mother?" My spindle dangled uselessly. I'd had little news of Helen, let alone heard from someone who had actually met her.

"I have," Hippodameia said, fingers flying. "I was present at their wedding feast in Troy. Later, Helen and Paris and their children visited my father in Lyrnessus—"

"Children?" I interrupted. I laid down my spindle and stared at her. "They have children?" *Of course they do,* I realized now. I should not have been surprised.

"They had three, but none survived. A roof collapsed and crushed them when they were still very young."

Perhaps I should have felt sympathy for my mother's loss, but I confess that I felt nothing. "And my brother, Pleisthenes?" I asked, picking up the spindle again. "Do you have any news of him?"

"I'm sorry to say that he was taken by an illness," Hippodameia said tenderly. "Such a beautiful boy. He resembled Helen —the same golden curls, the same hyacinth blue eyes."

A wave of grief for my dear little brother swept over me. "And my mother?" I pressed, unable to resist asking. "Is she still beautiful?"

"Everyone says that Helen is the most beautiful woman in the world. And it's true!" Hippodameia confirmed. "She's not like other women, whose beauty fades. Helen seems to become even more beautiful as the years pass. Everyone adores her.

But there's something about her, something undefinable, that is just as powerful as her beauty. King Priam swears there is no one like her. And Prince Paris is bewitched by her. He's as enamored as he was when he first set eyes on her. Every man in Troy is at least a little in love with Helen. Even when she was great with child, her beauty was incomparable. The Trojan men may be devoted to their wives, but it's Helen they think of when they're making love."

"And the wives don't hate her for that?" I asked incredulously.

"You'd think they would." Hippodameia smiled. "But they don't. They truly worship her. Her dearest friend is Andromache, the wife of Hector, Paris's oldest brother. Such a lovely woman, with her lustrous dark hair and her exquisite green eyes—any man would feel fortunate to have Andromache for his wife. But it's Helen whom everyone desires. The Trojans won't give her up. They'll fight until the last man falls dead before they surrender their beautiful queen."

How could it be, I wondered, that my mother was so universally adored? Surely her great beauty must have inspired jealousy among at least a few of the women and resentment among some of the men that they were being asked to fight and die for her. I couldn't explain it. Maybe no one could.

I gathered my courage and asked, "In the times you were with her, did my mother ever speak of me? Did she ever mention that she had a daughter?"

Hippodameia hesitated and dropped her spindle. "Oh, yes!" she assured me as she pretended to search for it. "She spoke often of you. It was 'My Hermione said this' and 'My Hermione did that.' You were always on her mind."

But that hesitation before she answered told me all that I needed to know.

RESTLESS, I STRAPPED ON sturdy sandals and set out alone through the Greek encampment. It had become like a huge city, the men's crude tents clustered on the beach near the ships, the officers' well-furnished tents and huts placed among the scrub growth, each group identified by the shield of its commander. The encampment was mostly deserted now, except for slaves and their overseers.

I passed a slave fixing the broken wheel of a chariot. His shoulders glistened with sweat. We glanced at each other, he looked as though he was about to speak to me, and then he quickly went back to his task.

I frowned and walked on, but I'd gone only a few steps when it struck me: *I know him!* I turned and hurried back.

The slave laid aside his tools and greeted me with a low bow. "Princess Hermione," he said, grinning.

"Zethus!" I cried. "What are you doing here?"

"Unfortunately for me, Princess, I'm here as a slave. After I left you with your father at Gythion, I joined a ship bound for Thebes. From there I planned to go on to Troy, but your great Achilles came marauding with his Myrmidons. I was captured and brought here. The overseer discovered my talent for working with wood."

"I still have the little wooden boat you carved for me."

He wiped sweat from his brow and glanced warily over his shoulder. The overseer, who'd been watching suspiciously, was advancing toward us. "I must stop talking to you, mistress, or I'll shortly feel the sting of his whip as well as the lash of his tongue." Zethus hefted his tools and the length of wood he was shaping for the wheel. "The next time we meet, perhaps you'll tell me what *you're* doing here."

"Yes, the next time," I promised. There was so much more I wanted to ask Zethus, but I knew it would not go well for him if I did, so I moved on.

I passed the mounds of earth where the ashes of hundreds of our dead lay buried, and followed a well-worn path toward the battlefield. The sounds of men shouting were louder now. When I paused to fill my leather water bag from the communal tank, I saw a white-bearded man, thin as bone, hobbling slowly along the same path. It was old Calchas, the seer.

"Where are you going, Hermione?"

"To watch the battle."

He shook a warning finger. "Come with me. We'll watch together."

"But you're going away from the fighting."

"That doesn't mean I can't see it. It's far too dangerous

for us to be there among them, but if you'll allow me, I can describe to you exactly what's happening."

His advice seemed wise. I followed Calchas into a small grove of fig trees. The seer lowered himself to the ground, leaned against a gray-barked trunk, drew up his sharp knees, and closed his eyes. I sat down nearby and waited.

The seer, his eyes now opened wide and staring, began to describe what he saw. "The savage battle has been launched. Those hoarse cries you hear are the Trojans," he said. "Our Greeks marched to meet them in silence. Clouds of dust swirl around them. Out of the blinding dust comes Paris, magnificent as a god, a leopard skin slung across his shoulders. He carries a bow on his back, a sword on his hip, two bronze-tipped spears in his hand. He strides forward, shouting out a challenge to any Greek who dares to face him in mortal combat, a fight to the death. And there, leaping from his chariot to meet the challenge, is mighty King Menelaus—"

"Menelaus?" I broke in. "My father intends to fight Paris?" I was shocked. Somehow I hadn't expected the rivals to fight —I'd thought the armies would do it for them. Blood pounded in my ears.

"He's eager for revenge. But what's this?" Calchas leaned forward intently. "Paris cringes at the sight of Menelaus advancing fearlessly straight for him! The prince's knees are trembling, his face is pale with dread, and he retreats back into the Trojan lines, hiding among his men. He will not fight Menelaus! Can you hear our own Greeks howling with laughter?" Calchas, too, was laughing shrilly.

A wave of relief swept over me. "I hadn't known Paris was so cowardly," I said. "Tell me, what's happening now?"

"His older brother, Hector, is calling him a curse to his father, King Priam, a disgrace to Troy and to himself. Paris is covered in shame! And he agrees now to meet Menelaus and to fight it out. Hector strides between the two great armies and makes the proposal: Paris and Menelaus will meet one on one in mortal combat, the winner to take Helen home. The two sides will then declare peace."

"Surely Father will win!" I cried. My earlier relief vanished. "He's a much better fighter, don't you think?"

"That's not for me to say." Calchas raised his bushy eyebrows. "Now old Priam is talking with Helen, who has been watching from a tower on the great wall of the citadel. Ah, Hermione, if only you could hear what I hear! Your mother speaks of how she regrets leaving her husband and her favorite child now full grown. You, Hermione! She's speaking of *you!*"

I was too caught up in thinking of Helen, my mother, and the tears she shed for me to listen to the seer's description of the men's preparations for their fight. The old seer grunted and struggled stiffly to his feet, his staring eyes focused on the faraway scene. I jumped up, too fearful for my father's safety to remain still.

"The duel has begun," he announced. "Menelaus hurls his spear—it strikes Paris's shield and goes straight through it, but

Paris leaps aside and avoids death's black cloud. Now Menelaus draws his sword and smashes it on his rival's helmet, but the sword shatters in his hand! Menelaus lunges, seizes the horsehair crest of the Trojan's helmet, swings Paris around, and starts to drag him off. But Aphrodite, daughter of Zeus, sweeps in and breaks the helmet strap, setting Paris free!"

I cried out, begging Zeus to intervene and help my father, but the great god ignored me. Calchas rubbed his eyes and sank down again beneath the fig tree. "The goddess has wrapped Paris in mist, snatched her favorite away from murderous Menelaus, and spirited him back to his bedroom in the palace."

"Aphrodite saved Paris?" I asked in disbelief.

"It seems so. But Helen is waiting for him. She's been watching from the tower, a witness to his cowardice. Aphrodite is there with her. The goddess of love, known for her ethereal beauty, appears now as an aged crone, commanding Helen to go to Paris's bed. Helen resists, and Aphrodite berates her, calling her a wretched, headstrong woman, and threatens to turn her over to the warriors to be stoned to death. Helen relents, and there she is, radiant, dressed in silvery white robes. Oh, Hermione, if only you could hear! She tells Paris that she wishes he had died in battle, brought down by Menelaus, 'that great warrior, my husband of long ago,' as she calls him."

"How does he answer her?"

The seer hesitated. "It's hard to believe what he tells her! Paris promises her that even though Menelaus won today, he's sure that *he* will win tomorrow—he will prove to her that he is the better fighter. In the meantime, Paris wants to make love!"

"But my mother turns him away—doesn't she?"

No answer from Calchas. I repeated, "Doesn't she?"

"No," he replied. "No, she does not refuse him. They lie in the great carved bed, lost in love." Calchas shook his head sadly. "Menelaus has fairly won the fight, but Helen will not come back, nor will Paris send her. It is Zeus's doing."

Would the gods never listen to me? I put my head down on my knees and wept.

THE GODS WERE ARGUING, Calchas said. "Zeus claims that your father won, but his wife, Hera, wants the fight to go on. To placate her, Zeus has sent Athena to provoke it." The fighting resumed when one of the Trojan archers, urged on by Athena, wounded Menelaus. "It's not serious," Calchas assured me. "Athena just wanted to break the truce between the two sides."

But I had to see for myself. I rushed back to our tents, and I was there when the king was carried in. I pushed through the crowd of men surrounding him and knelt by his side. With blood spurting from his wound, Menelaus lay pale and still. "Father!" I whispered, taking his hand.

He looked at me with feverish eyes. "Don't worry, daughter," he murmured. "Agamemnon has already sent for a healer."

Menelaus would recover, but the truce had been broken. The next day the Greeks donned their armor, and the Trojans readied for an assault. Agamemnon leaped into his chariot to take command of his armies. Orestes led a contingent of archers and their charioteers toward the battle. I watched him go without a chance to say goodbye. So much was still left unsaid between us.

Before the shining sun had set, the bodies of hundreds of Trojans and hundreds of Greeks lay sprawled across the dusty plain, their swords and spears and shields scattered uselessly among them. Neither side claimed victory. But for that day at least, Orestes was unhurt.

The Way of Men

THE KILLING WENT ON, day after day. At the end of each day's battle the Trojans silently gathered their dead and carried them back inside the city walls. Our dead were piled on wooden pyres and set alight. The funeral fires blazed through the night, and the next day the ashes were placed in a common grave under a mound of earth that stretched as far as I could see.

One evening, soon after sunset, an exhausted Orestes staggered into my tent, almost too weary to speak.

I led him to my couch. He wiped his sweat-streaked face with a muddy arm. I sent a servant for a basin of warm, scented water and a sponge to wipe his brow. Despite his dirty face, I had never seen him look so handsome. I offered him watered wine, which he refused, and a plate of cheese and nuts that I'd planned to eat for my own meal. He waved that away too.

"Not hungry," he said. "Not after all I've seen today." He

sat slumped, his head down, his hands dangling between his knees.

I sat close beside him. "What brings you here, Orestes?" I asked, puzzled. "What can I do for you?"

He raised his head and gazed at me searchingly. "Love me," he said. "Just love me, Hermione."

"Love you? But I do love you! You must know that, Orestes! I've loved you for a very long time—it's just that we've never spoken of it."

"I want to speak of it now, Hermione. I don't want to die without speaking of it. My charioteer was killed today, the deadly arrow shot by an archer on Troy's high wall. It missed me by a hair, due to my man's quick action. He gave his life for me. Tomorrow I'll have a new charioteer who may not be so loyal, or so quick."

"You're not going to die," I insisted.

It was a stupid thing to say, and we both knew it. Archers wore no armor and carried no shield, depending on their charioteer to carry them wherever they needed to go, maneuver them deftly, and get them away quickly. Death was everywhere. The odds were great for every man who rose at dawn that he would be dead by nightfall.

"But I wouldn't mind speaking of love anyway," I added.

We kissed and kissed again and lay in each other's arms until Orestes drifted off to sleep and I followed him there. I was still sleeping when my lover awakened with a start and leaped from my bed.

"The moon still shines brightly," I mumbled drowsily. "Must you go so soon, Orestes?"

"The day's fighting begins at dawn." He bent down and kissed me, and I flung my arms around his neck and held him close until he finally pulled away.

I shouldn't have been happy, with death's black cloud all around us — but I was.

WHILE THE MEN MADE terrible war, I spent my days in the tranquil company of Hippodameia, who now lived in a simple hut in Agamemnon's encampment. We often walked along the beach, the roar of battle in the distance, and spoke of the desires we shared with all young women for a home, a husband, children, those things that only peace could bring. When we sat and spun our wool, I felt free to confide in Hippodameia of my love for Orestes.

"He's always at his father's side and so caught up in the war that I rarely see him," I explained. "But those times that we're together, we're so close that we breathe each other's breath and dream each other's dreams."

Hippodameia talked about her husband, cut down by Achilles on her wedding day. "He was many years older than I," she said. "Even older than Agamemnon. His beard was almost white. I have no idea what sort of husband he would have made. Speaking the truth, I'd rather be with Achilles. He's young and strong. But I wonder if I'll ever be with him again."

"It's all in the hands of the gods," I reminded her, thinking of my own sweet lover, and she agreed that it was true.

One day we stood on the beach, gazing out at the dark, frothing sea, and watched a ship cutting swiftly through the tossing waves toward the shore. Ships often arrived, bringing supplies for the Greek armies. But this was no cargo ship letting down its anchor stone. A small boat was lowered with two occupants, and a pair of oarsmen rowed it toward the beach.

"It's Astynome! And that must be her father!" I exclaimed, and we hurried to greet them.

"Hail and welcome, priest of Apollo!" I called out as the father and daughter stepped onto the beach, lifting the hems of their robes above the ripples. Chryses acknowledged my greeting solemnly, but he did not look pleased.

Astynome, however, was beaming. "I wanted to come back, and here I am!" she crowed as we embraced. "Where's King Agamemnon?"

"On the battlefield. He'll return when the sun has set." Then I noticed her rounded belly. "I'll send a herald now to tell him you've come."

Her father clamped his arms sternly across his chest. "She's expecting a child, as you can see," he grumbled. "She tells me that Agamemnon is the father, and she wants to be with him."

"It's true," the girl said gaily. "I love him! I'm sure he'll want me back." Her attention shifted uneasily to Hippoda-meia. "Unless . . ."

"Agamemnon is kind to me, but he doesn't lust for me," Hippodameia assured her. "The king will welcome you, and I'll gladly go back to Achilles, if he'll have me."

I glanced from one girl to the other. It seemed that this might work out well after all. "Let's go to Menelaus's tent and wait for the men to come in from battle," I suggested, and after I'd called for warm water for them to wash their hands and had ordered food and drink, I sent a herald to find Agamem-non and tell him of their arrival. But I was not sure what to do about Achilles.

Since the day Agamemnon had demanded that he surren-der Hippodameia, Achilles had refused to join the battle. Even when Hector challenged him to fight man to man, Achilles refused to leave his tents. Great Ajax went out in his stead. The two warriors fought hard from sunrise to sunset. At night-fall, when there was still no winner, they declared a truce. Ajax awarded Hector his priceless purple war belt, Hector presented Ajax with his silver-studded sword, and the two embraced. Agamemnon ordered seven oxen to be sacrificed to Zeus. The oxen were roasted, and both men shared in the feast. The talk that night was of nothing but the glorious fight.

"How can it be glorious?" I'd asked Orestes during one of our precious times together. "I just want the war to be over."

"It's the way of men," he'd said.

CCCC

AGAMEMNON WELCOMED ASTYNOME delightedly. And now, he hoped, Achilles would welcome Hippodameia just as delightedly and agree to return to the battlefield.

Agamemnon sent for Odysseus and Ajax. "Take the lovely girl to Achilles, and give him my solemn oath that I have not once touched her in lust, have never made love to her," he instructed them. "Is that not true, my dear Hippodameia?"

"It's true."

To further entice Achilles to fight again, Agamemnon also promised to send him a trove of gifts: iron pots, bronze cauldrons, bars of gold, a dozen massive stallions, and seven weavers taken as prisoners on Lesbos. "And tell Achilles that once we're home in Mycenae, he will be my son-in-law, as true a son as my own Orestes, and he can have his pick of my daughters, Chrysothemis and Electra, as a wife."

Hippodameia's face crumpled. She wanted to believe that she would one day marry Achilles. Agamemnon, oblivious, kept adding even more treasure to persuade Achilles. "Seven beautiful cities surrounded by wonderful green vineyards and flocks of fat sheep! Just let him lose his anger and come and fight beside us once more."

"Achilles would never marry either of those girls, Chrysothemis or Electra," I assured Hippodameia when we were alone. "Agamemnon is just trying to persuade him to fight again. You mustn't worry about it. And, if it will make you feel better, I'll go with you to Achilles' camp."

When Hippodameia complained that she had nothing to wear, Astynome generously offered her one of the embroidered tunics she'd brought with her from Sminthos. Agamemnon sent a carrying chair so that she would arrive in style. I walked beside the chair, trying to distract her with idle conversation and keep her calm. For my part, I remembered how Orestes and I had escorted her from Achilles' camp to Agamemnon's months earlier, and how enraged Achilles had been then. I wished Orestes were with us now—he would be better than Odysseus, I thought, at dealing with Achilles' volatile temper.

"Wait here," Odysseus said when we reached the Myrmidons' tents. "When Achilles has accepted Agamemnon's promise of gifts, I'll send you a signal, and Hippodameia can come forward in all her beauty."

The wait went on much too long. Hippodameia and I grew restive. It was my idea to creep closer to Achilles' tent to find out what was happening. When we did, we found a feast in progress, the men lounging on carpets while Patroclus plucked a lyre and sang songs of bravery. Hippodameia and I crouched behind a rock to listen. The snatches of conversation I was able to make out sounded amiable. Achilles was being a good host. Wine goblets were emptied and refilled.

"What are they talking about?" Hippodameia whispered. "Can you hear?"

I put my finger to my lips. "Odysseus is describing the gifts Agamemnon is offering."

"All this is for you, Achilles," Odysseus was saying, "and your lithe and lovely Hippodameia will immediately be returned to you, untouched. But the Trojans have gained the upper hand. We need you to help us."

Abruptly the mood turned dark and ugly. "I refuse!" Achilles declared loudly. "Agamemnon has insulted my honor! I loathe him, I accept none of his gifts, and I will not fight for him, nor will my men. Tomorrow I sail to Phthia, and my loyal Myrmidons sail with me. Pyrrhus!" he shouted for his son. "Pyrrhus, escort these shameless dogs back to the tents of Agamemnon!"

Hippodameia and I stared at each other. What had happened? Everything had fallen apart. All the men were shouting. I grabbed her hand, and we rushed back to her carrying chair to wait for Ajax and Odysseus.

They burst out of Achilles' tent. "Let's go," Ajax growled. "There's no reasoning with him."

We stumbled back to Agamemnon's camp by torchlight, Hippodameia weeping and Pyrrhus snarling and snapping at our heels.

THE FIGHTING RESUMED THE next morning, still without Achilles and his men, and continued, day after blood-soaked day. Achilles did not sail for Phthia, as he had threatened, but neither did he leave his tents. Patroclus stayed with him, while Pyrrhus no doubt skulked nearby.

Astynome, her belly swelling, lounged contentedly in the

little hut near Agamemnon's tent, happy to be back with the man she adored and who, for his part, did seem fond of her. Hippodameia waited gloomily for Achilles to realize that he loved her, though he was behaving so badly. "I think he has no need for me," Hippodameia sighed plaintively.

I suspected she was right, but I kept silent and didn't share my thoughts with her. I, for one, would not have wanted to live anywhere near Achilles' son, Pyrrhus.

I'd heard Calchas say many times that the gods had decreed that Troy must come to defeat. Yet the battles were clearly going against our men. Whenever the Greeks gained the advantage, the goddesses intervened on the side of the Trojans. My father had recovered from his injury, though now he walked with a limp, but many soldiers lay wounded and suffering. Many more had been killed.

Astynome understood what was happening. "The gods will dictate the outcome of this great war. They determine *every-thing* that happens—not just the war. It's out of the hands of mere mortals. Hera obviously favors the Greeks. When she thought Zeus was helping the Trojans too much, she seduced him, and while he slept, she called on his brother, Poseidon, to come to the aid of the Greeks. And Poseidon actually came to the battlefield and led the charge until Zeus woke up, saw what was happening, and put a stop to it."

"How do you know all this?" I asked.

"It was revealed to me in a dream."

I envied Astynome her dreams. I learned nothing from

mine—they reminded me only of my desire for the end of the war and the beginning of a life with Orestes. Sometimes I dreamed of my mother. I wondered if the years had changed her heart, if not her beauty. I wondered if she dreamed of me.

Astynome hadn't been back long when Hippodameia decided to send a message to Patroclus, begging him to persuade Achilles to claim her. "Patroclus has always been a good friend to me," she said while she waited for an answer. "But I confess, I'm jealous of the bond between him and Achilles. Achilles cares more for Patroclus than he does for me."

She had almost given up hope when Patroclus himself brought her the answer she'd prayed for. "Achilles wishes you to come," he said, "but not until the three-quarter moon reaches full."

We joyfully gathered the things she'd need to take with her —she had only the gown she'd been wearing when she was taken prisoner, the embroidered tunic Astynome had given her, and a few plain chitons. On the day Hippodameia was to leave for Achilles' encampment, we ordered our servants to fill a large tub with scented water. Astynome joined us, and we took turns bathing. Our servants rubbed us with oil and dressed us in new gowns of finely woven brocade, sashed with tasseled silk, brought as gifts from Astynome's homeland.

Astynome was braiding Hippodameia's hair when Orestes appeared unexpectedly in my tent, his face drawn in sorrow. One look told us he'd brought bad news.

"Orestes, what is it?"

"Patroclus is dead."

Hippodameia shrieked, and I led Orestes to a bench and knelt beside him. Patroclus, he told us, had convinced Achilles that the Greeks were losing their battles: too many lay dead, too many more were badly wounded. Zeus himself had stepped in to help Hector, who broke through the Greek defenses and flung flaming torches at the Greek ships, setting them alight. The entire fleet was in danger. Patroclus persuaded Achilles to lend him his armor and let him lead the Myrmidons into battle.

"Patroclus argued that the armor would deceive the Trojans into believing that mighty Achilles was back in the battle again and send them fleeing," Orestes continued. "Achilles gave in and finally agreed to lend the armor, but he ordered Patroclus only to defend the Greek ships, nothing more! And then he was to come back to the Myrmidons' encampment."

Patroclus had put on Achilles' breastplate, helmet, and greaves and picked up his weapons—all but the spear, which was too heavy for any man to handle except Achilles himself, and Patroclus carried his own. He borrowed Achilles' horses, and Achilles filled his wine cup and poured out a libation to Zeus, praying for his friend's victory and safe return.

"Only part of the prayer was answered. Our ships were saved. Zeus gave Patroclus victory," Orestes told us, "but he didn't let him return safely. Hector killed Patroclus, but he couldn't have done it without Apollo's help. The god struck

Patroclus from behind and knocked the helmet from his head, broke his spear, and caused his shield to fall." Orestes shuddered. "He was defenseless against Hector. I witnessed the brutal carnage. With my own eyes I saw Hector strip Achilles' armor from Patroclus's dead body and put it on himself. Now the Greeks and the Trojans are fighting for possession of the body. Patroclus's soul cannot enter the House of Death until his body is given a proper burial."

Hippodameia's face was a mask of sorrow as Orestes described what happened. "Achilles knows?" she asked.

"He knew when his horses returned without Patroclus. Achilles has surrendered to the madness of grief, rolling in the dust, rubbing soot and ashes onto his face, and shouting out Patroclus's name."

"I'm going to find him," Hippodameia said.

"Don't." Orestes grabbed her wrist. "He's lost his sanity."

"Then I'll help him find it." She wrenched free and ran from the tent. Orestes started after her.

"Let her go, Orestes," I called out. "Maybe her love will help to heal him."

"There is no healing him, Hermione. He thinks of nothing but revenge."

That night, Orestes and I lay in each other's arms, whispering in the darkness. "What do you think will happen now?" I asked.

"More fighting. More death."

"I wonder if it will ever end."

"It will, my love, and soon. It's fated to end in the tenth year. The gods have decreed it."

"And then what?"

"You and I will go home to Greece."

"Together, Orestes?"

"Together, Hermione. I promise you! And we will marry, as our grandfather Tyndareus wished."

And I slept, believing it would happen just as Orestes promised.

Achilles' Rage

ASTYNOME CAME TO MY tent the next morning, after Orestes had gone to join Agamemnon. She sat down wearily, her eyes heavy with sleep, and yawned. "I didn't rest well."

"The baby?" I asked.

"No, the baby's fine. I had another dream. It was about Achilles' mother, Thetis, the sea nymph. When she heard that Hector had stripped Achilles' armor from Patroclus's body, Thetis came to comfort Achilles. She promised to get him a new set of armor."

I fetched Astynome some bread and a bowl of cheese mixed with nuts and honey. She always seemed to be hungry.

"She's on her way to visit Hephaestus, the god of fire," Astynome said between mouthfuls, "and he's creating invincible armor for Achilles. That much was in the dream. The rest I learned from Agamemnon. Achilles has promised to return to fight. He went to the trench where the Trojans were struggling to get Patroclus's body away from the Greeks, and he gave his fierce war cry. It was so ferocious that the Trojans left the body and fled behind their walls. Achilles leaped into his war chariot and chased the fleeing men, slaying any who failed to reach safety. They're terrified of him."

"With Achilles back in the battle, the war is truly almost over."

Astynome rose clumsily and helped herself to more bread and cheese. "I'd like to think so. But something else in the dream bothers me. I saw Achilles lying dead."

"But Achilles is invulnerable! He once told Hippodameia that his mother had dipped him in the River Styx when he was a baby, and that would make him immortal."

"Maybe. But maybe not," Astynome said. "All I can tell you is what I dreamed."

PATROCLUS'S BODY, RESCUED FROM the Trojans, was laid out in Achilles' tent. The mourning began, Achilles' wails louder than anyone's. I went to stay with Hippodameia during this difficult time.

"He sits by the body night and day, sobbing and wailing," she told me. "His mother came to him. I heard them talking. She warned him that, if he insists on seeking revenge, he'll certainly be killed. But he won't listen to her. His mind is made up."

I remembered Astynome's dream of Achilles lying dead, but I decided not to tell Hippodameia about it. If that was what Fate had decreed, it was useless to discuss it.

Hippodameia took me to the shelter where the Myrmidons' weapons were kept. "Thetis brought him this shield and armor made by Hephaestus." Here was what Astynome had dreamed about: a massive bronze shield, a breastplate that gleamed like fire, a helmet of burnished bronze with a bristling golden crest, and a pair of greaves made of flexible tin. Every piece was magnificently wrought, but Hephaestus's shield was a masterpiece, elegantly engraved with scenes of war and peace.

Hippodameia pointed out the scene of men with their scythes in a king's fields, bringing in the harvest, and the scene with a circle of girls carrying baskets of grapes while a young boy plucked his lyre. But my eye was drawn to a wedding party, where the bride walked through the streets by torchlight while choirs sang and young men whirled and young girls joined hands in a graceful dance. I gazed at this scene and felt that I was part of it.

"That's what I wish we were doing now—singing and dancing," Hippodameia remarked wistfully. "You and I and the men we love."

There were scenes of war and killing, too, on the gorgeous shield, but we weren't interested in them. We already knew too much of it.

We left the armory and found a place to sit beneath soft

white clouds adrift in an azure sky. Hippodameia's caged birds twittered merrily nearby, an odd contrast to the wailing of Achilles and his Myrmidons. We took out our spindles and wool and began to spin.

"I'm not sure I bring Achilles any comfort," she confessed. "I thought I could heal him, but I was wrong—his grief is so deep and his feelings of guilt are so overwhelming. But he also blames *me!* Achilles insists that if only *I* had died when he was taking me prisoner, Agamemnon would not have demanded me as his prize, his own honor would not have been insulted, and none of this would have happened. And so it really *is* my fault!" Her lip trembled.

"Don't believe him. It's not your fault, Hippodameia! It's what men do!"

Hippodameia tried to smile. "I know. Still, it's easier for him to blame me, isn't it? And now Patroclus is dead, and I mourn him as well. He promised that he would take me to Phthia and see me married to Achilles." The thread twisted through our fingers. "Now that will never happen."

I TOOK HIPPODAMEIA BACK to Menelaus's camp with me, unwilling to leave her alone with the Myrmidons. Astynome joined us. We three women clung to each other, knowing that our lives, too, hung in the balance.

Achilles vowed to avenge the death of his beloved Patroclus. Nothing would satisfy him but taking the life of Hector. We couldn't be present on the battlefield and didn't want to be; nevertheless, we craved to know what was happening. We found spindle-legged Calchas, with his wispy beard and hairless skull, and begged him to use his second sight to tell us. We sat on the ground in a circle with the old seer, his hooded eyes focused on a point in the far distance, and we strained to catch every word.

"The Trojans have fled behind their wall. Hector stands alone, shackled by his deadly fate, but holding his ground against Achilles. Hector begins to run. Some will say that he runs from fear. Others will say that he hopes to tire Achilles, who has sat stubbornly in his hut doing nothing for so long. Achilles gives chase."

Through Calchas's eyes we watched Achilles pursue Hector around the walls of Troy, once, twice, three times, and each time Hector tried to reach the Trojan gates, Achilles prevented it. Hector had no choice now but to stand and fight.

"Hector knows he is doomed. He pleads with his archenemy. 'Promise me that you will not defile my body but will return it to my people.' But Achilles, in his rage, denies him. The fight to the death begins."

So powerful was Calchas's description that we saw the duel as if we were actually present. We listened with our hearts pounding. We scarcely dared to breathe.

"Achilles hurls his spear. Hector ducks, and the bronze tip flies past. But the goddess Athena, hovering above the pair, snatches up the spear, and sends it back to Achilles! Hector takes his turn, hurling his spear. It strikes Achilles' shield with full force but drops away harmlessly. The two warriors grab their swords and race toward each other. Achilles, teeth bared, stabs Hector in the neck. Hector falls."

Calchas was silent, and we waited.

"Hector is dead."

We sighed, relieved that it was over. But Calchas held up his hand.

"Wait! Achilles hasn't finished taking his revenge. He strips Hector's body of the armor. He is bent on shaming Hector. He slits the tendons in Hector's heels, threads leather straps through the slits, and fastens the straps to his chariot. Now he whips his stallions into a frenzy, and they plunge headlong, dragging Hector's lifeless body through clouds of dust."

Hippodameia screamed and fainted. Astynome caught her. I grabbed Calchas's sleeve. "And Hector's people? Have they witnessed this?"

Calchas nodded. "They have. King Priam, mad with grief, vows to beg Achilles to return his son's body. Hector's mother tears her hair and cries pitifully. His people wail . . ."

And what about my mother? I wondered. *Is she crying too? Does she blame herself?* I imagined Helen there in all her loveliness, and for once I did not envy her beauty.

"Hector's wife?" I whispered. "Does Andromache know?"

"His lovely wife sits in her chamber and weaves at her loom. She has heard nothing and orders her women to prepare a bath for her husband for when he returns from battle."

Calchas paused, and a troubled look crossed his face. "Now she hears the wailing, and she knows."

I imagined that I could hear Andromache's anguished cry: "Oh, Hector, I am destroyed!"

HECTOR WAS DEAD, AND now Achilles turned his attention to the rituals that would guarantee Patroclus's safe delivery to the House of Death. All of us attended. As the body was placed on a pyre and consumed by fire, Achilles led the singing of chants that sent chills down my spine. The Myrmidons organized traditional funeral games, contests that would continue for days.

But still Achilles' hunger for revenge was not satisfied. Not content to let the body of Hector lie in peace, Achilles continued to abuse it. Every day for nine days he ruthlessly dragged Hector's body three times around the tomb in which Patroclus's ashes were buried. We marveled that Hector's body did not decay but remained perfect. Astynome knew why. "Apollo and Aphrodite are protecting it," she said.

Astynome, whose time was near for the birth of her baby, wanted to return to Agamemnon's camp, but Hippodameia begged us to stay with her for a little longer—"until Achilles loses his madness," she said—and so we did.

That was how we happened to be present when King Priam arrived at Achilles' camp. Somehow the old king had managed to avoid the guards—Astynome whispered that Zeus had sent Hermes, the messenger god, to protect him in his perilous mission. Achilles and those closest to him were gathered in his hut when the Trojan king entered unannounced, hobbled straight to Achilles, knelt painfully and clasped Achilles' knees, and pleaded for the return of Hector's body.

Everyone, including Achilles, was thunderstruck. Pyrrhus took one long step forward, his sword drawn, but then he seemed to hesitate and sheathed his weapon. I doubted that he had halted out of pity for Priam; more likely, one of the merciful gods had stopped him.

Achilles found his voice. "What have you to offer me, King Priam?"

"I bring a priceless ransom, a cart loaded with the gold and jewels in my treasury equal to the weight of my beloved son," King Priam answered, his leathery old cheeks wet with tears. "Now I put my lips to the hands of the man who killed my son."

Achilles' stony heart was softened by this sorrowing old king. He called for his serving women to wash and anoint Hector's body and wrap it in a brilliant purple cape while his men unloaded the treasure. Achilles himself lifted Hector's body onto King Priam's cart. He ordered a sheep slaughtered and bread and wine brought out for a meal. He had a bed made up for Priam and provided him with thick fleeces and warm blankets. He promised a truce until Prince Hector had been buried in Troy.

"Nine days to mourn him, a tenth to bury him, the eleventh to build the mound above him. On the twelfth we'll fight again," Achilles told Priam.

Astynome, Hippodameia, and I witnessed the whole scene. When it was finished, Achilles took Hippodameia by the wrist and led her off to his own sleeping quarters. She went with him without a backward glance, leaving Astynome and me to find a place to sleep in her tent. I lay awake, knowing that Pyrrhus was lurking somewhere nearby. I didn't trust him.

During the night, Astynome's labor began. I sent for Marpessa, who—old and crippled as she was—still served as midwife for women unlucky enough to give birth on the beach of Troy. Toward morning Agamemnon's son was born. Astynome named him Chryses, in honor of her father.

Love and Betrayal

THERE IS NO ACCOUNTING for the whim of the gods. I could think of no other explanation for what happened next. Those all-powerful beings had decreed that Achilles' good fortune would soon come to an end.

During the truce he'd granted to Priam for the mourning and burial of Hector, Achilles went to the place where the River Scamander joins the sea to bathe in the twin pools. Everyone seemed to have the same idea. The battles had exhausted us, and all our spirits needed refreshing. The pools were large, and Greek and Trojan women bathed in one pool while Greek and Trojan men were in the other. Admiring gazes passed in both directions. I saw Orestes, his beautiful naked body, and yearned to be with him again. He saw mine, and I knew he felt that same yearning.

Soon the lithe and lovely young women and the strong and

handsome young men were leaving the pools and slipping off in pairs into the trees. Orestes and I also seized the opportunity.

Among the bathers was a Trojan princess named Polyxena, daughter of King Priam and sister of Hector and Paris. Polyxena, round hipped and slender armed, had the large, liquid eyes of a doe. Her white hands were as delicate as a bird's wings. When Achilles locked eyes with Polyxena, he forgot all about faithful Hippodameia and led the Trojan princess to the privacy of the grove. I saw them there.

Before they emerged, Achilles had fallen madly in love with Polyxena and made up his mind to marry the sister of his dead rival. He sent word to King Priam that he would return the treasure he had accepted for the ransom of Hector's body if Priam would consent to the marriage.

When Hippodameia found out, she was infuriated. She raged and she wept; I tried to console her, though there wasn't much I could say.

Once again Achilles seemed to have lost all his sense and reason, but it wasn't until later that the extent of his madness was discovered. At some point in his infatuation, he revealed to Polyxena a secret he had never confided to anyone. We knew the story that when he was an infant, his mother, Thetis, had dipped him in the waters of the River Styx to ensure his immortality. But what no one knew was that the water had not touched that one small place where she'd held him, the heel of his foot. And so, to prove his love, he foolishly told Polyxena about his vulnerable spot.

Polyxena betrayed him. She immediately passed the information to her brother, Prince Paris. Paris, not a warrior like Hector but nonetheless skillful with bow and arrow, waited for his chance. Treacherous Polyxena made sure that he got it.

She lured Achilles to the temple of Apollo, where their marriage was supposed to be celebrated. Odysseus, suspicious of the whole affair from the beginning, went with Achilles, hoping to salvage the situation. Neither saw Paris hidden in the temple, waiting. Paris aimed his arrow at that small, vulnerable spot: Achilles' heel. Apollo ensured that the arrow found its mark. Some even said it was Apollo's arrow that killed him. Achilles died in the arms of Odysseus, who carried our hero's body back to the Greek camp and told us what happened.

We were stunned by the death of Achilles. The mourning began again. The wailing of the Myrmidons continued night after night, day after day. Agamemnon took charge of the funeral rites. Pyrrhus, convulsed with grief, vowed to slaughter every Trojan who came in his path. I held the distraught Hippodameia and wiped her tears.

Now, I wondered, when would the killing end? How could the Greeks now hope to win the war without Achilles?

Orestes and I discussed the situation when we found a chance to be together. "The oracles make different predictions to different people," Orestes said. "One says that the war can't be won without a special bow and arrows, and that these have to be gotten from an archer named Philoctetes on the island of Lemnos. Another says that a wooden statue of Pallas Athena must be stolen from its hiding place in the Trojan citadel. Yet a third claims that a certain bone must be found and brought to our camp. Or that Pyrrhus has to take a particular role in the fighting."

"Pyrrhus!" I snorted. "I can't imagine that dog face having a particular role in anything!"

"He's the son of Achilles—that's his role," Orestes reminded me. "He has taken up his father's armor and weapons, and Odysseus approves. But our soldiers are dispirited. More than ever they talk about going home. They haven't seen their wives and children for almost a decade."

"And your father? What does Agamemnon say?"

Orestes shrugged. "War is his life. He thrives on it."

MY OLD FRIEND, ZETHUS, brought me a gift. He had built me a loom, almost like the one that leaned against the wall in my mother's bedroom at Sparta—two uprights joined by a beautifully carved beam from which the warp strings hung suspended. The warp strings on my mother's loom had been weighted with gold discs. "I have no gold or silver, but these clay weights will hold the warp taut," he said. The shuttle that carried the weft thread was smooth and balanced nicely in my hand.

I thanked Zethus and praised his elegant workmanship. He grinned, pleased that he had pleased me. "I'm no longer a slave," he told me proudly. "I've been given new work. Odysseus has persuaded Agamemnon to build a very large wooden horse, big enough for our best Greek warriors to conceal themselves inside it. The plan is to leave it on the beach, and once the Trojans have hauled the wooden horse inside the walls of Troy, the Greeks will climb out and open the city gates, and our fighters will rush in."

The plan sounded ridiculous. "The Trojans surely are not so stupid as to bring a huge wooden horse into their city," I told him, laughing. "Even Odysseus can't believe that!"

"There's much more to the plan," Zethus explained. "Odysseus has worked it all out. The Greeks will call it a gift, saying that they're leaving it in honor of the goddess Athena. Then they'll burn the encampment, board their ships, and pretend to sail away. But they'll sail only far enough so that their ships are out of sight of the watchtowers. The Trojans will believe that the Greeks have given up and gone home. They'll think they've won the war, and while they're celebrating victory, a signal will be given to the hidden ships to return, and our men will overrun Troy and reclaim Helen and the king's treasure."

I still thought it was a mad idea, but Zethus wholeheartedly believed in it, and it seemed that Agamemnon and my father did too. Agamemnon dispatched warriors to the forests of Mount Ida to cut down fir trees to build the gigantic horse. Zethus, the most talented of the carpenters and woodworkers, was in charge of the actual construction. The work went on for days. The men sang as they labored. In the evenings they told stories around the fires. They accepted as true what the oracles had foretold: the war would end in its tenth year. As near as I could count, we were well past the middle of that year. The war would soon end and we'd return to our homeland. I wanted to believe it too.

Remembering how my mother's nimble fingers drew the bright-dyed weft thread across the warp, I stood at my loom and wove. I was no longer the unhappy child left behind by her mother, and I no longer cared whether I would ever be reunited with Helen. Soon Orestes and I would marry, and we would have children. While the men built their wooden horse, I wove a wedding veil.

Orestes and I were together as much as the fighting allowed. We hadn't yet spoken to our fathers of our wish to marry. They were too deeply involved in organizing their final assault on the Trojans to be interested in their children's love affair.

"This is how we'll arrange it," Orestes had proposed the previous night in my tent. "After the Trojans have been defeated, I'll return to Mycenae with Agamemnon as he expects, and tell him of our marriage plans, and you'll sail back to Sparta with Menelaus and Helen. I'm sure our two families, kingly brothers married to queenly sisters, will want to celebrate our wedding with the ceremonies and feasting it deserves. In the meantime," he said, "I've brought you a surprise." From a leather pouch he produced an intricately designed golden goblet made of two halves, neither of which would stand alone. "It's a wedding goblet. I'll keep one half, and you'll have the other. It was my idea, but Zethus made it for us."

"I didn't know Zethus could work in gold," I said, running my finger along the delicate etching of a wedding party. I was struck by the beauty of the goblet and overjoyed to have this promise of our future marriage. I thought it even more beautiful than the design Hephaestus had etched on Achilles' magnificent shield.

"Zethus can make anything," Orestes replied. "Now we must have a little ceremony and make our betrothal official."

He filled the two halves of the goblet with wine. We poured a few drops on the ground for the gods, pledged our love, and drank, each sipping a little from both halves, promising not to drink from it again until our wedding day. Orestes and I kissed and kissed again and again, until our passion was spent.

As I was weaving, Astynome came to my tent with her newborn baby, Chryses, and cooed to him while I worked. I told her what I was weaving, showed her my half of the wedding goblet, and confided the plans Orestes and I had made. But as I talked and wove, I made mistakes and often had to undo whatever I had just finished. Astynome laughed. "Maybe you should start with something simpler—like towels for a baby!"

"Astynome," I said, laying aside the shuttle, "you've told me that you often have dreams of things that may happen in the future. You learned in a dream that Zeus and Hera were arguing. You knew that Thetis was having new armor made for Achilles, and you even knew that Achilles would die. And so I wonder," I continued, "if you've ever dreamed of my mother. I haven't seen her since I was a child, and I hardly remember her. What is Helen like now? Do you know?"

"I don't dream about Helen, because Helen doesn't change." Astynome said. The baby was fussing, and she got up to walk with him. "She's the same now as she was the day she left Sparta, and the Trojans adore her as much today as they did when Paris brought her here."

"They're not angry at her because of the suffering she's caused? Doesn't Andromache blame her for Hector's death?"

"They don't see it that way. They don't think it's Helen's fault."

"But it *is* her fault!" I gave up my weaving efforts and took the baby from her. "And why do the Greeks not blame her?"

"You should ask your father that! And Agamemnon! Your father wants to get her back, and Agamemnon gave his word to help him. So did nearly all of your mother's suitors. They are honor bound to fight this war to the finish. The soldiers who serve under them have nothing to say about it."

She took little Chryses back from me, and we sat quietly while the baby suckled contentedly. Sighing, I said, "Well, if Calchas is right, it will end soon, and we'll all go home. It can't be soon enough for me." Then I made the mistake of asking Astynome if she would be going to Greece with Agamemnon.

"I don't know. I scarcely ever see him. He seems to have tired of me, and he ignores his new son. I don't dare ask." Her lip was trembling. "I have no idea what my future will bring, Hermione. I pray to the gods and await my fate, whatever it is. I've had no dreams about that." She struggled to sound brave, but I knew that she was frightened, for herself and her child, and there was nothing I could say.

THE GREEK ENCAMPMENT WAS astir. The great warrior and champion archer Philoctetes had arrived from the island of Lemnos. Philoctetes was another of my mother's former suitors, and when Menelaus had called for help, he was one of the first to respond. But an argument later came up with Odysseus—this happened fairly often, for Odysseus could be a difficult man—and Philoctetes was left behind on Lemnos. There he remained until an oracle revealed that he possessed the special bow and arrows needed to finally conquer the Trojans. Menelaus now believed that Philoctetes was the one man who could kill Prince Paris. Suddenly all was forgiven, and Philoctetes received a hero's welcome at the Greek encampment.

Philoctetes immediately challenged Paris to combat in archery. The two great armies gathered on the plain to watch. I went looking for Calchas to describe what was happening in this fateful duel. The aged seer was aching in his bones, but he had always been fond of me, and he agreed to go with me to our usual spot in the small grove of fig trees, and to tell me what his second sight revealed.

"The air shimmers with excitement. This is the duel the Greeks have been waiting for. Wagers are made on how many arrows Philoctetes will shoot in order to kill the Trojan prince. Menelaus has mounted a special stand from which to observe the contest. A hush falls on the crowd. Philoctetes looses his first arrow, but it misses its mark. Paris's arrow also goes wide. Philoctetes puts his second arrow to string—and it strikes Paris in his bow hand! Paris manages to shoot again, but poorly. Philoctetes' third arrow pierces Paris's eye, and a fourth strikes him in the heel, in the same manner as Paris wounded Achilles."

I wondered if my mother was watching, and what she was thinking, what pain she felt as her lover lay gravely wounded. "Is Paris dead, Calchas?"

"No, not dead, Hermione, but he is dying. Paris has asked his friends to carry him to his former lover, Oenone. Years ago he cast her aside for Helen. When they parted, Oenone told him, 'If ever you are badly hurt, come back to me, for only I can heal you.' Now Paris begs her to heal his wounds as she once promised him, but she refuses, taking her revenge. Tomorrow all of Troy will grieve for Paris."

"And Helen?" I asked. "Calchas, can you tell me what will happen to my mother now? Is she ready to come home with my father and me?"

Calchas was silent for a long time before he answered. "She will be claimed by both Deiphobus and Helenus, brothers of Paris," he said. "Priam will award her to Deiphobus, who will find her attempting to escape and force her to marry him. Unless Menelaus can reach her first."

16

The Wooden Horse

THE WOODEN HORSE WAS ready. We gathered on the beach to admire it. It was enormous, large enough to conceal at least twenty warriors inside, with a secret trapdoor on the horse's flank and a message carved onto its side: "In grateful thanksgiving for a safe return to our homelands, we dedicate this offering to the Goddess Athena."

With the warriors hidden in its belly, the wooden horse would be left where it stood on the beach. Our belongings had already been loaded onto the ships; what remained of the Greek camp would be set on fire and burned to ashes. Only one man, designated by Odysseus, would be left behind to light a beacon when the plan had been set in motion, signaling the ships to return. Zethus had been chosen to be that man. I saw him just before I boarded Menelaus's ship. He'd come to say goodbye.

"I wanted one last chance to speak to you, Princess Hermione," Zethus said. "I expect to be killed. Odysseus has ordered me to allow myself to be captured by the Trojans. I don't know if King Priam will recognize me as his bastard son who sailed for Greece with Paris ten years ago."

I remembered how I'd found Zethus asleep in my father's stables in Sparta. Zethus, who helped me understand what had happened to my mother. Zethus, who had given me the little carving of a ship, built me a loom, made a wedding goblet for Orestes and me. He'd done so much! But I had questions. "You've been with us all these years, Zethus, but where is your heart? Why are you helping us? Aren't you a Trojan? And why does Odysseus, who is suspicious of almost everybody, trust *you*?"

"I swore my loyalty to the Greeks many years ago. I've been a slave, but I was treated well. I've helped to build the wooden horse, and now I'll help to get it inside the walls of Troy."

"That doesn't answer *why,* Zethus."

Zethus looked uncomfortable. "Because of my devotion to you, Princess Hermione. I would gladly give my life for you. And now I bid you a last farewell."

He bowed and rushed away. Speechless, I watched him go.

MY FATHER WAS THE first to climb up a rope ladder into the belly of the horse. Next was Odysseus, who'd concocted the whole plan. Pyrrhus followed; he would lead the fight once they'd entered Troy. The choice of Pyrrhus as leader shocked me, though he was his father's son and no doubt Menelaus and Agamemnon sought to honor him.

I watched Orestes climb the ladder. We had said our goodbyes the night before as we held each other, whispering words of love, and I had promised not to weep when he was gone. The wooden horse was a risky plan, and I knew well that I might never see Orestes—or my father—alive again. But I kept my promise and, dry eyed, went with the others to board Menelaus's ship. At nightfall the camp was set on fire. As our ships put out to sea, we watched the flames leap skyward. But we didn't sail far—only to the island of Tenedos, just out of sight of Troy on the mainland—and prepared to wait there aboard the ships. Hippodameia was with me; she still grieved for Achilles and worried what her fate would be.

"We're all fearful," I said. "I wish I could have persuaded Astynome to bring her baby and come with us. She has such amazing dreams. She could help us." But Astynome had chosen to board one of Agamemnon's ships—a mistake, I thought.

Calchas had also boarded Agamemnon's ship; I couldn't summon him and his second sight to describe the scene to me as it unfolded. Only later, when it was all over, did I learn in fragments what happened the next day in Troy.

The Trojans awoke to discover that the Greeks had gone, their camp nothing but smoldering ashes, but that they'd left a huge wooden horse on the beach outside the city gates. King Priam and some of his sons went down from the citadel to look at this strange object and to read the inscription on its flank.

Fierce disagreement erupted. One of the princes wanted to haul the wooden horse into the city, because it was a gift to the goddess Athena. Another argued that Athena often favored the Greeks and that the horse should be left where it was. At the very least, he insisted, they should break into the body of the horse to find out what was inside. The two sides argued until Priam decided that the horse was to be brought into the city.

All day the Trojans struggled with the wooden horse, putting logs under it as rollers and using ropes to drag it. It was too broad to pass through the city gates—four times it became wedged tight, and four times they labored to free it. Even after they knocked down parts of the wall, their difficulties were not over. The arguing went on.

Princess Cassandra, Priam's mad daughter, warned them of the danger. "It's a trap!" she told her father. "Beware of the gifts given to you by Greeks!" But no one ever believed Cassandra—that was her curse.

Still, there were others who were suspicious of this wondrous wooden horse. One of the Trojans hurled a spear at it; the spear pierced the wood and stuck there, quivering—and caused the Greeks inside to quiver as well!

There were cries from many Trojans to burn the horse, to destroy it.

The Trojans had not yet discovered that their sacred wooden statue of Pallas Athena, which everyone believed was safely hidden, had been stolen. Wily Odysseus, in disguise, had sneaked into Troy a day earlier and taken it, knowing that the loss of the carving would weaken the Trojans and their will to defend their city.

Unaware of the theft, Priam remained adamant. The wooden horse must stay, lest Athena be offended by their treatment of it, and it must be hauled all the way up to the citadel. While this enormous task was being undertaken, Priam's guards marched in, dragging Zethus in shackles, just as was planned. When Priam recognized his son by Cassandra's maidservant, he ordered him freed. Zethus successfully convinced the skeptical Trojans that he was on their side, explaining that if they had not brought the horse into the city, Athena would surely have ruined them.

Zethus played his role well. Priam was deceived by this artfully concocted tale. He ordered a feast to celebrate the Trojans' victory over the Greeks. Women gathered flowers from along the banks of the River Scamander, wove them into garlands, and hung them around the neck of the wooden horse. They spread a carpet of blooms around the horse's hooves. The Trojans cheered.

Meanwhile, the Greeks, barely able to draw a breath in the stifling belly of the horse, waited tensely for Odysseus to give the order to attack. They argued in whispers. "It's not yet time," Odysseus insisted.

Pyrrhus, determined to begin the attack, was barely prevented from assaulting Odysseus to have his way.

Voices outside the horse tormented the men crowded inside. Helen, accompanied by her new husband, Deiphobus, walked around the horse three times, speaking loudly. Menelaus could hear her clearly. He had not arrived in time to prevent her marriage, and that further inflamed him. She seemed to be taunting him, as though she knew he was there. Odysseus had to restrain him from opening the trapdoor and leaping down to confront her.

The wait went on.

A day of feasting and revelry celebrating the Trojan victory ended toward midnight, and the people of Troy fell into a deep and untroubled sleep.

But to us onboard the ships, waiting anxiously out of sight and knowing nothing of what had transpired, that day had seemed endless. A bright moon rose. No one on the ships could even think of sleeping. We, too, were waiting. I thought about Zethus, wondering if he was safe. I was fearful for my father, fearful for Orestes, and worried what would now happen to my mother. The past ten years had brought us all to this night.

We crowded onto the deck and peered into the darkness, watching for Zethus's signal fire. The moon rose high, and shards of moonlight glittered on the black water. At last the lookout on the mast reported a flicker in the distance. On his ship Agamemnon lighted a basin of wood chips as an answering signal. If the gods favored us, Zethus would see the light and find a way to pass the word to the men who had spent a long day and two long nights in the belly of the wooden horse. At Tenedos the anchor stones were raised, and the Greek ships sliced silently through the foaming sea toward Troy.

INSIDE THE GATES OF the city, Zethus spotted Agamemnon's signal and crept close to the wooden horse. He spoke softly to the men hiding there: "The ships are coming."

Odysseus calculated how long it would take the ships to sail from Tenedos to the harbor north of the beach where the remains of our former encampment still smoldered, and how much longer for the men to march from the harbor to the city. Zethus confirmed their arrival. The Greeks opened the trapdoor and scrambled down the rope ladder. With Pyrrhus in the lead, one group silently slit the throats of the sentries and hurried on to Priam's royal palace. A second group opened the gates, closed up after the Trojans had hauled the wooden horse inside. Greek soldiers poured through the gates and spread out over the sleeping city, killing as they went.

Pyrrhus, consumed by rage, reached the royal palace, seized Priam by the throat, and slew him. He dragged the king's butchered body to the tomb of Achilles and left it there. He found Hector's widow, Andromache, on the rampart, clutching her infant son, Astyanax. Pyrrhus grabbed the little boy by his foot, whirled the screaming child over his head, and flung him onto the rocks below. Taking the sobbing mother as his prize, Pyrrhus dragged Andromache away.

Now Polyxena had to die. She'd betrayed Achilles—as he lay dying he'd called for her to be sacrificed—and Pyrrhus was quite ready to kill her. "Achilles loved her. My father deserves to have his spoils too," he said.

Polyxena saved Pyrrhus the trouble and stabbed herself on Achilles' tomb.

Menelaus, torn by conflicting feelings of love and hate, cared about nothing but finding Helen. He ran to the house of Deiphobus. My father may have intended to murder his unfaithful wife. I myself had heard him swearing to Odysseus, "She must die!" But what actually happened when he found my mother I could only try to imagine.

Helen was holding a bloody dagger, and Deiphobus lay dead at her feet. Menelaus dropped his sword, undone at the sight of her: the most beautiful woman in the world. Perhaps she knelt and clasped his knees, a supplicant, calling herself a whore, a lost woman. Or maybe she simply stood there, looking at him, waiting for him to put his knife to her throat.

"Menelaus," Helen said. "Please forgive me. I have wronged you."

He looked into her hyacinth blue eyes and loved her as much as he did when he first married her.

"Helen, I forgive you."

They gazed at each other. He raised my mother's hand to his lips. I don't know what happened between them, only that my father led her out of Troy, followed by servants carrying chests of her jewels and gowns. Nearly everyone else was killed that bloody night.

My heart fluttered as my father brought my mother to his ship. She looked exactly as she had when I'd last seen her, at our palace in Sparta, entertaining our guest, Prince Paris. It was true: her beauty had not faded. Menelaus raked his fingers through his beard, no longer fiery red but threaded with gray. He couldn't take his eyes off her.

I walked toward her, my hands outstretched and trembling. A sob caught in my throat. "Mother."

"Hermione?" she asked with a little smile. I expected her to weep, to show some feeling—joy, sorrow, some kind of emotion—but she didn't. I could tell that she wasn't sure she recognized me. Her smile was pleasant but distant. She touched my cheek lightly with her fingertips. "I'm so happy to see you," she said. Then she turned all of her attention back to my father.

I swallowed my disappointment. I had hoped for so much more.

Book III
After the War

Promises

AFTER TEN LONG YEARS of endless fighting, Troy had been destroyed, all the treasure seized and divided, the walls of the city torn down. The city itself was now a smoking ruin.

A huge feast was being prepared near the harbor to celebrate our victory. The scene was chaotic. I hurried toward Agamemnon's ship, searching for Orestes. I caught a far-off glimpse of him and tried to make my way through the crowds to reach him, eager to be in his arms once more. I called his name, but my voice was drowned out by the shouting and laughter and singing.

One of Father's heralds intercepted me as I fought my way through the surging crowds. "King Menelaus and Queen Helen desire your presence, Princess Hermione."

"Tell them I'll come in a little while," I said, still trying to keep Orestes in sight.

"I'm ordered to bring you *now*, Princess."

Reluctantly, I went with him.

I found my mother and father deep in conversation with Pyrrhus. What could they possibly have to discuss with him? I'd already heard too many reports of his cruel murder of Andromache's child and his brutal seizure of her as his concubine. I'd never liked Pyrrhus, and the more I saw of him, the less I could bear to be anywhere near him. He was grinning at me now in a way that unsettled me. It was more a leer than a smile.

I acknowledged my father and my mother with a bow. They were holding hands.

"We have excellent news for you, dear Hermione," Father said. That same little smile played on my mother's lips. Her eyes were fastened on my father, as though she couldn't get enough of him. "We have arranged for your marriage to Pyrrhus, son of Achilles."

I opened my mouth and closed it again. I felt as though I were suffocating. My legs were weak as water. Pyrrhus reached out to steady me, keeping me from toppling over. I slapped his hand away. He sickened me! I loathed him! How could my parents possibly think to have me marry him? I hadn't yet had a chance to tell them that it was Orestes I loved, Orestes who loved me, Orestes I wanted to marry. Surely Helen hadn't forgotten that her own father had pledged us when we were infants!

I fought down the impulse to flee or to cry out or even to

protest. Better to say nothing now, I thought; to wait until later and then slip away during the night while everyone was sleeping and search until I found my love. I knew he was searching for me, too!

Pyrrhus stared at me with glittering eyes, his lip curled in a sneer. I stared back at him, expressionless. But he was much stronger than I, even in a staring contest, and I was the first to look away.

THE GOLDEN DISC OF the sun slid into the dark sea. Agamemnon, in a triumphant mood, came to our ship to talk with Menelaus. Orestes hadn't come with his father. I was told that he was busy preparing the ships for the journey back to Greece. Agamemnon was in a hurry. A brisk wind had risen, and he wanted to cut short the celebration and set sail at once.

"It will move us speedily away from here and back to our homeland," Agamemnon told my father. "We can celebrate when we arrive in Greece."

Menelaus had other plans. "First, sacrifices must be made to Athena. Then we'll sail."

"Athena was more helpful to the Trojans than she was to us," Agamemnon argued. "She deserves no sacrifices."

Soon the two brothers were shouting at each other, their faces red with anger, their words full of spite. Agamemnon stormed off.

The night was cloudless, and the shore was bathed in moonlight. I was determined to leave my father's ship and find

Orestes. I had to tell him about Pyrrhus. I needed his help in making my parents understand that I could not marry Achilles' son. I was about to slip away when a lookout climbed down from the mast and reported sighting the white sails of Agamemnon's ships in the distance.

Orestes was certainly with them, bound for Mycenae. We'd had no time to speak, to kiss, to renew our promises. Sick at heart, I rushed to find Menelaus and Helen, but they'd withdrawn into Father's private quarters. I was shut out.

The white sails had disappeared. Orestes was gone.

I spent the night pacing, agonizing. Maybe my mother could help—she knew what love was! She more than anyone! Helen didn't emerge from Father's quarters until midmorning, stretching luxuriously. She seemed surprised to find me waiting for her.

"You look awful, Hermione," she said. "Didn't you sleep well? It's important to get a good night's sleep if you want to preserve your looks." She peered at me closely. "Aren't you happy to be marrying Pyrrhus? Having the son of our great Achilles as your husband should please you very much. He's as handsome as Achilles ever was! Your father and I have decided that you should marry him as soon as possible. We'll have the ceremony right here on the shore, and then you can sail with him, back to Phthia, or wherever those Myrmidons of his live. You'd like that, wouldn't you, Hermione?"

I could hardly believe my mother was speaking to me this

way. We hadn't seen each other in nearly ten years, and I'd gotten along without her all that time. I was now a grown woman, and she was treating me as though I were still a child. And why would my father think a cruel, arrogant man like Pyrrhus would make me a suitable husband?

"No, I wouldn't like it at all, Mother!" I said, too loudly. "And neither would you! You left your husband to run away with a handsome man who possessed neither heart nor soul, and from what I hear, not much courage, either! Thousands of people have died because of what you did, and now you think you can come back into my life and tell *me* what to do? You believe you know what's good for me!" I was shouting, but I couldn't stop. "You don't even know me, Queen Helen. You and I are complete strangers. The man I love sailed away from here last night. We plan to marry, as Tyndareus intended! Tyndareus, your father! And now I don't know if I'll ever see Orestes again, and you're forcing me to marry a man I hate!"

I was sobbing, tears spilling down my cheeks, my nose dripping. It was true that I hadn't slept the night before, my clothes smelled sour, and my hair was a mass of tangles. My mother looked at me with pity. Had she heard a word I'd said?

"Poor Hermione," she said, shaking her head in distaste. "Too bad you were destined to look like your father, instead of like me." She turned away, leaving me distraught.

An Unwilling Bride

KING MENELAUS SENT OUT heralds to the ships that had not yet sailed, announcing that my wedding to Pyrrhus would take place that evening. More animals were slaughtered and prepared for the spit, amphoras of wine were unloaded from the remaining ships, and baskets of ripe fruit were carried in from the fields that hadn't been reduced to ruin. *Others may celebrate,* I thought; *I will not.*

I was numb. I could not think what to do. Stumbling along the beach in a daze, I encountered Astynome carrying her baby. She also appeared dazed.

"Astynome, I thought you'd gone with Agamemnon," I said.

"He left us behind. He told everyone that he's now in love with Cassandra. He took her as his concubine, but his servants say he plans to rid himself of Clytemnestra when he gets home to Mycenae, and then marry Cassandra. Not long ago he promised to marry *me.*"

"Don't envy Cassandra. Clytemnestra can be very unpleasant when she's angered."

Astynome knew that Orestes had sailed with Agamemnon's fleet, but she hadn't yet heard that I was being forced to marry Pyrrhus. We fell weeping into each other's arms, cursing our fates. Together we decided to leave the baby in the care of a serving girl and to search for Hippodameia. With both Patroclus and Achilles dead and no place to go, Hippodameia had stayed on with the Myrmidons, who were using her shamefully.

"Oh, my dear friends!" Hippodameia cried when we found her, and the weeping began again. "How could things have turned out so badly for all of us?"

My two friends were horrified that I was to marry Pyrrhus that evening. "He's a brute," Hippodameia said. "He ignores me, thanks be to the gods, and spends most of his time abusing Andromache. Pyrrhus believes he's entitled to mistreat her, because she's Hector's widow. Poor thing—she looks half-dead, and I believe she wishes she *were* dead. She can't bear even to look at the beast who murdered her little boy."

"Yes, he is a beast," I said. "And soon that beast will be my husband. My only hope is that he will exhaust himself with Andromache and leave me alone as well."

Never had there been three more miserable women, and we decided to find Andromache and make it four. We found her crouched by Pyrrhus's ship, her clothes torn, her face smeared with ashes. She stared at us with vacant eyes. She was like a wounded animal. I reached out, but she drew away from me with a sharp little cry.

"Andromache," I whispered, "I'm Hermione, daughter of Menelaus, soon to be the unwilling wife of Pyrrhus. I mean you no harm. Maybe we can help each other."

Tentatively she accepted my hand, and her gaze met mine briefly before it darted away again. I'd never seen such pain in a woman's eyes. I noticed that her lip was swollen and one of her eyes blackened. Had Pyrrhus done that to her?

Astynome spoke up. "Let's go bathe in the pools!" she said.

It was the custom for a bride and her friends to bathe together before a wedding. I dreaded the ordeal ahead of me, but I welcomed a chance to be with these sympathetic women.

We discovered that Andromache's feet were shackled. "I know how to free her," Hippodameia said. She called a guard and smiled at him beguilingly. He unfastened Andromache's fetters, and we helped her to her feet. "We'll bribe him when we come back. I know this guard. He's not a bad human being. I trust him not to tell Pyrrhus we were here."

We had little to say as we walked to the pools, past the burial mounds covering the ashes of the dead Greeks. Smoke curled up from the ruins behind the walls of the defeated city. The watchtowers had been toppled. The main gate was like a gaping wound. There were no sounds of human voices, but screeching vultures swooped low over the bodies that lay rotting within the walls. Andromache shuffled along unsteadily between us, staring at the bloodstained ground.

The pools fed by the River Scamander were deserted. Andromache stood stiffly, her arms at her sides. She hadn't spoken a word. Three of us removed our chitons and slid naked into the hot water.

"Andromache?" Hippodameia called out. "Come join us!"

Andromache didn't move, and Hippodameia climbed out and whispered to her. Hippodameia, whose husband had been murdered by Achilles on her wedding day, could surely see into Andromache's heart better than anyone. Reluctantly the wretched woman removed her torn robe and lowered herself into the pool. Her body was covered with bruises.

We hadn't brought our serving women. We washed our own garments and spread them on the rocks to dry. We sponged our bodies and washed each other's hair. I closed my eyes and sank up to my neck in the soothing water, but whenever I thought of Orestes, despair crept over me. I'd lost him, and, unless the gods intervened, before the day ended I'd be wed to a man I despised.

"I confess that I'm glad Pyrrhus is marrying you," Andromache murmured close to my ear, speaking to me for the first time. "Maybe he'll leave me alone for at least one night. Because I hate him even more than you do. He killed my beloved husband and murdered my adored child. If ever I have a chance to kill Pyrrhus, I swear I will do it."

My eyes flew open, but Andromache turned away again and wouldn't look at me. The pleasure of the hot bath was finished for me. I climbed out of the pool, ran naked to plunge into the second pool, and endured the shock of the cold spring water. I grabbed my chiton from the rocks, still damp, and dressed hurriedly. The sun was already past the midpoint. "I have to leave," I told the others.

"We're coming with you," Astynome said.

"We will not let you face this alone," added Hippodameia.

Andromache grimaced. "I can't go with you, Hermione. I must return to my fetters or endure another beating." She kissed my cheek.

HELEN WAS WAITING FOR me at Father's ship, and she was displeased.

"You stupid girl!" she said sharply. "This is your wedding day, and you disappear! We have to find a decent peplos for you to wear, and a proper veil. Why is your hair looking so bedraggled?" She glanced at Astynome and Hippodameia and frowned. "Who are these girls you've brought with you, Hermione?"

"I'm her friend," Astynome said.

"As am I," said Hippodameia.

"They'll be with me at the wedding," I explained to my mother. "If you insist upon forcing me to marry Pyrrhus."

Helen sighed. Her delicately arched eyebrows rose. "Hermione, do you understand nothing? Women do as men command

—that's the way of the world. We really have very little choice of whom we marry. Isn't that true?" She looked from one to the other of my friends.

"It's true," admitted Hippodameia, and Astynome nodded.

"My father chose Menelaus from among all my suitors and married me to him. The choice wasn't mine—I scarcely knew him!" Helen said.

"You chose to leave him and to run away with Paris," I could not resist reminding her.

"It was the work of Aphrodite," she said. "I'm not sure it *was* my choice. And it was certainly *not* my choice to marry Deiphobus after Paris was killed—Priam insisted, and Deiphobus forced himself upon me."

"Now he is dead too—and by your own hand!"

"Did I kill him?" Helen frowned. "First he was there, threatening me, and then he lay dead on the floor and I was holding a bloody knife. But did I choose to kill him? I'm not certain I did," she said, shaking her head. "I don't remember. Perhaps the gods intervened."

"But it was your choice to return to Father?"

"Oh, yes." My mother smiled. "This time it is. I'm happy that he still wants me as his wife after all that has happened."

I wondered if she was telling the truth.

"Then why are you forcing me to marry Pyrrhus? I was promised to Orestes by your father. I love him, Mother, and Orestes loves me! Surely you can understand that."

"I understand it, but I can do nothing about it, and neither can you. It doesn't matter what your grandfather promised—he's long dead. Your father pledged you to the son of Achilles even before the ships sailed from Greece for Troy."

Had he really done that? Was *this* true? And if it was, as my mother claimed, why had he not said anything to me in all this time?

"Menelaus owes it to the memory of the great warrior to honor that pledge," Helen was saying, though I scarcely listened. "Breaking that promise would only lead to more violence, and there's surely been enough of that. Now bring your friends, Hermione, and we'll prepare for your wedding. Who knows—you may even come to care for Pyrrhus. Stranger things have happened."

I gazed into her eyes of hyacinth blue and gave up. "I will obey, Mother, and do as you and Father command. But I will *never* care for that brute."

Glumly, I went with my mother, my two friends trailing along silently behind us. It seemed odd to be with Helen. She had not expressed a single word of regret at leaving me behind, or one word of pleasure at seeing me after such a long separation. Was she happy to be with me? What did she think of me, of the woman I'd become?

I walked beside Helen, feeling tongue-tied. There was so much in my heart that I wanted to say to her but I could not. It had been ten years since we'd lived together. We were different people now. I didn't know her. I wasn't sure I ever had. I had no idea what she was thinking. She was so cool, so remote.

All the fleets except Agamemnon's lay anchored near the teeming beach. The smell of roasting meat drifted through the air. Musicians were tuning their instruments. Only days earlier this had been a desolate place, the shelters of a temporary city built for war pulled down and burned, leaving only smoking ash. Now the ashes had been buried and tents erected again, fitted out with carpets and fine furnishings looted from the conquered Troy. It had all happened so swiftly, carried out by Trojans now enslaved by the Greeks.

My mother led me into her quarters, where she'd laid out several gowns and veils from the trunks she'd brought from Troy. "I wove them myself," she said, holding up one elegantly decorated peplos after another. "There should be something suitable here for you. And for your friends, too," she added, glancing at Hippodameia and Astynome.

My mother sent several of her serving women to dress me and to fix my hair. She also left necklaces and bracelets set with lapis lazuli, earrings of amethyst, and other jewelry. I chose a peplos of finely spun wool dyed a delicate yellow and treated with oil that gave it a rich luster, and a gossamer veil stitched with spangles of hammered silver and small discs of gold. There were also well-made sandals of soft and supple leather. The loom Zethus had made for me and the veil I'd been weaving for my dreamed-of wedding to Orestes were already on Pyrrhus's ship. I prayed that my half of the wedding goblet was safely hidden there too.

Astynome dismissed Helen's serving women, telling them

that she would arrange my hair herself. It had grown long, and when Astynome finished combing it smooth and fixing little curls across my forehead, it shone like burnished copper.

"Hermione," Hippodameia said, watching us, "you have no idea how beautiful you look. I think Helen is jealous of you."

Hippodameia began then to recall her own wedding, interrupted so brutally by the arrival of Achilles. "I'd spent the day with my mother and aunts and sisters. They walked with me to the megaron where my father and the man I was to marry were making their sacrifices to the gods. I remember the scent of flowers. How nervous I felt when I saw the man who was to be my husband! His eyes were kind. But at that moment Achilles stormed in with his henchmen and the murders began."

"And yet, in spite of what he had done, you came to love him," I remarked, wondering how that could be possible.

"Yes," Hippodameia admitted, "I did. There was goodness in Achilles as well, and when I discovered that goodness, my feelings toward him changed." She took my hands in both of hers and looked earnestly into my eyes. "Pyrrhus is his son. If you can, try to find the goodness in him, too. You may not love him, but it will make your life bearable."

Though I did think she was wrong—I saw no hints of goodness in Pyrrhus—I thanked her.

Astynome arranged my shimmering veil, and when the heralds had twice come for us and we could not delay any longer, the three of us went out together to the beach where the rites would take place and my father would hand me over to my husband. It was to be a hurried affair. Menelaus was eager to take Helen home to Sparta; Pyrrhus would tolerate no more delays before returning to Phthia.

Pyrrhus had never looked more handsome; I gave him that. He wore a beautiful white tunic banded in blue and belted over a kilt fringed with tassels, and a necklace of amber beads that were favored by warriors. His long, wheat-colored hair was freshly washed and oiled. He had grown a beard. But handsome as he was, he was not Orestes.

I must stop thinking about Orestes, I told myself. *My lover is gone.*

Animals were sacrificed, and libations of wine were poured on the ground. I scarcely heard the words being spoken. My father, smiling, joined my hands with Pyrrhus's.

My lover is gone.

The feasting and drinking went on until after the stars appeared. I looked for Hippodameia and Astynome but couldn't find them. Queen Helen, luminous in her beauty, was the center of attention, just as she had always been. She was playing a lyre and singing in a pure, silvery voice, her golden hair streaming, marble-white skin glowing in the torchlight. Every man listened as though no one else in the world had ever sung such songs.

Pyrrhus led me back to his tent. We walked in silence. We had nothing to say to each other. I was surprised to find Andromache there, though I should not have been. She huddled in a corner, watching us warily. Pyrrhus grasped her by the shoulders and steered her out of the tent. "Tonight I lie with my wife," he said. She went away silently. I knew she was relieved.

My husband took me angrily, forcibly, with no regard for my feelings. I closed my eyes and submitted, weeping for Orestes.

My lover is gone. Gone. Gone.

19

Leaving Troy

THE REMAINING GREEK FLEETS prepared to sail for home.
Odysseus had already departed with his ships. Menelaus's
fleet was ready to set out for Sparta. Helen had agreed to take
Astynome, along with her baby, as her servant. Astynome had
confided to me that although she had accepted this offer, her
goal when she reached Sparta was to find her way to Agamemnon in Mycenae. I considered that foolhardy. Not only was
Clytemnestra not likely to welcome her as a replacement, but
Agamemnon had declared his love for Cassandra. Hippodameia begged to be allowed to come with me, and when I asked
permission from Pyrrhus, he did not deny me. I would have at
least one friend — two, if Andromache could be counted.

Someone else had joined us: a Trojan named Helenus, twin
brother of Cassandra, brother of Hector and Paris, though
not nearly as handsome as Paris. Helenus had been the rival
of Deiphobus to marry my mother after Paris was killed, but

luckily for Helenus—or Helen might have stabbed him instead —Priam chose Deiphobus. Helenus was said to have the gift of prophecy, taught him by his sister, Cassandra, but people believed *his* prophecies, unlike hers.

"Helenus will make a useful servant," Pyrrhus said. "I need someone to make accurate predictions."

Maybe it would be good for Andromache to have her husband's brother nearby. Or maybe not—that depended on many things. Helenus was unlikely to forget that Pyrrhus had also murdered Priam, Helenus's father, and countless other noble Trojans. I marveled that my husband could sleep at night with so many in his household who no doubt wished him dead.

We were ready to set sail. I had looked in vain for Zethus. No one seemed to know what happened to him after he'd fulfilled his duty, signaling the Greek ships and then letting the men inside the wooden horse know when the troops had arrived. I had to assume he'd been killed in the turmoil and bloodshed that followed. I greatly feared that his body lay rotting within the walls of the ruined city.

THE GODS HAD DECIDED to toy with the Greeks once more —or perhaps the men had misjudged the winds. Pyrrhus had told me he expected to reach Phthia in three days. Menelaus had given a similar estimate of the time it would take his ships to get to Sparta. But they hadn't counted on the violent tempests that swept the Chief Sea, scattering the ships and drowning many men who, until the water finally closed over their heads, had clung to the belief that they'd soon be with their wives and children again.

Now, after a long and violent voyage, Pyrrhus's ships— what was left of them—arrived at Iolkos, the main seaport in Phthia. I was very glad to be on dry land after days of relentlessly churning seas, towering waves, and winds that tore at the sail. The Myrmidons had reached their homeland at last, and when we stepped onto the shore, even the most hardened among them kissed the ground.

We camped at Iolkos while the ships were unloaded and Pyrrhus's share of the Trojan treasure was piled onto donkey carts. That night the men celebrated, and after much wine had been drunk, Pyrrhus summoned a ship's captain, a man named Leucus, and ordered him to burn all the ships bearing Pyrrhus's emblem, the horns of a bull on a rayed star.

Leucus was not a Myrmidon but came from the island of Skyros, where Pyrrhus had spent his boyhood. "All of them?" Leucus asked, and hesitated, frowning.

"Yes, all of them!" Pyrrhus shouted angrily. "Are you questioning my command?" He struck Leucus squarely in the face. Blood spurted from the captain's mouth. His front teeth were now gone.

Leucus didn't flinch. He gave the order to the men, who ran drunkenly from ship to ship with flaming torches, setting fire to the entire fleet. I watched the leaping flames with a sinking heart and understood that Pyrrhus was destroying our connection to the rest of the world.

The blackened hulls of the ships were still smoldering when Pyrrhus led his war-weary troops on the long journey overland toward the heart of Phthia. The rough path, sometimes not much more than a goat track, wound through the mountains. There were no carrying chairs. Hippodameia, Andromache, and I struggled to keep up with the soldiers and the donkey carts. Helenus did what he could to help us, until Pyrrhus grew suspicious of the Trojan's nearness to Andromache and ordered him to stay away. Runners dashed ahead to scattered villages to alert the inhabitants to our approach. Peasants emerged from their huts to greet the battle-scarred warriors, trying to recognize the men they hadn't seen for ten years.

I saw no young children in these villages, only hollow-eyed women and a few stooped old men; the younger men and boys had left their homes long ago to follow Achilles into battle. There were tears of joy as women welcomed their husbands, and half-grown boys and girls shrank from fathers who were strangers to them. There were tears of grief, too; many women wailed and scratched their faces when they realized their husbands were not among those who had come back.

The villagers quickly organized themselves to prepare a feast, slaughtering their fattest animals and bringing out dust-covered wine jars saved for years for this occasion. After we'd eaten and drunk our fill and stories had been told and retold, we moved on to the next village, and the next, Pyrrhus's army of Myrmidons shrinking as the men reached their homes.

I'd lost count of the days when at last we crossed a broad plain marked with stands of leafy green trees, sparkling springs, and a fast-moving river. Pyrrhus pointed out the citadel on the crest of a high hill. "Pharsalos!" he shouted. "Capital of Phthia, the kingdom of the Myrmidons!"

Walls constructed of huge, rough boulders—walls twice as thick as those at Sparta and Mycenae—encircled the citadel and extended down the hill to surround the town below. Outside the walls lay abandoned fields, once planted in grain but now overrun with thistle, and we entered the sleepy lower town through unguarded gates hanging on broken hinges. The narrow, crooked streets were unpaved and dusty, and the mud-brick houses, even the large ones of the wealthier citizens, were neglected and crumbling, the sagging roofs in need of thatching.

"It's nothing like Troy," murmured Andromache, walking beside me.

The inhabitants watched us warily, unsure how to respond to this stranger who announced himself as Pyrrhus, king of Phthia. No one rushed out to bow or to clasp his hands.

Pyrrhus's face darkened. "Has no one told them their king has come home at last?"

"They've been too long without a ruler," I said, hoping to tame his growing anger. "It will take a little time for them to get used to having a king again."

We reached the top of the steep, winding path to the citadel. "So far from the sea!" Hippodameia exclaimed, breathless from the climb.

"My grandmother, Thetis, lived here with Peleus," Pyrrhus growled. "She was born of the sea, and yet she made this her home for many years. And my father was born here!"

Achilles had indeed been born in Pharsalos, but as a boy he'd been sent by Thetis to live in the palace of the king of Skyros. Achilles had not yet reached full manhood when he lay with the king's daughter, and Pyrrhus was the result of that union. Pyrrhus grew up in Skyros; he had never before seen Pharsalos, and the people of Pharsalos had never seen *him*.

We wandered through the moldering chambers of the palace. Small animals had taken up residence in nearly every room; birds fluttered from their nests near the ceiling. Sheepherders had no doubt used the place as their own and kept their flocks here with them. I'm not sure what I expected, but certainly not this. Compared with Agamemnon's magnificent citadel at Mycenae and Menelaus's beautiful palace at Sparta, this was not much better than the tents and crude huts in which we'd lived on the beaches of Troy.

"Welcome to your new home, Hermione," Pyrrhus said sourly. He was surely disappointed too, but his pride wouldn't allow him to show it.

I wanted to weep, but I'd learned that tears were usually pointless and accomplished nothing. Instead, the next day I sent for workers from the town to clean out the birds' nests and dung piles. The sleeping fleeces were infested with vermin and had to be taken out and burned; fortunately, there were plenty of sheep to provide fresh ones. Most of the cooking pots had been stolen from the kitchens. I found clay bowls and the two-handled drinking cups piled on shelves thick with mouse droppings. The bowls were chipped and cracked, and many of the cups were missing one handle.

I took a few cups to show to my husband, who was sucking marrow from a bone pulled from the previous night's fire in what had once been the megaron. He had spent the morning having the donkey carts unloaded and the goods put into one of the storage rooms that could be secured.

"These cups are not usable," I pointed out. "Perhaps there are some silver goblets among your treasure." The image of my half of the beautiful wedding goblet floated into my mind, and I brushed it away.

Pyrrhus snatched a damaged cup from my hands and knocked it sharply against the wall, breaking off the second handle. "Good enough now, I think," he said, and handed it to me with a smirk.

If this was to be my home, then I would do whatever was possible to transform this crumbling heap of stone, this maze of dismal rooms, dark corridors, and gloomy halls, and make it livable. I asked Pyrrhus to hire masons from the town to repair the damaged walls. "Helenus can oversee the work," I said, and grudgingly my husband agreed.

But no one in the city of Pharsalos, or in the kingdom of

Phthia, seemed to know anything about the proper decoration of a royal palace. I doubted that I could find artists who knew how to paint wet plaster with the scenes I remembered from my home in Sparta, or artisans skilled in laying tiles on the floors and finishing the wooden columns of the great hall —even if I could convince Pyrrhus to pay for it.

Long ago my mother had ordered tables and chairs and couches when she was expecting Prince Paris to visit Sparta. Remembering that, I ventured down to the lower town with Ardeste, my new maidservant. Ardeste had grown up in Pharsalos; she knew the town well and found craftsmen for me. When I explained what I wanted, they bowed and smiled, but they had no idea how to do those things. I had to settle for something much simpler, much cruder.

Sometimes I blamed poor Ardeste for not finding the kind of craftsmen I wanted. Sometimes I took out my frustration on some unlucky fellow who had never built anything more elaborate than a sheepfold.

And I argued constantly with Pyrrhus.

"Are you mad, Hermione?" he shouted at me. "You are no longer living the luxurious life of the spoiled daughter of a rich king, thinking you have only to snap your fingers and whatever you want will be yours!"

"Who are you to talk?" I shouted back at him. "You took your share of the Trojan treasury, and I know that Menelaus handed over part of the spoils as my dowry. So please don't tell me that I have to live like a pig farmer's wife!"

My efforts to improve the palace and make it livable helped me to forget, if only briefly, that I loathed my husband. Pyrrhus was no better than I'd expected him to be. We settled into a cool but practical relationship in which I saw to the running of his household, with the assistance of Hippodameia. He was free to swagger around as king of Phthia with his faithful horde of Myrmidons, terrorizing the villages and exacting tribute from the villagers. I had found not one scrap of affection in my heart for Pyrrhus. We had as little to do with each other as possible. I was quite happy that Andromache shared his bed, but on those nights when he was not with her or one of his other concubines, he came to my bed and I received him. It was my duty to provide him with sons.

Then Andromache announced that she was expecting a child.

No doubt I should have foreseen this. In the beginning, after Hector was killed by Achilles, I had felt enormous pity for Andromache. As if her husband's death weren't terrible enough, Pyrrhus had flung their little son to his death on the rocks below the walls of Troy. Pyrrhus brutally compounded the savagery by seizing Andromache as his concubine, dooming her to whatever misery he chose to inflict. I'd seen the bruises on her body and the marks made by her shackles. Who would not have pitied such an unfortunate woman?

Now she was carrying a child. She seemed pleased—almost content.

"Pyrrhus could not be happier," Hippodameia told me

when Andromache gave birth to a son. To my own surprise I suffered pangs of jealousy.

I, too, wanted a child, but not Pyrrhus's child—Orestes'. When I was alone, I took my half of our wedding goblet from the place where I'd hidden it. I could not imagine that I would ever forget him, and painful as it was, I vowed that I would not. Every day, I touched my lips to the rim where his lips had once been and renewed my vow: *Someday, Orestes, we will be together again. We will marry, and we will have a child.*

Hippodameia sensed my yearning. "Andromache has had a life marked by tragedy, but I think she has prayed to the goddesses to deny you a baby."

"Do you believe it could be so?" I thought Andromache and I were friends, and it hadn't occurred to me that she might turn against me.

"Oh, yes," Hippodameia said. "I do."

"Why would she want to deny me a baby?"

"So that she can replace you as Pyrrhus's wife."

"But surely she doesn't love him! It's not possible! She once swore to me that she'd kill him if she ever had the chance!"

"Andromache doesn't love him," Hippodameia said, "but she does want to be queen."

From then on I was highly suspicious of everything Andromache said and did. I watched her closely. She was only a concubine, yet after the birth of her baby boy I noticed that she occupied a special position in the royal household. She had given Pyrrhus a son, and I had given him none. I was ready to blame her.

Then I received another shock: Hippodameia was pregnant. Her belly was already swelling.

"Who?" I asked. "Who is the father?" I hoped she'd say it was Helenus.

But she looked away, avoiding my eye. I knew the answer.

20

Murder and Revenge

PYRRHUS AND HIS MYRMIDONS had left Phthia, marching west. Helenus had made a prophecy, and Pyrrhus had decided to consult the oracle at Zeus's shrine at Dodona to learn what it meant. They'd been gone for nearly three months. Life in the cheerless palace was more tolerable without Pyrrhus. One day when I'd retired to my bedroom to escape the wails of infants that were not mine, I was at my loom when Ardeste announced the arrival of a visitor. Visitors were rare, and I was eager to learn who had found his way to the citadel of Pharsalos.

"He doesn't wish to give his name, mistress. But he sends you this." Ardeste held in her palm a small wooden carving of a horse, a miniature of the huge wooden horse at Troy. *Zethus!* Could it be? I dropped my shuttle and, without bothering to see to the condition of my hair or my well-worn peplos, ran to greet him in the anteroom.

Zethus strode toward me, his hands outstretched in greeting. I was so pleased to see him that I wanted to embrace him, but I stopped myself and welcomed him in the formal manner our positions required.

"Let me call for refreshments, Zethus, and then you can tell me what brings you here." I reminded myself to be patient and wait before plying him with the questions I ached to ask.

Ardeste and one of the young serving girls set down a platter of sesame cakes and a jar of wine mixed with water and herbs. When the serving girl paused to clean up a few drops of spilled wine, Ardeste hurried her away, glancing curiously over her shoulder for another look at Zethus.

Finally we were alone.

"I was afraid you were dead, Zethus! I imagined you lying murdered in the streets of Troy!"

"But as you see, mistress, I am very much alive," Zethus said. "I had no idea where you were, but if one asks enough questions, one eventually finds out what one needs to know. That's how I learned you had married Pyrrhus of Phthia."

"You can be sure I had nothing to say about it! My marriage was the will of King Menelaus and Queen Helen. My father promised me to Pyrrhus without my knowledge." I sipped some wine. "How *did* you find me, Zethus?"

"Fate surely had a hand in it. I left Troy with Orestes in Agamemnon's fleet, but Fate later separated us, and after I had wandered for months it brought me to Iolkos. There I heard reports of a red-haired princess, the bride of Pyrrhus, who had passed through the port on her way to the faraway city of Pharsalos. This red-haired princess was sending messengers far and wide in search of rare woven carpets and finely wrought furniture with inlays of ebony and ivory. You can find such elegant work in the area of the Mycenaeans and equally well-made goods in other parts of the country too, but"—Zethus hesitated and then continued—"it's not well understood by the less artistically talented Myrmidons."

"It's true," I agreed. "The Myrmidons can build a strong wall of immense boulders and hammer out every kind of bronze weaponry on their stone anvils. Do you remember Achilles' spear, so heavy that he was the only one who could lift it? But their craftsmen lack the skill to paint a glorious scene on the wall they've built or to hammer a delicate golden goblet."

I was thinking, of course, of the wedding goblet Zethus had made for Orestes and me. Happy as I was to see Zethus, I wanted news of Orestes far more than I wanted a discussion of walls and weapons, but I checked my impatience and waited for the right moment to ask.

"That's one reason I've come here—to offer my services as an overseer," Zethus was saying. "I know artisans who can make exactly what you want, or I can guide craftsmen who have talent but lack experience. And, if you'll allow me, I can do some of the work myself."

I felt as though I'd just been offered a desirable gift, but I doubted Pyrrhus would be pleased if I accepted it. "My husband already complains that I spend too much," I confessed.

I'd begun thinking of how I was going to introduce Zethus and his plans to Pyrrhus when Zethus leaned forward with a serious, almost regretful, expression. "That's only an excuse for coming here, Hermione. I've brought news that may not yet have reached you."

The sudden change in his mood put me on guard. "What news is that, Zethus?"

He shifted uneasily and sighed. "Agamemnon is dead. Clytemnestra, too."

"Agamemnon and Clytemnestra dead? How can this be? What happened?" I sank back, stunned, afraid to ask the next question. "And Orestes?" I whispered. "He, also?"

Zethus shook his head, and I was weak with relief.

"Orestes is alive. But I believe he wishes with all his heart he were dead."

I poured more wine into our goblets, my hands trembling so much that I spilled some. "Tell me, Zethus."

"Allow me to begin at the beginning. Orestes didn't sail from Troy on Agamemnon's ship, but on another ship in his father's fleet," Zethus said. "Everything happened very quickly—he wanted to find you, but his father kept him engaged. Then he asked me to come with him, and I was willing. We left at once and managed to avoid the storm that tormented the rest of you. As we were nearing the Greek mainland, Orestes bribed the captain of our ship to change course and take us to Gythion. There we found a boat to take us up the river to Sparta. Orestes wanted to ask Menelaus's permission to marry you. He expected to find you there with your parents.

"The royal palace at Sparta was nearly deserted. No one greeted us. A white-bearded servant told us he'd heard that Menelaus's ship had been blown off course. The servant was hopeful that Menelaus and Queen Helen would arrive soon. We thought you were with them, and Orestes was prepared to wait. Every day, he sent a boatman to Gythion to ask for news of Menelaus and Helen—and of his beloved Hermione.

"The little news we had was discouraging. Many of those returning from Troy had been lost in the tempests. At last, two seamen who'd survived the voyage told us that Menelaus and Helen had escaped the worst of the storms and landed safely in Egypt. Orestes still assumed you were with them, and he rejoiced. But the seamen added that you had married Pyrrhus and gone with him to Phthia. The rejoicing turned to grief. The next day Orestes left Sparta—just walked away. I went with him.

"Slowly we made our way toward Mycenae, staying among the shepherds in the hills, sleeping on the ground, sharing their simple meals. His disappointment at losing you was hard to bear. Then, when we reached the city of Tiryns, we met a troupe of traveling bards and musicians. Not recognizing

Orestes, they recited the story of Agamemnon's murder by his wife and her lover."

"Clytemnestra killed Agamemnon?" I interrupted. "I cannot believe what you're saying, Zethus!"

Zethus nodded. "The bards told us that it happened this way. When Agamemnon's fleet sailed for Mycenae, a servant who'd spent every night on the palace roof, watching for the signal fire, rushed to tell Clytemnestra that Agamemnon had left Troy victorious and was on his way home. The queen had good reason for wanting advance warning of the king's return. She'd taken a lover, Aegisthus. It was well known that she resented Agamemnon for murdering her first husband, Tantalus. And she was furious that he'd been willing to sacrifice Iphigenia. She would not forgive him for that."

"I was there when Iphigenia lay on the altar," I whispered. "I heard Clytemnestra curse Agamemnon. But who is Aegisthus?"

"A former king of Mycenae who believed he'd been cheated of his throne. Aegisthus nursed a deep hatred of Agamemnon and Menelaus and their father, too. He'd refused to join the expedition to Troy. And Clytemnestra had another reason to be enraged. She'd found out that Agamemnon planned to bring Cassandra home to marry her. So, with Clytemnestra angry and alone at Mycenae, Aegisthus easily seduced her. Together they plotted to kill Agamemnon when he returned from the war.

"But Agamemnon had ordered his court minstrel to send him a message if Clytemnestra took a lover. Unfortunately for the minstrel, Aegisthus caught him spying and had him taken to a deserted island and left to starve."

The court minstrel! I remembered him—my round-faced, big-bellied music tutor when I'd stayed in Mycenae with Clytemnestra before the war began. Now the birds had picked his bones clean. "So Agamemnon never learned about Aegisthus?"

"Exactly. When the servant on the rooftop reported to Clytemnestra that her husband was coming home, she arranged a royal welcome. She rolled out a purple carpet to greet him. Her slaves prepared a warm bath for him while servants laid out a splendid feast in the great hall.

"While she waited for Agamemnon's arrival, Clytemnestra had woven a large net. Now, as he stepped out of his silver bathing tub, she threw the net over him and ensnared him. Aegisthus stepped up and struck him with a sword, Agamemnon stumbled backward and fell into the tub, and Clytemnestra seized an ax and beheaded him. Cassandra cowered in fear outside the palace, trying to convince anyone who would listen that death lay within. Of course, no one believed her. Clytemnestra found Cassandra and murdered her as well.

"We heard that Agamemnon's body was buried in a rude grave outside the palace walls and that Aegisthus had made himself king—riding in Agamemnon's bronze chariot, sitting on his golden throne, wearing his purple robes and his jeweled diadem, and sleeping with Agamemnon's wife in his splendid bed."

Zethus paused uncertainly, and I begged him to go on. "I must know everything that's happened. You said that Clytemnestra has also been killed."

"This is not an easy story to tell," he said, "and I beg your indulgence if I sometimes find it difficult." I nodded, and Zethus collected his thoughts. "Orestes was in a mad rage, determined to seek revenge," he continued. "I understood his anger, and I urged him to make a pilgrimage to the oracle at Delphi, to ask what he should do. I proposed to go with him, but he refused. That was when he made me promise to look for you and to give you a message: 'Tell Hermione that I will die with her name on my lips.' The next day he disappeared. That was many months ago. I searched for him in Mycenae, without success. Eventually, as I've said, the hand of Fate guided me to Phthia and Iolkos. I have no idea if Orestes went to Delphi, but I do know this: he has killed Aegisthus, for which no one blames him. But he has also killed Clytemnestra."

"Great Zeus!" I cried. "Orestes has murdered his mother? It cannot be!"

"It's true—he has. And the penalty for matricide is very grave indeed, no matter what treachery she committed. It's forbidden by every god and by every court of law. Even if Orestes has escaped punishment by the court, he will not escape the torment of the Furies."

I fell silent then, too shocked for speech and filled with black foreboding. I shuddered at Zethus's mention of the Furies, the three terrible serpent-haired, bat-winged, dog-headed Angry Ones who punish the most serious crimes. They were said to hound the perpetrator and drive him mad—sometimes to suicide.

"Where is he now?" I managed to ask, nearly choking on the words. "What will happen to him?"

Zethus shook his head, avoiding my eyes. "I don't know."

I walked to the window and stared out at the countryside beyond the town walls, my thoughts disordered, my body trembling as though with a fever. A cloud of dust rose in the distance. From the cloud a column of men and horses emerged, moving toward the citadel. I was sure that Pyrrhus and his Myrmidons were coming home from their journey. They'd been gone for three months or more; I'd hoped it would be even longer.

Hippodameia, who had given birth to a daughter while Pyrrhus was away, would no doubt be pleased to see him. Andromache would be pleased as well. The rivalry between the two for his attentions would start again. The intensity of it surprised me. For my part, I was much happier when Pyrrhus ignored me; it was always a great relief to have my husband away from Pharsalos on one of his expeditions and a burden to have him return. He could not have returned at a worse time, when I was struggling to digest the terrible news of Orestes. But whether I was pleased or not made no difference. It was likely that Pyrrhus would not welcome Zethus as a friend, that he'd be suspicious of him, and of me. I hesitated, unsure what to do.

I wondered if Pyrrhus knew about the murders: Agamemnon and Cassandra by Clytemnestra, Aegisthus and Clytemnestra by Orestes. It was the kind of story that spread quickly, yet Pharsalos was so far from everything that news was slow to reach us. Dodona was even more remote.

So many deaths, so much blood! But bloodshed had never bothered Pyrrhus. He had proved he was capable of any sort of murder. I gazed out the window at the cloud of dust moving steadily toward the town. My head began to clear a little. I loved Orestes, no matter what he had done. *Oh, my poor Orestes! Whatever torments you are enduring, I wish I were there to share them with you!*

I would go to him.

Years ago my mother left her husband to be with another man, an act that caused a war lasting ten years and leaving thousands dead and a city in ruins. But Helen blamed it on Aphrodite. The goddess had promised her to Paris. She had no choice in the matter! But I would have no such excuse. I would leave Pyrrhus of my own free will.

What will happen now, I wondered, *if I follow my heart and go in search of Orestes?*

Of course, I knew: Pyrrhus would come after both of us, and he would kill us—not because he loved me, but because I was *his*.

It didn't matter. I had made my decision.

I turned away from the window. "Zethus, you've been my friend since I was a child."

"It's true, mistress. I was your friend then, and I'm your friend now."

"Not long ago you pledged your devotion to me."

"My devotion and my life."

"Then help me to get away from here. Take me to find Orestes."

Zethus hesitated, studying a spot on the wall. "I'll do whatever you ask of me. But what you're asking is very dangerous. Dangerous for *you*—it doesn't matter about me. Pyrrhus won't willingly let you go. If we leave without his permission or his knowledge, he'll come for you, or he'll send his Myrmidons to capture you and drag you back. I won't be able to save either one of us. Even if we can elude them for a while, the terrain is difficult. Most people will be afraid to risk helping us. There are wild beasts to be avoided—I saw them as I came here. And even if the gods are on our side and we make suitable sacrifices and do everything just right, there will be perils at every step—"

"I know all that, Zethus!" I interrupted impatiently. "Please don't give me a list of everything that could possibly go wrong. I must find Orestes. You're my only hope of finding him."

Zethus nodded. "Mistress Hermione, I'm here because Orestes asked me to search for you. I told him that I thought it would be nearly impossible to find you—nevertheless, I did.

It will be nearly impossible to take you away from here, but I'll do whatever I can. When do you want to leave?"

The distant rattle of drums and blare of horns announced Pyrrhus's arrival at the gates of Pharsalos.

"My husband is already at the gates, back from his visit to the oracle of Dodona. We'll make our plans and seize the first opportunity."

"And hope that Pyrrhus doesn't decide to murder me in the meantime," Zethus said grimly.

21

Plan for Escape

I URGED ZETHUS TO leave the citadel immediately and find quarters in the lower town. "Pyrrhus has spies everywhere, so no matter what you do, he'll know about your visit before the day is over. I'll tell him about our plans to decorate the palace, and you'll have a chance to look for artisans. Everything will look quite normal. We'll meet again soon. Now go—quickly."

By the time the heralds reached the citadel to announce Pyrrhus's return, everything was ready for him: a sheep had been slaughtered and spitted and was roasting over a fire, water was heated for his bath, the robe I'd woven for him had been laid out in his dressing room—very much like the way my aunt, Clytemnestra, had prepared for the return of my uncle, Agamemnon, though I had no intention of murdering my husband. I was leaving him, but without the help of Aphrodite. There would be no goddess to put everyone into a trance until I got away. I would have only Zethus to rely on.

The royal household gathered in the courtyard to welcome Pyrrhus: Andromache with her little son on her hip, Hippodameia with her newborn daughter in her arms, a number of cooks, guards, and servants.

With a false smile and modestly lowered eyes, I greeted my husband. He barely acknowledged me, responding in his arrogant manner. After he'd bathed and his servants had dressed him in his new robe, I led him into the gloomy megaron, the walls blackened years ago with smoke from the hearth.

Pyrrhus was in an ebullient mood, unusual for him. He ate heartily, enjoying the roast meat and the bread, staining his fingers red with the seeds of a pomegranate. Wine elevated his mood even more. He admired his bastard son, setting him on his knee, and paid scant attention to his bastard daughter. After the children had been carried away by their nurses, Andromache and Hippodameia quietly took their places on stools nearby.

The time seemed right to tell him about the arrival of Zethus and my plans to improve the palace: hiring plasterers and painters and tile makers, all to work under Zethus's guidance.

"You recall how cleverly Zethus designed and built the wooden horse! Imagine how pleasant this megaron will be, the walls painted with scenes of our glorious victory at Troy!" I said brightly. Before he could begin to grumble about the cost, I leaned closer. "What an excellent way to impress your people," I suggested. "It will give them pride, to see their king and queen living as splendidly as any in Greece."

"No need to make any changes here," Pyrrhus said, tearing into a meat-laden bone. "We're moving. I'm building a new city with a citadel and a palace."

"Moving?" This took me by surprise. "Where? What do you have in mind, Pyrrhus?"

He scowled. "If you will just let me enjoy my meal in peace, I'll tell you all you need to know." He continued to rip meat from the bone, reached for a chunk of bread, and then drained his wine goblet and pounded it on the table to be refilled.

I waited silently, exchanging glances with Andromache and Hippodameia, who appeared as startled as I was. Finally, his appetite sated, his wine goblet full again, Pyrrhus talked loudly about his journey westward.

"We set up our tents in the mountains of Epirus, near the oracle of Dodona. There I met some of my father's people, who led us to the shrine with the sacred oak tree and the priests with unwashed feet who interpret the rustling of its leaves. Months ago Helenus prophesied, 'When you find a house built upon a foundation of metal, with walls of wood and a roof of wool, there you will build a city.' The oracle said that our tents made of blankets draped over our swords stuck in the ground and supported by branches exactly matched Helenus's description! The meaning is absolutely clear. I will send Helenus to begin to build our new city on that precise spot. It's to be called Bouthroton."

"But that's so far away!" I exclaimed.

"Far away from what?" Pyrrhus asked irritably.

Better to have said nothing, I realized. "Just . . . Sparta," I stammered. "My parents. I'd like to visit Menelaus and Helen."

"Really? You want to visit the whore and the man who can't keep his own wife in his bed?" Then he added with a malevolent smile, "Or is it your murderous cousin Orestes you're so eager to see again?"

He knows. Stunned, I opened my mouth and closed it again, unable to utter a word.

"Helenus foresaw the murders, which included his sister Cassandra," he said. "It's hard to say what's more appalling: the queen's murder of her husband, or the son's murder of his mother."

Pyrrhus drained his wine goblet for the third time—or was it the fourth? A servant refilled it without waiting for him to pound the table. "Your family, Hermione!" he said sarcastically. "Your mother's sister and your dear cousin of whom you are so deeply fond—both murderers! I wonder what Menelaus has to say about this. And your mother, too, if your father hasn't yet punished her for what *she's* done. As he should! If it hadn't been for Queen Helen, none of this would have happened. She's the one who deserves to die, as does any woman who betrays her husband."

My face burned with hurt and anger, but his remark sent a chill through me. "Surely you can't blame my mother for this!" I replied sharply. "Helen had nothing to do with

Clytemnestra's betrayal and murder of Agamemnon, or with Orestes' vengeance!"

"But it does show a certain pattern among the women in your family to cuckold their husbands, doesn't it?" I didn't like the way his mouth twisted or the way he leaned toward me, his face too close to mine. I hated his sour breath on me.

I knew it was a mistake to argue with him, and yet I couldn't stop myself. "And when husbands betray their wives with concubines, that's a very different matter, I suppose? Men are free to sow their seed wherever they wish, and women must accept it! *I'm* supposed to accept it!"

I saw the alarmed expressions on the faces of Andromache and Hippodameia, Pyrrhus's favored bedmates. They stared at me, mouths forming O's, and they knew, as I did, that there were others as well. I wondered about their true feelings, but I no longer cared enough about either woman to want to ask them.

The anger rang in his voice like the clash of a bronze sword on a bronze shield. "My ill luck to have married a whore like her mother in every way but one — her looks. At least Helen is beautiful!"

For little more than a heartbeat I was rigid as stone. Then I inclined my head slightly in the direction of Pyrrhus's glaring eyes and reddening face and swept out of the megaron.

"Bitch!" he shouted. A wine goblet flew past my head and smashed. Wine ran down the wall like blood.

I kept going.

"You're not even a decent whore, Hermione!" he bellowed after me. "Andromache knows how to please a man. Hippodameia does too. You eat my food and drink my wine and give me nothing in return."

His cruel words bounced off me like pebbles off a wall, but I knew that I would pay for *my* words, for speaking out. I sat in my bedroom, trembling, waiting for whatever punishment he chose to deal.

My husband had no love for me; I was merely part of the spoils of war, as Andromache was. But she had given him a son, even Hippodameia had produced a daughter, and he often threw it in my face that I was barren. *Of no value,* he had told me more than once; *worthless.*

My punishment was longer coming than I'd expected. As the night wore on and he didn't appear, I hoped that he had decided to stay with one of his concubines and I could go to sleep. But I was wrong. Pyrrhus strode shouting into my bedroom and seized me.

"I've been thinking about your visitor," he snarled, forcing me down on the bed. "Zethus is your lover now, isn't he?" he roared. I denied it. "Now that you've lost your pretty Orestes, you've turned to a common carpenter." Pyrrhus shouted at me, called me vile names, had even viler names for poor Zethus, and vowed that he would castrate him and make him a slave.

There was no reasoning with him. Madness ruled him. His

anger had inflamed his lust. I shut my eyes and bit my thumb to keep from screaming.

I HEARD THE SERVANTS stirring outside my room when at last Pyrrhus finished with me and stumbled off to his own bed. My bones ached, my whole body hurt, and I was exhausted, but sleep was out of the question. I ordered a warm bath and sank into it gratefully. My maidservant, Ardeste, rubbed me with oil. I saw in her eyes that she had heard more than I wanted her to know.

She dressed me in an embroidered peplos and fastened a narrow belt of gold links around my waist. "Mistress," she whispered, "I can help you, if you wish."

I looked at her. "Help me? In what way, Ardeste?" *Is this a trap? Is she another of Pyrrhus's spies?*

"In the servants' quarters last night we heard Pyrrhus raving, spewing hatred of you and your friend. Zethus should leave Pharsalos without delay. It's dangerous for him. I can take a message to him."

I studied my servant carefully. "How do I know I can trust *you*, Ardeste? This household is infested with spies."

"We have a saying here in Pharsalos," she replied. "'There are more spies than fleas.' But in the end you have to trust someone. You've known me since you first came here with Pyrrhus, and you are well liked by the people. Achilles is remembered as a brave and wonderful warrior, but many who had nothing to fear feared him anyway. Pyrrhus is much like his father in the wrong ways. Everyone is afraid of him except his Myrmidons, who claim to love him. Escape while you can, mistress. I'll come with you, if you wish."

I thought hard about what Ardeste was telling me. She was right—if I intended to escape and set out to find Orestes, no matter what terrible thing he had done and how terribly he was being punished—then I had to do it now. Ardeste, her back to me, knelt by my bathing tub and dipped out the water, waiting for my decision.

"What do we need to do to get ready, Ardeste?" I asked.

"I'll find Zethus," she said. "It won't be difficult—everyone will know of the stranger in town. We'll arrange to meet. I grew up here, and I know the place well. There's a cave where he can wait for us. It's well hidden. We won't be found there." She sponged out the last of the bath water and replaced the jar of scented oil on a shelf. "You will not be able to travel as a queen—there will be no carrying chair. Do you think you can manage?"

"I lived in a military camp on a beach for ten years," I said. "I know how to get along very well without luxuries."

She pinched back a smile. She probably didn't believe me. "I'll bring you plain tunics and sturdy sandals. And a shawl to cover your head. Everyone will recognize your red hair."

"I once stole a scarf from a marketplace to cover my hair." It was my turn to smile, remembering how old Marpessa helped me to travel on the women's ship to Troy.

Ardeste said, "On the night we leave, you must give Pyrrhus

a drug that will induce the most pleasant dreams and leave him unable to pursue you. I'll bring you a powder made of ground poppy seeds to mix with his wine. Be sure to give some to Andromache and Hippodameia. I'll make certain that the Myrmidons with him also drink some."

I hoped I could do what she suggested without arousing suspicions. I closed my eyes for a moment, and when I opened them again, my mind was clear.

"Find Zethus," I told her. "Tell him our plan. We'll leave tonight. The longer we wait, the harder it will be."

Book IV
Flight

The Journey Begins

ARDESTE LEFT FOR THE lower town carrying a market basket, but shopping was only an excuse to look for Zethus. My plan was to sleep, having had no chance the night before. But just as I lay down, Hippodameia drifted into my room. She was in a talkative mood.

"I was worried about you, Hermione," she said sympathetically. "Pyrrhus seemed so angry last night."

"Yes," I agreed, hoping to keep the conversation short. "He was."

"He's that way sometimes. But I think it was hearing about the visit from your friend that set him off. Pyrrhus is like Achilles — very jealous. I wonder how Zethus found you here. We're so far from everything."

The direction this conversation was taking made me uneasy. No matter what I said, it would surely be repeated to Pyrrhus. My old friend Hippodameia was not only sleeping with my husband—she was more than welcome to him—but she also might be spying for him. I wondered why women couldn't be kinder to one another. Maybe it was a matter of survival.

Now my survival was also at stake.

I yawned deeply and suggested that we talk later, after I'd rested, and Hippodameia reluctantly drifted out again. But still the gift of sleep did not come. Then I heard Ardeste's soft footsteps.

"I found Zethus and told him everything that happened," she whispered. "He was distressed to hear of your argument with Pyrrhus. I explained our plan and showed him the way to the cave. He'll meet us there tonight." She told me how to mix the poppy-seed powder into the wine so that it wouldn't be detected. "We must be sure that everyone gets some. It won't take much. And as soon as the drink begins to do its work, we'll leave."

"How long will the drug keep its effect?"

"Long enough, I hope."

I TUCKED THE PACKET of powder into a fold in my peplos and held it in place with the gold-link belt. I was uneasy, my hands trembling no matter how I tried to control them, and I wondered if Pyrrhus would sense my anxiety and question me. But he was more intent on carousing with his Myrmidon chieftains and as usual paid little attention to me. The weather had become cooler, and a fire blazed in the hearth at the center of the megaron. Pyrrhus had ordered a banquet, and the smell of baking bread and roasting meat hung in the air.

Ardeste moved among my husband's friends, pouring wine into their goblets. She avoided looking at me directly. A blind minstrel plucked his lyre and sang the men's favorite stories of victorious battles. They listened intently, cheering loudly at their favorite parts. Then, unexpectedly, Pyrrhus called out to me.

"Hermione, my beauty! Bring your lyre and honor us with a song, to welcome your husband home!"

"My beauty"? I thought. *Is he serious?*

He had never called me that, and he had never asked me to play for him. I wondered if he suspected something. I hadn't touched my lyre, made from the shell of a tortoise, in many months, and I was not sure I could even do this. But, I reasoned, the men had been drinking and they wouldn't know if I performed well or not. The blind minstrel smiled and nodded in my direction. I hurried to my room, made sure the packet of powder was still secure, and took down the lyre.

The men were waiting. I plucked the strings, badly out of tune—enough to make me wince—but Pyrrhus seemed not to notice, or to care. "A love song!" he cried, with that sneering smile I detested.

I stumbled through the beginning of the one song I could

remember that might be considered a love song, and then—almost miraculously—the blind minstrel picked up the tune and led me through it, while I added a few notes, singing along with him. Pyrrhus seemed surprised by this unusual performance, but the men were well pleased and called for more.

The minstrel began another song, a favorite of the men. I took advantage of their distraction to empty most of the powder from the packet into a large ewer of wine mixed with water and flavored with a little pine resin. The Myrmidons were fond of the slight bitterness of the resinated wine, and it served to mask the taste of the poppy-seed powder.

"Drink well, my good men of Pharsalos!" I cried merrily, smiling and moving among them with the ewer, pouring the wine into their goblets. The blind minstrel, sensing my presence, shook his head, refusing the wine. "Perhaps you'll want it later, poet!" I said, and poured more wine into his cup. "Drink up when your songs reward you with a thirst."

Andromache and Hippodameia turned up their noses when I attempted to fill their goblets. "I don't like the taste of resin," Andromache complained. Hippodameia agreed. "It's too bitter."

"True women of Greece are quite fond of it," I reminded them—reminding them at the same time that they were not Greeks. "It's a taste you would do well to acquire." Then, with a smile and an arched eyebrow, I whispered, "And it will surely enhance your pleasure, both given and received, in lovemaking." I glanced meaningfully toward Pyrrhus, who had drained one full goblet of the drug-laced wine and was ready for another.

Glumly, the two women held out their goblets, and I filled them. "Come now, drink up, my friends!" They sipped tentatively, made faces, and decided that the best thing was to drink it down in one swallow. I nodded, smiled, and moved on.

The potion Ardeste and I had administered was taking effect, gradually at first, and then, with another round of wine, more quickly. I watched their eyelids grow heavy; their speech was slurred. A few of the Myrmidons who had imbibed more than the others were actually nodding off. Pyrrhus yawned hugely. Moments later I heard him snoring. Andromache and Hippodameia had put their heads down on the table. Only a few of the guards were still awake, but they, too, had become drowsy.

It was time to go.

Ardeste moved quietly toward the door. I paused for a few moments, circling the megaron where the fire had burned down to glowing embers, and then I followed her. She had a simple woolen peplos for me, a plain rope belt, and a fringed shawl. I changed into sturdy sandals and rolled my soft leather slippers into a bundle with the embroidered gown I'd just taken off. "Bring it with you," Ardeste advised. "You may find an occasion to wear it later in our journey."

I added my wedding veil with the silver and gold ornaments, as well as the lapis lazuli and amethyst jewelry, necklaces and bracelets, armlets and ankle rings, that my mother had given me for my wedding—not with the idea of wearing any of it, but to use in trade. I also took my mother's silver spindle and, of course, my half of the wedding goblet.

We left the palace by a side door, heads modestly lowered and faces covered, and walked toward the servants' quarters, to avoid the suspicious glances of any outside guards who might have been around, though I suspected they'd all come into the megaron to enjoy the feast, leaving the palace unguarded, and were now asleep with the others. We circled behind the servants' quarters to the small postern gate. From there a steep, narrow path plunged almost straight down through the scrub growth. Loose soil and crumbling rock skittered out from under our feet, and we began to slide, grabbing at brush and young saplings to break our descent. We reached the bottom with cuts and scrapes to our hands, elbows, and knees. My peplos was torn.

A thin sliver of moon darted behind a cloud. We were somewhere outside the walls that encircled the town, and Ardeste admitted that she was lost. "I've been to this cave a few times," she said as we groped and stumbled through the darkness. "But that was in broad daylight."

I was frightened, but I was also exhilarated. I had not felt so free in all the months since I'd married Pyrrhus. But as the night wore on, I was more aware of how tired I was. I tripped over tree roots and once or twice I fell, sprawling in the dirt.

An owl hooted, then hooted again.

"It's Zethus!" Ardeste exclaimed, and imitated the same low call.

We'd been circling the hidden mouth of the cave without realizing it, but now we followed the sound of the "owl" until we found Zethus. We crouched in the damp cave ripe with the scent of animal dung and discussed what to do next. Bats flittered in and out through a small hole in the roof, on their nightly search for a meal of insects. The triumph I felt at escaping from the gloomy palace was rapidly being replaced by anxiety. The drug would soon lose its effect, and Pyrrhus and his men—and the two women—would wake up and realize that I was gone.

I could only imagine my husband's rage.

"We can't stay in this cave," Ardeste agreed. "But where do we go now?"

"Why can't we stay here, for at least a day?" Zethus asked. "The mouth of the cave is well hidden. I had a hard time finding it. So did you. And you made sure that everyone in the megaron drank well?"

"Oh yes," I assured them, until I remembered the blind minstrel. "Except the bard," I said. "He's the only one I don't remember seeing actually put the cup to his lips."

Ardeste groaned. "The bard sees everything! Not with his eyes, but with his ears. He misses nothing. I will guess that he heard us both leave, knows we left together, and senses exactly which way we went. And Pyrrhus will demand that he report it all."

"But that may not give Pyrrhus enough information to find you," Zethus argued. "The question is, are we safer if we stay here quietly for a day and leave tomorrow night, or is it better to go now, before they wake up, and put as much distance between them and us as we can?"

I listened to the two of them discussing what we should do, my head sunk in my hands. "We haven't even decided where we're going," I said wearily. "Maybe we should talk about that first."

It was pitch-black in the cave, and I couldn't see the expressions on their faces, but I could guess from the sudden silence that they were staring worriedly in the direction of my voice.

"You're right, Mistress Hermione," Zethus said gently. "It's not enough simply to run away from Pyrrhus and Pharsalos. You must run toward someone and someplace."

"Orestes," I sobbed, for the tears had come in a rush, and I could scarcely speak.

"Yes," Zethus said, "Orestes. I propose that we begin with the oracle at Delphi. But first we'll rest a while, then leave before the stars begin to fade."

23

The Road to Delphi

I HADN'T REALIZED HOW hungry I was. Zethus had brought a jar of water from a spring and a loaf of bread. We squatted on the floor of the cave and tore at the bread with our hands while we talked.

The Delphic oracle was the most famous in all of Greece. I remembered that Menelaus and Agamemnon had consulted the oracle before going to war against Troy. They must have been certain that they were meant to proceed with their intentions, or they would not have done so.

Zethus believed this oracle would help us to find Orestes. "Delphi lies to the south. If the gods favor us, eventually we will find our way there."

I had to trust him.

"One foot in front of the other," Zethus said, "from the time Dawn reaches her rosy fingers into the great vault of the sky until Helios completes his journey, for as many days as it takes."

It wasn't safe to delay any longer. We crept away from the shelter of the cave and began our journey. We stopped first at a humble thatch-roofed hut on the edge of the town, the home of Ardeste's cousin, the wife of a sandal maker. Ardeste would introduce us as servants in the royal household who had been wrongly accused by Pyrrhus of theft and were now forced to flee.

Zethus and I waited near a goat pen while Ardeste awakened her cousin. There was no love for Pyrrhus among the villagers, and the cousin was glad to offer us fruit and cheese. She gave me an extra shawl and tunic, warning of the coming cold weather. She quickly saw through my disguise—my hair gave me away—but she and the sandal maker promised to say nothing to the soldiers who were sure to rush down from the citadel searching for us when the drug wore off and Pyrrhus realized what had happened.

The cousin also insisted that we take her old donkey, called Onos. "He'll make your journey easier. In two days' time, you'll reach Thaumakia. When you do, slap him on his rump and he'll find his way home."

Ardeste and I took turns riding Onos. We made good progress through the rough and hilly countryside, crossing several streams on foot and one fast-rushing river by means of a stone bridge. We followed one of the streams to a lake with several small villages on its banks. The lake teemed with fish, and though we hadn't the means to net them ourselves, the villagers who were bringing in their catch offered us some. Zethus made a fire and roasted the fish on a green branch. No royal feast ever tasted better.

That night we found an empty fisherman's hut and fell into an exhausted sleep. The next day we reached Thaumakia, a bustling center of commerce where we felt free to wander the streets without continually looking over our shoulders to make sure we weren't being followed. Now we had to make a decision. Ardeste had promised to send the little donkey back to her cousin in Pharsalos, but we'd found Onos so useful that we wanted to keep him.

"I'll make sure he gets back to my cousin when our journey is over," Ardeste said, though we all knew that she would not be returning there.

As we walked, Zethus picked up small pieces of wood and began carving, transforming the bits into exquisite little figures. When we met a tradesman carrying a load of wine jars, we asked him to deliver the carving of a donkey to a certain sandal maker in Pharsalos.

I wanted to cut one of the silver spangles from my wedding veil and send it to the cousin in payment for Onos, but Zethus opposed this. "It would be like giving Pyrrhus an arrow, pointing in the direction of our travel," he explained. "Everyone will ask how this silver piece got into the hands of an ordinary sandal maker," Zethus argued, "and it will not take long for Pyrrhus and his spies to think of an answer."

I disliked cheating Ardeste's kind cousin, but there seemed no way around it. Someday, I told myself, I'd make it up to her.

Toward evening we followed a stream into a village of thatched huts set in a grove of oak and plane trees. Flowering shrubs and fruit and nut trees heavy with apples, figs, pomegranates, and almonds surrounded the huts. Zethus traded a carving of a tree for a basket, which we filled with fruit. It was such a pleasant place that Ardeste and I wanted to stay, but Zethus convinced us it was too early to stop for the night. "We need to get as far from Pharsalos as possible in the shortest time possible," he said, and Ardeste and I consented, though we were so tired we could scarcely manage to put one foot in front of the other as Zethus had told us we must.

We passed through mountainous terrain so rough that even Onos balked. There was an easier route, but Zethus persuaded us that the mountain path made following us much harder.

Sheep and goats grazed in the high pastures. A lonely shepherd was glad to share his cheese and soured milk in exchange for some of the nuts and fruit in our basket. After we'd eaten our fill, the shepherd played his syrinx, hollow reeds cut to different lengths that produced a series of tones when he blew across the open ends. His mournful music floated in the frosty air.

"The sheep like my songs," the shepherd told us. "It calms them."

The music may have calmed the sheep, but it reminded me of Orestes and of my longing for him and made me sad.

The next day we helped the shepherd move his sheep to a lower pasture, and that night, Zethus offered to stay awake to watch over the flock while the shepherd slept. Once or twice I was awakened by the howling of wolves. In the morning we discovered that Zethus had fallen asleep and the wolves had made off with two of the lambs. The shepherd was angry, and though Zethus apologized and offered to pay for the lambs, the shepherd cursed him, shouting that we had brought him misfortune. Words didn't pacify him. He began to pelt us with pebbles. We snatched up our few belongings and fled, stones flying past our heads.

After more days of hard travel through craggy mountains, we came upon a *herma,* a pile of stones marking a boundary. Each of us added a stone to the pile, honoring the messenger god Hermes, who was also the protector of travelers, and left a small honey cake as a sacrifice. We were footsore and tired, but Zethus urged us on, promising we'd reach the town of Trakhis, a port on the sea of Malis, before nightfall.

As he promised, as the sun was sinking behind the western mountains we stood on the shore of a small sea that led eventually to the Chief Sea.

Ardeste had never before seen the sea and was amazed at the sight of the large body of water crowded with fishing boats. But she was most interested in the reeds that grew abundantly near the shore. She gathered some of the thickest reeds and persuaded Zethus to make her a syrinx like the one the shepherd had played.

A group of good-humored fishermen had unloaded their overflowing nets, built fires on the beach, spitted the biggest and best of their fish, and invited us to share their meal. Zethus carved several small wooden fish and gave them to the fishermen who'd fed us. Bands of minstrels roamed the shore, singing old songs that brought tears to the eyes of the fishermen when the wine jar had been passed around again and again. The poets entertained their rapt audience with stories about the war with Troy, the glorious battles fought and won, or fought and lost. They described in rich detail the exploits of the great warrior Achilles, and of his triumphs and his death. They told of the wooden horse, the death of Hector, and the killing of King Priam at the hands of Pyrrhus.

We listened, eager to hear more, but not daring to look at one another. The wine jar made another round, and the poets enthralled their listeners with the story of Menelaus and his beautiful but wanton wife, Helen, now at home with him again in Sparta. There was no mention of their daughter, Hermione. I stared at my hands as the oldest poet, white-haired and stooped, got to his feet and began to relate the story of Clytemnestra and Aegisthus, of the return of Agamemnon from the war, and of his murder. Tears coursed down my cheeks as his voice rose to tell his spellbound audience of the revenge that Orestes took on his mother, Clytemnestra, his father's murderess.

The fishermen, too, were stirred. The hour was late, they had spent long days at sea, and their heads were fogged by weariness and wine. There was a sharp chill in the air and a biting wind had risen, early signs of the coming winter. The poets and minstrels wrapped themselves in their robes and went off to find shelter. The fishermen talked of making their way home, but only a few of them left. Those who stayed began to argue among themselves about the fate they believed Orestes deserved.

"Orestes is young," some of them reasoned. "The prince was avenging the murder of his father. Clytemnestra was not only an adulteress but a murderess. What son would not seek vengeance?"

But the older fishermen, those with grizzled beards and flesh that showed the toll of years at sea, weren't so willing to forgive Orestes. "He should have allowed the courts to try Queen Clytemnestra. It's a son's duty to defend his mother, no matter what she's been accused of."

Back and forth went the argument, growing more heated. They were shouting at each other when a bearded man carrying a curiously made staff stepped forward and called for quiet. I hadn't noticed him before; he seemed to have appeared out of nowhere. He removed the wide-brimmed hat that marked him as a man of humble birth, but his speech was as eloquent as any learned man's. The fishermen stopped quarreling and waited respectfully to hear what he had to say.

"Orestes is receiving his just punishment from the Furies,"

the traveler told them. "The Angry Ones give him no peace, no rest. I have heard that Orestes has lost his mind. He covers his head and raves. They say that he goes without washing himself or eating, and tries to injure himself. His sister Electra stays with him and cares for him. But the other sister, Chrysothemis, has no pity. She calls for him—and Electra, too—to be stoned until they're dead."

I couldn't bear it. Before Zethus could stop me, I jumped up and cried, "But what hope is there for Orestes?"

The men turned to stare at me. I heard the murmurs, "Who is she?"

I shook off Zethus's hand and rushed over to the speaker, pulling at his sleeve. "What will become of him?"

The traveler's eyebrows arched. "I only report to you what has already happened," he said. "To learn Orestes' fate, you must ask the oracle at Delphi. She may tell you where he is and what will happen in the future."

"Thank you," I murmured, and stepped back, embarrassed. I had called attention to myself, and that was a mistake.

Zethus had a firm grip on my arm. "My sister is somewhat excitable," he explained to the crowd. "Her illness makes her so. I'll see that she gets some rest."

The traveler nodded but had nothing more to say. The fishermen were still staring. Zethus was practically dragging me away from the beach. "Hermione," he whispered fiercely, "you must not do such things! The last thing we want is for someone to recognize you! We're no longer in Phthia, but that doesn't mean Pyrrhus isn't going to try to find you. Now let's try to arrange for shelter for the night. We'll be on our way at first light. We can't stay here any longer."

The night had grown much colder. I was shivering. The traveler stepped out of the shadows and motioned for us to follow him. With a few quiet words to Zethus he directed us to an empty hut, where we spread our fleeces. I lay down, wrapped myself in my woolen robe, and listened to the murmur of their voices as the two men talked softly. Ardeste was already asleep. I tried, but I wasn't able to make out their words. Then I sensed that the traveler was bending over me, and immediately I received the gift of sleep.

Long before the stars had faded, Zethus was up and urging us to leave our snug beds. Frost covered the ground in a white mantle. "What were you talking about last night with that man?" I asked. "And who is he?"

"We were in the presence of Zeus's messenger god, Hermes, and didn't realize it. He called himself Hodios and claimed he was only a traveler, but later I realized that's one of Hermes' names. He advised me on how to reach Delphi and the best way to approach the oracle. But he warned that in winter the oracle goes silent. Apollo's brother Dionysus takes up residence at Delphi throughout the winter. But Dionysus is the god of wine and ecstasy, and he doesn't have mighty Apollo's power to predict the future—he's interested only in drinking and dancing, and he'll be no help at all. Hermes urges us to hurry if we want to reach Delphi in time to speak to the oracle. He said that he'll visit us often during our journey."

Ardeste was awake now too, rubbing her eyes sleepily. We gathered our belongings and prepared to leave. I noticed that the reeds Ardeste had collected along the shore had disappeared, and in their place was a beautifully made syrinx.

"Hermes made it last night while we were talking," Zethus said. "He cut reeds to the proper lengths, bound them together with wool, and stoppered the ends with beeswax. 'Nothing to it,' he told me when he'd finished. 'I invented the syrinx, though my son Pan likes to take credit for it.'"

"The lyre, too," I said. "My mother told me that when I was a child."

"There's something else," Zethus said as we left Trakhis. "Hermes believes you're the one to help Orestes. But he warns that it won't be easy."

THE PATH LEADING SOUTH toward Delphi was poorly marked and sometimes disappeared entirely. Several times we thought we'd lost the way. I watched for Hermes, who was known to move with the speed of wind. But no one resembling the traveler appeared. I wondered if he'd forgotten us.

Just before sunset we entered a small village, and since Zethus now judged we'd come far enough from Pharsalos and it seemed safe to do so, I cut off one of the silver spangles from my wedding veil and offered it in exchange for food and a place to sleep. While Zethus bargained with a villager, I noticed the sandals on the feet of a shepherd carrying a little lamb on his shoulders. The unusual sandals were made not of leather but of palm and myrtle branches. It was only as the shepherd was passing that I saw the small wings on the sandals and realized it was Hermes in still another guise. But when I turned to speak to him, he had disappeared.

The same thing happened the next day. We took care to leave stones at each *herma* as we passed, and made sacrifices of honey cakes sold by vendors near every pile of stones. We never recognized the messenger god until he had passed us, and when we turned, he was gone. Hermes wasn't like the other gods, who stunned or dazzled when they came down among us mortals; instead, he always appeared so ordinary that we failed to notice him.

When we'd first begun our journey, we slept in the open, in a grove of trees or beside a mountain stream. But now a chill wind blew steadily, the sun was often cloaked in clouds, and we had to seek shelter each night. I worried that we'd arrive at Delphi too late to consult the oracle.

Finally we reached the southern slopes of Mount Parnassus within sight of Delphi and joined the streams of suppliants on the road leading to the oracle. All were hoping to receive answers to their most important questions before winter set in and the oracle departed. Ominous clouds clung to the mountaintops, and I wrapped my shawl more tightly around me and tucked my fingers in my armpits to warm them. An unwashed, reeking beggar approached us, filthy hand extended, and Ardeste offered him a few dried figs from the last of our provisions. He greedily gobbled up the fruit and shuffled away. I was about to chastise her for giving away our last bit of food, but before the beggar disappeared into the crowd I glanced at his feet. His sandals had little wings.

"My lord Hermes! Wait!" I shouted after him, thinking perhaps he could give us some news of Orestes, some guidance on what to do next.

But again it was too late. The messenger god had already disappeared.

24

The Oracle Speaks

THE CROWDS AT DELPHI were dense and impatient. We decided that Ardeste and Zethus would take the donkey and wait for me while I joined the long column that crawled slowly toward Apollo's shrine, the altar for sacrifices, and the place beyond it where the oracle sat on a three-legged stool over an opening in the earth. More suppliants had joined the line behind me. An old couple seeking advice about suitable husbands for their four daughters had come to Delphi in the past when their four sons were seeking wives, and they were eager to tell me what to expect.

"The oracle is known as the pythoness," the wife said. "Three women take turns speaking in her voice. They're women from surrounding villages past childbearing age whose lives are untainted by scandal or gossip."

"She's named for the serpent Python who guarded the spot believed to be the center of the world," the husband explained.

"When Apollo was still a little child, he shot an arrow that killed the serpent."

The column crept forward. Others continued to join it. The couple chattered on. Vapors rose from the cleft and swirled around the pythoness and put her into a trance, they said. While the oracle was in the trance, Apollo possessed her spirit, and she prophesied. The husband said that the pythoness's speech was like the ravings of a madwoman, impossible for ordinary people to understand, but that the priests of Apollo stood nearby to explain what she was saying.

"She never answers yes or no to a question," the wife said, "and she always speaks the truth, but it's often hard to know exactly what she means."

"You must figure it out for yourself," the husband advised.

I felt very uneasy. During the fighting, Apollo was on the Greeks' side and then the Trojans'. Apollo had helped Paris shoot the arrow that wounded Achilles in his one vulnerable spot.

What help could I now expect from Apollo's oracle?

The column of suppliants wound back and forth like a serpent with its tail far down the slope of Mount Parnassus. Slowly, slowly, the crowd edged forward, climbing the steep path toward the oracle. Dark clouds blotted out Helios in his flaming chariot, and we shivered in the icy wind that clawed through our woolen robes. My feet were cold. My limbs ached. I was hungry. I wondered where Zethus and Ardeste were waiting. My eyes grew heavy. I slapped my cheeks to keep myself awake, to keep moving forward, nearer to the pythoness, until I was close enough to observe the faces of those who had asked their questions and had received answers. Sometimes the look was one of relief, or encouragement; occasionally I saw joy in a face, but just as often I saw profound sorrow. I tried not to think about what my own expression would reveal when my turn finally came.

The other suppliants waiting to speak to the oracle had brought animals to sacrifice to Apollo, and I had only a necklace of gold beads, each bead in the shape of a Greek warrior's shield. This may not have been the right sort of offering. I looked around uneasily at others, all with the proper kind of offerings of meat. Behind the old couple was a goatherd with a ram, a doe, and three bleating kids, and as my nervousness grew I decided to barter some of my beads in exchange for two of his animals. Surely he didn't need so many.

The goatherd listened gravely to my proposal, and after some thought he nodded, holding up two fingers. I unstrung two beads from my necklace, and he handed me a rope and walked away. I realized that I was holding the rope with all five animals, and the beads were still in my hand. "Wait!" I called after him. "You forgot the beads!"

Then I noticed his winged sandals as he disappeared.

When I reached Apollo's shrine, below the oracle's stool, a priest led my goats away to slaughter. I'd been waiting for a long time, but before I felt quite ready, I was standing before the pythoness. I knelt and clasped the bony knees of an ordinary-looking woman, neither beautiful nor ugly. Her eyes were her most striking feature. She seemed to be looking at me, but I couldn't tell if she actually saw me. I licked my lips and stated my request.

"I love Orestes, prince of Mycenae," I told the pythoness, trying not to stammer. "But my beloved has committed a grave deed. His mother murdered his father, and he in turn has killed his adulterous mother and her lover. Now he is pursued by the Furies, who have driven him to madness."

"I know all this," the pythoness interrupted sharply. "Apollo advocated avenging the murder of Agamemnon, telling Orestes when he came here that if he did not exact retribution, he would be an outcast of society and prevented from entering any shrine or temple. I instructed him to pour libations of wine next to Agamemnon's tomb, to cut off a lock of hair and leave it on the tomb, and then to contrive a way to punish Aegisthus and Clytemnestra for what they'd done. But I also warned him: the Furies do not readily forgive a matricide. I gave Orestes a bow made of ox horn to fend them off when they became too much to bear. There is nothing more I can do."

The oracle's words needed no interpretation. She wasn't raving, and her eyes looked straight into mine.

"If there's nothing more you can do for him, then please

tell me what I can do," I pleaded. "I believe I can save him, but first I must find him."

"You are married to Pyrrhus. He will be displeased."

"Yes, he'll be very angry," I admitted. "He's always very angry."

The pythoness answered sternly. "You have been promised to two men, a cruel one whom you despise, and a kind one who has committed the gravest of deeds. You will find Orestes, and yet not find the man you are looking for. He has two sisters. Trust one, but not the other."

"Which one should I trust?"

"The one who earns it."

"But who is the man I'll find, if not Orestes? How do I help Orestes once I find him? And what shall I do about Pyrrhus?"

Abruptly the pythoness began to speak in a tongue I couldn't understand. A priest came forward to interpret. "The pythoness says a long road lies ahead of you, and you must follow the road to its end. She has nothing more to say to you."

He pushed me firmly away. It was not at all clear to me what I was to do. A second priest was already accepting the offerings of the old couple with the four daughters.

I searched for Zethus and Ardeste among the surging crowd, and I was relieved to hear them calling me from where they waited with the donkey. I saw the questions in their eyes. "Later," I said.

We had started down the slopes of Mount Parnassus on

a rough path somewhat parallel to the main path leading up when I twisted my ankle on the loose stones and injured it. Zethus insisted that we stop to rest on a jutting rock. Far below us was a bustling port on the shores of a sea so large I couldn't see the opposite shore. Small fishing boats bobbed among bigger ships anchored in the harbor.

"What is this town?"

"Krisa," Zethus said, "ruled by King Strophius. This is the Sea of Corinth."

I knew about Krisa. Orestes had come here as a child to stay with his best friend, Pylades. He'd often spoken of it. I wondered if he'd come here when he consulted the pythoness at Delphi.

Ardeste volunteered to continue on down to the beach to trade some of my silver spangles for fish. "Shall I inquire about some sort of lodging for the night, mistress? You shouldn't walk far with your injured ankle."

Zethus insisted on staying with me, hovering nearby but leaving me with my thoughts: *What man does she think I'll find? What about Orestes' sisters? How will I know whom to trust?*

A fleet of black ships had entered the harbor. They were so close that I could also make out the emblem painted on the bow: the horns of a bull on a rayed star. Pyrrhus's emblem.

I called to Zethus. "What are these ships? Where did they come from? Pyrrhus destroyed what was left of his fleet when we first arrived in Iolkos."

Zethus squinted at the ships. "I don't know, but I'm afraid he has come searching for you."

I shuddered. Pyrrhus must have learned where I was going, asked questions, perhaps even tortured people to tell him. I thought of Ardeste's cousin, the wife of the sandal maker, and worried what she may have suffered until she'd been forced to confess that she had helped me escape.

Ardeste returned, breathless from her climb up from the beach. Her eyes were large and frightened. In her basket were grilled fish and a loaf of bread, but my hunger was forgotten when we heard her news.

"Those are Pyrrhus's ships! I heard the fishermen talking. He went to Iolkos, looking for you. The blind minstrel directed him there. As you know, the minstrel hears everything, his sense of smell is better than an animal's—he knew we'd left together, and he deliberately sent Pyrrhus and his Myrmidons off in the wrong direction, to Iolkos. That bought us time, but not enough."

"But the ships? What have you heard about them? I saw his entire fleet go up in flames!"

"The fishermen said that Pyrrhus and his men seized ships from merchants at Iolkos and sailed to a port on the Saronic Gulf, left the stolen ships there, and crossed the narrow strip of land to Corinth. Then Pyrrhus demanded that Corinthian merchants surrender their vessels. "No one dared to defy him. Pyrrhus had his emblem painted on the stolen ships and sailed for Krisa."

"And now he's come here to claim me! I hardly think I'm worth his trouble. He's convinced that I'm barren. It's Andromache who gave him a son."

"He's enraged," Ardeste said. "Not only at you for leaving him, but at Apollo, too. He blames Apollo for his father's death."

Hordes of men were streaming off Pyrrhus's pirated ships and onto the beach below us. I could easily pick out Pyrrhus himself, preparing to climb the path to the oracle. Behind him the seamen were attempting to herd a pair of fat oxen up the path still crowded with cold, weary suppliants.

"He may be too late to speak to the pythoness before the time of prophesying ends until spring," I said. "I wonder what he'll do then."

"Hard to imagine," Zethus said. "But when he hears that somebody has been trading silver spangles for food, he'll guess that it's you."

"I spoke to a fisherman willing to let us stay as long as we wish in his hut a little way from the beach," Ardeste said.

"Then let's go now," Zethus said. "We'll be safer there."

He helped me onto Onos's back, and we picked our way cautiously down the steep, uneven path toward the beach. I was careful to keep my hair covered, hoping that no Myrmidon would happen to recognize me.

Word was being passed along from the oracle's priests that this was the final day of prophecy. Whoever had not reached the pythoness by sunset would be turned away. I was relieved that I'd had an opportunity to consult her, even if I still didn't understand the prophecy I'd received. *Follow the road to its end*. But what road? And to what end?

The clouds parted. Helios's flaming chariot was already low in the western sky. Pyrrhus had no doubt heard the warning and surmised that he would not arrive in time—unless he eliminated all those suppliants ahead of him. He shouted an order, and his men charged ruthlessly through the anxious crowd, shoving aside any who blocked the path and sending them tumbling down the steep slope.

Pyrrhus forced his way to the head of the line, and his oxen were led away for slaughter. "I demand satisfaction for the death of my father, Achilles!" he bellowed. "It was Apollo who killed him, disguised as the cowardly Paris — Apollo's and not Paris's arrow that found its mark in my father's one vulnerable spot! And I demand the return of my lawful wife, Hermione!"

We were close enough to hear Pyrrhus raving, but not close enough to hear the pythoness's response. Whatever she said to him, Pyrrhus flew into a rage and issued another command to his Myrmidons. With fierce cries they surged forward and invaded Apollo's sacred shrine. They plundered it, seizing gold and silver and gems brought there as offerings. Myrmidons seized the butchered carcasses of the two fat oxen and carried them off. At another order from Pyrrhus they set fire to the shrine. It was a shocking sight, a scene of complete chaos.

"What can Pyrrhus have been thinking?" Zethus murmured. "To insult the great god Apollo in such a way!"

Tongues of flame consumed the sacred shrine. Pyrrhus raised his arms toward the orange-tinted sky and shouted curses at Apollo as the sun began to slip below the horizon. The pythoness seated on her tripod and the priests of Apollo surrounding her appeared unable to move, as if they'd turned to stone.

The sun disappeared, and the pythoness stirred. The priests pressed forward. One of them drew a sacrificial knife from his belt and plunged it into Pyrrhus's chest, stopping his beating heart.

The Long Road

PYRRHUS WAS DEAD, HIS Myrmidons in disarray. Before nightfall the pythoness ordered Apollo's shrine to be rebuilt and my husband's body to be buried beneath the threshold, in accordance with custom.

The Myrmidons wandered around aimlessly. The priests of Apollo, the wielder of the sacrificial knife, and the pythoness had all disappeared. Shocked and in a daze, I climbed onto the back of little Onos and let him carry me down to the town of Krisa by the light of a moon sometimes blocked by scudding clouds. We found the fisherman's hut that Ardeste had arranged for us. Zethus left Onos to graze in a patch of greenery. We ate the grilled fish and bread and poured a libation to the gods in thanksgiving for our safety. Not wishing to be haunted by Pyrrhus's ghost, I also poured a libation and cut off the ends of my hair, as was expected at the death of a spouse.

Above us on Mount Parnassus smoke still curled up from

the ashes of Apollo's shrine. Naturally, everyone in Krisa was talking about what had happened. A new set of priests, those serving Dionysus, had arrived to celebrate the coming of winter with drinking and ecstatic orgies. Soon the people dismayed by the terrible behavior of Pyrrhus turned their attention to the return of Dionysus. Despite the death of their leader, even the warlike Myrmidons allowed themselves to be caught up in the festive atmosphere, though I was afraid the copious amounts of wine they consumed would soon turn them vicious again.

Flakes of snow drifted down from the black sky. Our borrowed hut was damp and too small for three. The days were short with only a little weak sun, and the nights long and dark and very cold. I wanted to leave as soon as possible. We talked about traveling south, where it might be warmer.

Was that the long road I was supposed to follow? I didn't know.

Something else was troubling me: it was obvious that Zethus and Ardeste had become lovers. I was sure of it. I hadn't found them in each other's arms, but it was possible to sense these things. The way she looked at him. The way he "accidentally" touched her arm when they passed. How she said his name. He was too concerned for her comfort. When he served her a piece of the fish he had finished grilling, it was a better portion than he took for himself. There was a change in the sound of her laughter—what was there to laugh about?—and a lilt in her voice when they spoke to each other.

This had happened subtly, over time. I didn't know when it first began, but I envied them. I was jealous. Not that I wanted Zethus for myself, for I did not. He had been a loyal friend for a very long time, but I had never been drawn to him in the way that a man and woman are drawn to each other, as Orestes and I were. I wanted that kind of love, but I wanted it with Orestes.

The two came back from a nearby spring carrying animal skins filled with water. Ardeste had borrowed a bronze cauldron from the wife of a wine merchant she'd met in the marketplace. I had not had the luxury of a bath in a long time, and she promised that I'd have one that night. Zethus heated the water over our supper fire and waited outside the hut while I bathed. I invited Ardeste to bathe in the water after I'd finished.

"May Zethus then take his turn, mistress?" she asked, and I grudgingly allowed that he might. I disliked myself for the resentment I felt, but I couldn't help it.

Later, Ardeste carried the cauldron back to the wine merchant's wife and returned to our crowded little hut with a jar of wine and three clay goblets, a gift from the merchant.

"I have good news, mistress," she told me as she poured the wine. "The merchant's wife has offered us a second hut, smaller than this one but close by. You could then have this hut all to yourself, and we can share the other hut."

"'We'? You mean you and Zethus?"

"Yes, mistress." She lowered her eyes. "So that you'll be more comfortable."

I slammed down my goblet too hard, and wine splashed everywhere, but I didn't care. "Absolutely not! We're not staying here any longer." My tone sounded petulant, childish, even to my own ears. "We must make our plans and leave."

They glanced at me and then looked away, saying nothing. I had to get over this. I needed both of them, and I was afraid of my behavior driving them away.

PYRRHUS HAD ARRIVED AT Krisa with ten stolen ships, each with fifty of his Myrmidons as oarsmen—a total of five hundred men, plus their captains. Ashore, these oarsmen were again warriors, and with their king dead, they rampaged through Krisa. The Myrmidons were barbarians, interested mainly in killing and plundering. Their name means "ant people," descended from Zeus, who turned himself into an ant and mated with a princess of Phthia after turning her into an ant as well. But without Pyrrhus the men didn't know what to do or which way to turn. They drank and brawled and made nuisances of themselves among the people of Krisa, who'd grown sick of them and wished them gone.

Although most cared nothing for Pyrrhus's wife, I didn't feel safe with the Myrmidons around, for I was sure there were some who would find sport in capturing and tormenting me. Dressed in my ragged tunic and well-worn robe with a shawl covering my red hair, I avoided them. No one paid me any attention.

I visited a healer, an old crone who wrapped my injured ankle with herbs soaked in wine, and after a few days the pain disappeared and I felt strong again. I walked along the beach, so deep in thought that I scarcely noticed the long, steep road leading up to the citadel. Servants and tradesmen trudged up and down. I stopped a man carrying a load of wood on his back and inquired if by chance Prince Pylades was at the citadel.

"He is not," said the man, barely pausing. "But King Strophius is waiting for you."

I wanted to ask how that could be, but he was already too far away. Then I glimpsed the wings on his sandals.

I rushed back to the hut and asked Ardeste's help. We searched through the bundles I'd packed when we prepared to flee from Pharsalos. Somewhere in the depths, with Helen's silver spindle and my golden wedding goblet, Ardeste located the embroidered peplos she'd advised me to bring, predicting that I might find an occasion to wear it during our journey.

I dressed in my fine peplos and the jewelry that I hadn't yet needed to trade for food and shelter and offerings. Ardeste combed and plaited my hair.

I set off to climb the steep path to Strophius's citadel. My mother never went anywhere without at least three of her women, but I was not Helen, and I preferred to go alone.

A herald ushered me into the megaron. The walls were beautifully painted and the furnishings as grand as any I'd seen. I waited nervously as the herald announced me. "Hermione of Sparta!"

The old king glared at me from his throne. He appeared so cold and unfriendly that I regretted coming. "You're here to talk to Pylades," he said after a silence heavy as iron. "He's no longer my son. I've disowned him."

"Disowned him, my lord?" I hadn't expected this.

"I have, for participating in the murder of Queen Clytemnestra. There is no forgiveness for a matricide. Orestes and Electra should have been stoned until they were dead, and Pylades with them. Only then would justice have been served. May the Furies torment Orestes for the rest of his days."

I gasped. Zethus had not mentioned Pylades' involvement in the slayings. But how could Strophius wish death for his own son? "I've heard that Orestes went to Delphi to consult the oracle after he learned of Agamemnon's murder," I said as calmly as I could. "Did he also come here to Krisa, my lord?"

"Yes, he came here," the old king said, sighing. "I hadn't seen him since he left for Troy with Agamemnon. Such a fine boy he was then! He often stayed with me. I loved him like my own son. But now I hardly recognized him. He'd just learned of his father's murder; he was angry and confused. Powerful Apollo informed him that if he failed to avenge his father's death, he would become an outcast. The pythoness instructed him to go to Mycenae and even told him what to do when he got there. Pylades went with him, though I begged him not to be a part of this. I disagreed with Apollo, and I disagreed with the pythoness. But Pylades wouldn't listen to me. My son was an accomplice in the killings. Electra, too. They deserve to die."

The old king sobbed. Tears streamed down his craggy cheeks.

Perhaps he wasn't as hardhearted as he'd seemed at first. I tried to reason with him. "King Strophius, Clytemnestra was an adulteress and a murderer. She killed Agamemnon, your dear friend! Surely you believe in vengeance—and Apollo himself called for it."

"It's up to others to take revenge, you foolish girl! I know all about you. You're in love with a man who murdered his own mother. The courts would have taken care of the matter. It was not for Orestes to take it into his own hands, and now they are bloodied forever. And my son's are too. A matricide cannot be forgiven."

No argument was going to change the old king's mind. But before I left, I needed the answer to one more question. "Where are they, my lord? Where are Orestes and Pylades?"

"In exile, I'm told. Ask Electra—I hear that she is at Mycenae. All I know with certainty is that, whether my son lives or dies, I will never see him again."

Strophius closed his eyes and turned his face away. I murmured a few words of farewell and fled from the palace.

ARDESTE AND ZETHUS WERE not in the hut when I rushed there to repeat what I'd heard about Orestes from King Strophius. The embers on the hearth were cold. The shelf where Ardeste stored our food was empty. I was shivering and hungry. Disappointed, too, because I had so much to tell them, and there was now so much to do. I had to find a way to get to Mycenae.

A bearded face peered in at the door, startling me. "Queen Hermione?"

"Who asks?" I inquired suspiciously.

"Leucus. I've come to offer my services," he said, and smiled.

Until he smiled, I hadn't recognized the captain who'd been in charge of burning the ships at Iolkos. He would have been a handsome man if he weren't missing his front teeth, knocked out by Pyrrhus when the captain had dared to question the order to set the ships alight. He'd grown a beard since I last saw him, and it had changed his appearance.

"Leucus! What are you doing here?"

"Now that I no longer serve Pyrrhus, I'm in a position to serve *you*. My loyalty to Achilles kept me in the service of his son. Orestes was also my friend," Leucus continued. "He spoke often of his love for you. He left with Agamemnon, not knowing you'd be forced to marry Pyrrhus. I wish I could have helped then. Perhaps I can help you now."

My mood lifted as we talked, and I asked him to describe what had happened at Pharsalos after I fled.

"When we woke up from whatever trance the gods had placed on us and discovered that you were gone, Pyrrhus was in a rage, as you might expect. He was determined to leave at once with the Myrmidons to look for you, and he swore to kill you once you were found. I hoped to find you first and help you escape—you did not deserve to have a husband like Pyrrhus. Before we left, he sent Helenus to build the new palace at Bouthroton. Andromache went with him, and they took Hippodameia along."

"Andromache is with Helenus?" This was astonishing news! Pyrrhus valued the Trojan's ability to prophesy, but he'd been extremely jealous of him. It was hard to imagine that he'd sent Andromache off with the brother of the husband Achilles had slain. "How did this come about?"

"I can't explain it," Leucus said. "Maybe Pyrrhus tired of her. And she's known Helenus for most of her life. She may have been happy to go."

"I wish Pyrrhus had tired of *me*."

"That wasn't likely," Leucus said. "Pyrrhus regarded you as the prize to which he was entitled, though he often complained that you were stubborn and difficult to control. And he knew how much you wanted to be with Orestes, so it became a contest. But now the contest is over. One contestant is dead, the other in exile."

"And now you *do* have a chance to help me, Leucus!" I described my meeting with Strophius. "I must go to Mycenae to see Electra. She may know where to find Orestes!"

Leucus soon came up with a plan. We would recruit fifty Krisan fishermen as rowers, seize one of the ships Pyrrhus had stolen from a merchant in Corinth, and sail it back to its rightful owner. From there we would make our way overland to Mycenae.

"This has to be done in secrecy," he cautioned, "so as not to arouse the suspicions of the Myrmidons. They're a brutish lot. I know, because I've sailed with them for years."

We were deep in conversation when Ardeste and Zethus returned, fingers interlaced, glowing with the happiness that love bestows. Guiltily they apologized for the cold hearth and empty breadbasket. Zethus rebuilt the fire, and Ardeste began to prepare a simple meal.

We discussed the plans while we ate. Leucus had restored my hope of seeing Orestes again, and I swallowed my envy and agreed to let the lovers have their separate hut until we left.

"I've come to know many of the fishermen here," Zethus said. "I can speak to them without attracting too much attention."

"You can probably do it more easily than I can," said the captain. "The fishermen believe I'm a Myrmidon."

Zethus soon discovered that it was not as easy as he'd expected. The Myrmidons were everywhere, roaming the streets of Krisa and making trouble, and the fishermen feared that the Myrmidons would steal their wives and lovers as soon as their men set sail for Corinth. Nevertheless, Zethus recruited thirty-nine fishermen who relished the idea of taking the ship from under the noses of the Myrmidon guards.

But Leucus was worried. "We're still short by eleven men,"

he said. "Enough rowers if we have good weather, not enough if a winter storm strikes." He was worried, too, that one of the fishermen would give away the plot and our plans would be ruined.

We couldn't wait any longer, even if we didn't have the rowers we needed. Winters in Krisa were severe. Local women had told Ardeste about the storm that swept in last year as female worshippers of Dionysus were going up to Mount Parnassus to dance and sing as they did every year at this time. "Many women froze to death, buried in snow," Ardeste reported. We'd leave before the weather worsened and before word of our scheme leaked out.

Leucus scouted the ships anchored near the beach and chose one of the smaller vessels. He and Zethus secretly provisioned it. Hunched against the cold, we silently slipped aboard, Zethus coming last, leading Onos. Leucus himself raised the anchor stone, and the fishermen leaned into their oars and rowed us away from the beach, into the deep water. But Aeolus roared out of the north, a fierce blast of wind that drove our vessel back toward the rocky shore. The fishermen rowed desperately to keep the ship from foundering. Waves smashed against the rocks, hurling up a spray that fell on us like freezing rain. I wrapped myself in a thick woolen robe and prayed for the storm to end. Ardeste had never been on a ship, and she was ill from the moment we left Krisa. The donkey lowered his head and endured.

After long days and nights of buffeting winds and sleet, our ship entered the quiet harbor at Corinth. The true owner of the ship recognized it as one seized by Pyrrhus and painted with Pyrrhus's emblem, and he and his men rushed out shouting, armed with sticks and rocks. Leucus did what he could to calm them, and I offered the merchant a gift of silver spangles in addition to the return of his vessel. Our fishermen-sailors headed into the city of Corinth to reward themselves with a night or two of carousing before they considered how to make their way back to Krisa.

And I had to decide what long road to follow now.

Mycenae

THE CORINTHIAN OWNER OF the ship we'd returned offered us the hospitality of his home. The food and drink he served were the best available. The bed was comfortable, and I was weary to the bone, but the gift of sleep would not come to me. I tossed restlessly. Should I go to Mycenae to speak to Electra, asking her help in finding Orestes? Or should I go first to Sparta and ask my parents for their support in searching for him? My father might help me, but I was not sure about my mother. Helen and I barely knew each other when she came back into my life. No doubt she understood her sister Clytemnestra's hatred of Agamemnon. He'd killed Clytemnestra's first husband, and he would have killed Iphigenia if Artemis hadn't intervened. My mother might even have felt that Clytemnestra was right to rid herself of her cruel husband. If that was true, she wouldn't support Orestes, and she wouldn't help me. Better, then, to go to Mycenae, and not to Sparta.

Finally, my mind made up, I slept.

When morning came, the four of us set out along the road from Corinth to Mycenae. It was midwinter, but as we made our way southward, the weather became milder. When we couldn't find lodgings in a town or village, we lay down our fleeces, wrapped ourselves in our woolen robes, and huddled close to Onos the donkey for warmth.

After several wearying days of travel we reached Mycenae and entered the city through the main gate. The citadel loomed high on a hill above the city. People conducted their business, tradesmen came and went, vendors in the agora watched over their wares spread out on ground cloths. The tantalizing smell of cooking drew hungry customers. Yet this was not the lively, noisy place I remembered from my visits here with Menelaus and Helen.

Perhaps the low-hanging gray clouds muffled the sounds I associated with the city. There was no music of lyres and syrinxes, no vivacious chatter among women with baskets on their arms haggling with women selling eggs and cheese, brooms and wine jars. There was no passionate arguing among the men, no shouts of laughter from the children. No one smiled. They finished their errands and hurried away, heads down, eyes on the ground, not stopping to talk with their neighbors.

We bought lentil stew from one woman stirring a steaming pot and bread from another, then carried our food to the shelter of a large canopy. A family was having their meal nearby, an old man, a younger man, his wife and their baby, and their little boy. The boy reminded me of Pleisthenes. The last time I'd seen my brother, he was about the age of this boy, and it broke my heart to remember him. Safe by his mother's knee, the boy smiled at us, and I smiled back. Encouraged, he dashed away from his mother and came to gaze curiously at us. I asked him the usual questions—his name, how old he was. His mother retrieved him, and a tentative conversation began among us.

The old man asked where we'd traveled from, and Zethus, adept at conversations with strangers, explained, "We've been to Delphi to consult the oracle. Now we're on our way home to Sparta."

It was not the truth, but it didn't matter. The mother remarked that King Menelaus and Queen Helen had returned to Sparta at last. "You're fortunate that your king and queen have come home to you," she said. "Not like what happened here in Mycenae. We haven't yet recovered."

"A pity," Ardeste said sympathetically, and glanced at me. I kept silent.

The boy's father joined the conversation. "A terrible tragedy," he said. "Agamemnon should never have been murdered by his faithless wife. And no one could tolerate her lover—Aegisthus the usurper is the one thing on which we all agree. Agamemnon should have killed them both and taken back his throne. That would have settled the matter."

"And what of Orestes?" I struggled to get the words out. "Has he come back?"

"Oh, he came back, all right, and avenged his father's murder! He and his friend, Pylades, made short work of those two adulterers," the boy's father said.

"Orestes should not have done what he did," his wife said. She dipped bread into the stew and gave it to the boy, who stuffed it into his mouth. "He must be punished. His sister, too. Electra is as guilty as Orestes, for she urged him on."

Her husband interrupted. "I say he did the only thing he could do. Now we've heard that Apollo has sent him into exile."

She frowned at him. "And I say he should have let the law take its course."

"Apollo's word is above the law. Exile is punishment enough."

"So you say," his wife said irritably.

"But you feel sorry for Electra, don't you?" the husband asked. "Never allowed to leave the citadel! They say her brother receives his torment from the Furies, and Electra from her sister, Chrysothemis."

The old man—I took him to be the grandfather—listened to the conversation, shaking his head sadly. "As you can see, we disagree among ourselves," he said. "It's been many

months since the murders. Some people call Orestes a hero
and say that killing Clytemnestra was justified. Others take
the opposite view, that a son's duty is to defend his mother,
no matter what terrible thing she has done, even murdering
his father. Everyone in Mycenae has an opinion, and the city
is divided. Relatives don't speak to each other. Friends no longer converse. We've become a city of silence. After the murders we refused to allow Orestes to sit at our tables, to share
our meals, even to speak with any of us. Now we, too, are
afraid to speak to each other. Only to strangers." He smiled
sadly.

The younger man had begun to gather their belongings, the
mother shifted the baby to her hip and took the boy's hand,
and the grandfather reached for his walking stick. "May your
visit to Mycenae be pleasant," the old man added. "And your
journey home a safe one."

After they'd gone, we sat staring at each other. We, too,
were silent.

RAIN WAS THREATENING, AND Zethus went to inquire about
lodging. When he came back, he'd located rooms for us and a
place to tether Onos. On our way to the rooms, Leucus told
us that he planned to leave for Sparta the next day. This came
as a surprise. I'd assumed he would stay with us, and I was
disappointed.

"Why Sparta?" we asked.

"To look for Astynome. The last I saw of her she and her child were sailing with Helen and Menelaus as Helen's servant. Astynome hoped to make her way to Mycenae to find Agamemnon. She still believed he intended to marry her. I warned her that he would not. But Astynome would not believe it. She thought she could change his mind. I prayed that she stayed in Sparta once they arrived, and didn't come to Mycenae, and that she wasn't here during the terrible murders."

"But what have you to do with Astynome?" Zethus asked curiously.

Leucus smiled sheepishly. "I fell in love with her from the day Agamemnon took her as the spoils of war. I loved her when Apollo insisted that Agamemnon return her to her father, and I loved her even more when she came back to Agamemnon pregnant with his child. When the child was born, I wished that he were mine. I have never stopped loving Astynome, and it's my fondest hope to find her and persuade her to marry me."

Love, I thought, deeply moved by his story. *People will do anything for love.*

The next day as Leucus prepared to continue his journey to Sparta, I thanked him and told him how grateful I was for his help, and gave him a gift to deliver to my mother: her silver spindle. I had carried it with me ever since she'd left me and run away with Paris.

"Let her know that I'm well. Tell her that Pyrrhus is dead, if she hasn't heard." I hesitated. Should he tell her I was searching for Orestes? I decided against it. "Tell her—tell her that I'm still her daughter."

Leucus dropped the spindle into his bag and heaved the bag onto his back. We wished him well and watched him go.

"I hope he finds Astynome," Ardeste said, sighing. "And that she consents to marry him." Zethus patted her shoulder affectionately, and the lovers smiled into each other's eyes.

AFTER LEUCUS HAD GONE, I unpacked the embroidered peplos I'd worn to visit King Strophius. It had gotten wet during the stormy voyage from Krisa and looked bedraggled, but I put it on anyway and fastened my bracelets, an ankle ring, and earrings. Then I draped myself in a woolen shawl. It would have to do. "I'm going to the citadel," I announced.

I was determined to go alone, though both Ardeste and Zethus insisted it was too dangerous. "You don't know what you'll find up there," Zethus said, and Ardeste added, "This is not the same as visiting King Strophius."

They argued persuasively. I reminded them that they were my servants and I would make my own decisions, and they reminded me that as my servants they were bound to protect me. In the end it was my choice. Ardeste and Zethus would stay at our lodgings with the donkey. If I hadn't returned by sunset, Zethus was to come looking for me.

Ardeste rearranged the shawl to cover my red hair. "You don't need to announce yourself from a distance of fifty paces," she said.

I had spoken boldly, but I was uneasy, and my heart beat much too fast as I climbed the road to the citadel, past the tombs of Clytemnestra and Agamemnon and probably of Aegisthus as well, though I didn't stop to look for it. I recognized the two standing lions carved in the rock above the Lion Gate, the main entrance in the massive wall surrounding the palace and a complex of buildings. Only one man was visible in the guard house; he glanced at me without interest. The sprawling citadel seemed nearly deserted.

When I'd visited Mycenae with my parents as a child, and later stayed here with my aunt and my cousins, the citadel had bustled with activity. Laborers had carted in oil, wine, and grain from the surrounding olive groves, vineyards, and fertile fields, and artisans had worked at blacksmithing, pottery making, and wool dyeing. But now there seemed to be no one at all. The granary and storage rooms were deserted. I followed the broad path that used to be paved with smooth marble slabs. Now the path was uneven, many of the slabs broken or missing. Where were the artisans? The guards? The heralds?

A woman emerged from the main palace. Thin and dark haired with a nose as sharp as a hawk's beak, she so closely resembled Clytemnestra that I nearly spoke my aunt's name. The woman stared at me with narrowed eyes. "Who is it?" she demanded.

I was unnerved. Her voice sounded almost exactly like Clytemnestra's. Could this be her ghost?

"Hermione of Sparta, widow of Pyrrhus." My mouth was dry as dust. I removed the shawl that hid my hair.

The woman stepped closer, arms folded across her chest. "Hermione, of course! Who else has hair like yours! I'm Chrysothemis, in the event that you didn't recognize me. What brings you here?"

Chrysothemis! Though I was not pleased to see my cousin, I was relieved that I had not encountered her mother's ghost. "I've come to offer you and Electra my condolences. I've heard that terrible tragedies have befallen your family."

"I don't doubt you've heard about it—everyone has!" she said sarcastically. "We make quite a family story, don't we?" She scanned me from head to foot. "I'm sure Electra will be happy to see you."

She hadn't invited me into the palace. She also hadn't mentioned Orestes. It would surely have been better to wait, but my desire to know was stronger than my patience. "And your brother, Orestes?" My voice sounded high and tense to my own ears, and I wished I hadn't asked.

"He's been exiled," Chrysothemis said coolly. "Surely you've heard that as well, Hermione."

"I have," I admitted. "But I hoped his exile had ended and he'd come home."

"I doubt he'll ever come home. He's not welcome here."

I felt as though the ground had dropped away beneath me. "But—"

Chrysothemis had turned away and was walking back into

the palace. "You might as well come in, Hermione. I'll take you to Electra myself."

I followed Chrysothemis through a series of mostly empty rooms and past the megaron—the splendid hall where Agamemnon had once sat on his throne inlaid with ivory and gold and received visitors from all over the Greek world. There was no sign that a fire had burned recently on the central hearth. It, too, felt deserted. At the end of a dim corridor Chrysothemis stopped at a thick door guarded by an enormous man with muscles like boulders and legs like tree trunks. He was the largest man I had ever seen. I thought he must be from the ancient race of giants known as Cyclopes, though he didn't have their characteristic single eye in the middle of his forehead. Nevertheless, he was a terrifying sight.

"Open the door, Asius," said Chrysothemis, and the giant pushed open the great wooden door with his fingertips as though it were weightless. "A visitor, Electra," Chrysothemis called, and I stepped inside. The door slammed shut behind me. I felt as though I were being sealed in a tomb.

The room was small and dark and sparsely furnished. Electra, weaving at a loom on the far wall, turned to look at her visitor. She was taller than I remembered, and more beautiful, even in the dim light. She looked so much like Orestes that she might have been his twin—the same thick, dark hair in abundant curls, the same large, expressive eyes, the same sweet mouth. She stared at my hair and broke into a smile. "Hermione, can it be you?"

There were tears in her eyes and in mine, too, when we embraced. We hadn't been close as children, no doubt because she was a little older at an age when even a year or two seemed like a great deal. Now we were grown, and the petty issues of childhood seemed to vanish like smoke.

"I've wanted so badly to see you, Hermione! I hoped you'd find me here."

When Electra smiled, it was like seeing Orestes' smile again.

"This is where you live?" I asked, taking in the small, ill-furnished room. "These are hardly the quarters of a princess."

"They suit me," she said with a shrug. "I can't bear to go to those parts of the palace where my mother lived with her lover and where . . . everything happened," Electra said. "So I've moved here. These are the quarters of a scribe who left long ago. Chrysothemis calls herself queen and has taken our mother's bedroom. She's made it into a kind of shrine." She shrugged again. "I choose not to go there."

I gestured to the giant outside the door, raising my eyebrows. "My guard," she explained.

"To protect you?"

Her laugh was bitter. "To prevent me from leaving."

The door creaked open again, and an elderly servant carried in a tray of dried fruit and jars of wine and water. She set down the tray with a thump and went to perch on a low stool near the door, her sharp old eyes fixed on us.

"In the old days a banquet would have been made ready for

Electra's Story

ELECTRA SPOKE SOFTLY, KEEPING a watchful eye on the old servant. "During the war with Troy I stayed in Mycenae with my mother and Chrysothemis," she said. "A fierce hatred for Agamemnon had taken root in my mother's heart. Then Aegisthus came, and Clytemnestra welcomed him as her lover. I despised Aegisthus and everything about him—how he rode my father's horses, drove his chariot, wore his gorgeous robes, sat on his golden throne. And slept in the royal bed with my mother.

"When the war ended, we learned that Agamemnon was coming home. I had no idea then that my mother planned to murder him. I even helped her prepare the banquet for him. I wondered how she'd explain the presence of Aegisthus, but it didn't occur to me to warn my father. I just assumed he'd take care of the intruder in short order.

"When Agamemnon arrived with Cassandra, his beautiful concubine—some said she was second only to Helen in beauty—his bath was ready, his robes laid out, a royal feast spread on the table. When I heard the shouting and the screams, I was terrified. I hid from the tumult. Suddenly it was over, and Agamemnon was dead. Cassandra, too. My mother and Aegisthus buried my father outside the walls of the citadel and resumed their lives, as though nothing had happened. But then they worried that Orestes would come seeking vengeance.

"And he did. He'd consulted the oracle at Delphi. Apollo urged revenge and the pythoness told him what he had to do. His friend Pylades agreed to come with him to Mycenae.

"My mother hired mourners to pour libations on Agamemnon's tomb to appease his ghost, and I accompanied them, to pour libations in my own name. I didn't know that Orestes and Pylades had come, but Orestes had left a lock of his hair on the tomb, as he'd been told to do, and he and Pylades hid in a thicket to watch. When I found the lock of hair, I knew it belonged to my brother. Orestes leaped out of the thicket, calling my name. What joy it was to see him again! And what grief we shared at the murder of our father!

"We worked out a plan," Electra continued. "I went back to the palace and told my mother that I had poured the libations and she had nothing to fear from Agamemnon's ghost. A little later Orestes and Pylades appeared at the Lion Gate, disguised as strangers. Clytemnestra didn't recognize him. In a false voice he told her that her son had died in Krisa.

Pylades showed her a bronze urn, claiming it held Orestes' ashes.

"Clytemnestra pretended deep sorrow and invited the two 'strangers' into the palace. But she couldn't hide her delight when she told Aegisthus that Orestes was dead and would not come to seek revenge! Their happiness came to a quick end. I was there when it happened. Orestes drew his sword and slew Aegisthus. When Clytemnestra recognized Orestes, she tried to soften his heart. 'My son!' she cried. 'I nursed you as an infant. Remember your duty to your mother!' Oh, she sounded so piteous!

"Our mother's words had no effect on Orestes. I ran forward to stop him—wasn't it enough to be rid of Aegisthus? But Pylades held me back. 'Let it happen,' he said. With one stroke of his sword, Orestes struck off her head."

Winds began to howl around the palace as Electra spoke. A storm was breaking. Electra listened to it for a moment and then continued her story.

"I was too shocked and horrified to move, but Chrysothemis came upon the bloody scene and ran screaming from the palace. Drenched in blood, Pylades and Orestes carried the bodies outside the walls and buried them. Soon everyone had heard what happened. The citizens of Mycenae swarmed into the streets, shouting insults. Then the Furies swept in, howling and swinging their scourges, their attacks so fierce and relentless that Orestes could not defend himself, even with the bow of ox horn the pythoness had given him. They pursued him night and day. When Orestes lay down to sleep, they lay beside him, hounding him. When he sat down to a meal, they sat with him, screeching their accusations. It drove him mad.

"Chrysothemis was always my mother's favorite. My sister is most like her—ruthless. She remains fiercely loyal to the memory of our mother and refuses to help our brother, but I stayed with him." Electra sighed, her eyes closed. "In caring for my brother, I fell deeply in love with his friend, Pylades."

The old servant's head drooped toward her chest. "She's been sampling the wine again," Electra whispered. "She thinks I don't know. I know, too, that the woman is a spy. She goes straight to Chrysothemis and reports everything I say or do. Fortunately, she's also rather deaf."

We watched her for a while. Her mouth fell open and she snored lightly.

"Do my parents know about the murders?" I asked.

"They heard the news from a fisherman as they were on their way home to Sparta from Egypt, and they came to Mycenae to find out what they could. But Helen was afraid the anger of the people would be turned against her for causing the deaths of so many Greeks, and she kept out of sight. When the case was taken before the court, Menelaus called for Orestes to be punished severely. The court agreed, ruling that he must be stoned to death, and I with him—because I had not tried to stop him and then sheltered him afterward.

"Our sentence was later commuted to death by suicide.

By then, Pylades and I had fallen in love, and he swore to die with us. But as we were about to leap together from a cliff into the sea, a plot to murder Helen was uncovered. She had many enemies who blamed her for ten years of war. An angry mob was about to set fire to the palace with her in it when magnificent Apollo appeared, wrenched the torches from their hands, and forbade them to kill Helen. At the same time he made his pronouncement: Orestes would not die for the vengeful murder of his mother. The crowd was stunned and fell back."

Tears were pouring down my cheeks, but Electra hadn't yet finished her story.

"Orestes went again to Delphi, a laurel wreath on his brow to show that he was under Apollo's protection. Still the Furies refused to leave him alone. Apollo angrily threatened to shoot them down, but they scorned his threats. Nothing cows them, not even the great and powerful Apollo! Hermes tried to help him escape, but Clytemnestra's ghost goaded the Furies to keep up their relentless torment.

"Apollo decided to send Orestes into exile. I went with him. He shaved his head, hoping that Clytemnestra's ghost wouldn't recognize him, but it always did. Each day he sacrificed a pig, and while the ghost gorged on the pig's blood, he washed himself in the running waters of a stream to rid himself of guilt. But a mother's blood carries such a powerful curse that much more was demanded of him."

"But what more could he possibly do?"

Electra smoothed the edges of her peplos, avoiding my eyes. "Orestes bit off his own finger."

Bit off his own finger! My legs weakened, and I thought I might faint.

"For a third time Orestes went to Delphi. He threw himself on the floor of the temple, raving and threatening to take his own life if he could not be rid of the Furies. Apollo promised the torment would end if Orestes made his way to the land of the Taurians, seized an ancient carved image of Artemis from her temple, and brought it to a shrine near Athens. He and Pylades sailed for Tauris. I wasn't allowed to go with them. It's a long journey through dangerous waters, and the Taurians are a cruel and uncivilized people. My sister Iphigenia was taken there many years ago by Artemis to save her from sacrifice."

"I was there at Aulis," I reminded Electra. "I saw the antlered doe Artemis left in Iphigenia's place on the altar."

"Yes, I remember," she said. "My sister sometimes speaks to me in dreams. She's a virtual prisoner, forced to preside over the sacrifice of any strangers who set foot in Tauris, and she's willing to do almost anything to escape. I worry that Orestes and Pylades will be captured, Iphigenia won't recognize them, and she'll unknowingly sacrifice them, too."

I was sick with despair. "You may think I'm foolish, Electra, but I truly believed my love would save him," I said. "I still believe it."

"Oh, my dear friend!" She took my face tenderly in her hands. "My brother is much changed. He may not know you. He may even strike out against you. At first he spoke of you nearly every day, but the Furies have destroyed his mind. Even I have had a difficult time with him, and in the end he sent me away—I, who was with him throughout his ordeal, who never left his side."

Electra leaned close to the old woman, who groaned and muttered. Satisfied that she slept soundly, Electra continued. "But now you've come, and you've given me new hope. Seizing the wooden image of Artemis from the shrine is not an easy task, even with Pylades' help. Getting it to Athens won't be easy either. But I believe they'll succeed. I propose that we find a way to go to Athens, make offerings to Apollo every day, and wait for them to come."

Eager as I was to see Orestes, I had doubts. "But how will we know that they haven't been captured by the Taurians and even sacrificed by Iphigenia?" I asked. "How will we know they've succeeded in taking the image? Or arrived safely in Athens? And that's only half of it! You're a prisoner here yourself—a giant at your door and a servant spying on you. How do we go about setting you free, Electra? There are too many things that can go wrong."

"Hermione, we can't simply stay here and do nothing! We must try!"

I didn't remember my cousin being so daring when we were

children. I had underestimated the strength of her love for Orestes, and for Pylades.

"All right, then. We'll ask Ardeste and Zethus for help," I said. "You and I can sit here and weave fantasies, Electra, but my friends are practical people. They weave real plans. I'll leave now, but I'll come back in a few days, and I promise I'll have a way to get you out of here."

The Giant Guard

I WAS AWARE OF the giant's eyes on me as I left Electra's quarters and made my way through the dim corridor. The courtyard was still deserted when I left through the Lion Gate. The storm had passed, and before sunset I was down in the city and telling my story to Ardeste and Zethus.

"I'm sure we can arrange this," Ardeste said confidently, as I had expected she would. "I'll go with you to the citadel. We'll see that the old servant gets plenty of wine, and as soon as she's asleep, Princess Electra and I will exchange clothes. Then, with Electra dressed in my tunic as your servant, you two will leave together. I'll stay behind, dressed as the princess and pretending to work on her loom."

"And then what?" I thought the plan was unlikely to succeed, and I didn't hesitate to say so. "How will *you* get away, Ardeste? The old woman will wake up and see through your disguise, even if the guard does not, and if the servant is a spy, she'll rush to tell Chrysothemis. It will not go well for you when she finds out."

"The old woman won't wake up. That shouldn't trouble you. We'll arrange it the same way we did with Pyrrhus and a room full of Myrmidons—with the seed of the poppy. I bought a small supply at the marketplace today. Just to be prepared," she added with a smile. "If I leave a half-empty wine goblet with a few grains dropped in it, I'll wager she'll drink it down without giving it a thought. It's a habit among servants, finishing off the last few drops. I confess that I've done it myself on occasion."

"You've already bought the poppy seeds, Ardeste?" I asked, though I'd known Ardeste long enough that I should not have been surprised. "But how will you get past the giant? I doubt that he's stupid."

"As soon as you're safely out of the room, I'll change clothes again, this time exchanging Electra's peplos for the servant's tunic. When she wakes up, she'll find herself dressed like a princess. I can mimic the way she walks. I'm sure I can fool the guard." She turned to Zethus, who was listening open-mouthed to his lover's ambitious plot. "You must wait for us on the road to Athens, and we'll be on our way."

I had no confidence that Ardeste's elaborate plan could work. If one part failed, the rest would surely follow. "What do you think of this idea, Zethus?"

"I never argue with Ardeste," he said, shaking his head.

"She's usually right. And I agree that we have to do something, and do it soon."

BUT WE HAD NOT taken the weather into account. The winter storms had begun, with pouring rain, thrashing winds, and mud everywhere. We were to rescue Electra and be off for Athens, but for three days the storms raged. We paced and fretted, until on the fourth day the clouds parted and Helios again smiled on us.

"You have the poppy-seed powder?"

Ardeste patted the slight bulge under her tunic.

Zethus embraced Ardeste, and I guessed what they were thinking: if our plan came to a bad end, this could be their last embrace. With one final backward look, Ardeste and I set out together. We climbed the road to the citadel and passed through the Lion Gate. I pointed out the empty guard tower, the granaries, the storage rooms, and the workshops of the artisans and described the location of the postern gate in the wall behind the palace.

"We're surely being watched," I said, "or I'd take you there and show you exactly where it is."

Chrysothemis did not come out to greet us. No one did; perhaps no one was watching us after all. But when we reached Electra's quarters, Asius was on guard. "You're right," Ardeste murmured. "He's huge."

The giant regarded us with the same empty expression

he'd shown on my earlier visit, even when I greeted him and called him by name. He pushed open the door. "Visitors," he boomed. Even his voice was oversize. Then we were inside, and the heavy door closed.

Electra was again at her loom, the elderly servant in a corner spinning wool. Electra welcomed me and sent her servant for wine and refreshments. I introduced Ardeste and hastily explained the plan before the old woman returned.

We were nervous, but we spent a long time in idle talk, recalling incidents from childhood, Orestes' talent with bow and arrow, and the games we used to play. Electra could hardly sit still. She sipped at her wine. "Ugh! This wine is terrible! Pero!" she called to the servant. "Bring us new wine, and clean goblets."

I looked at my cousin admiringly. She was playing her role well. When the old woman had gone out to fetch a different wine, Ardeste produced the poppy-seed powder and sprinkled a little into each of the goblets from which we had barely sipped. When Pero returned with the new wine, Electra said, "Please take this awful stuff away."

We waited, to see if she'd decide that the wine in the goblets she'd carried out was not so awful after all. Soon she returned with three more goblets and another jar of wine and resumed spinning. But it was not long before the spindle dropped from her fingers.

While the old woman slept, I helped Electra out of her peplos, Ardeste removed her tunic, and the two exchanged garments. But now we encountered a problem: Electra was tall, and Ardeste was not. Ardeste's tunic wasn't long enough, and Electra's peplos dragged on the ground, even when Ardeste pulled it up as high as she could around her waist and cinched it tight with the belt.

"It will have to do," she said, and added Electra's gold bracelets and necklaces and draped a shawl over her head.

Ardeste, posed at Electra's loom, would wait for a chance to find her way to the postern gate. Electra knocked on the door and called to Asius, "My guests are leaving now." I prayed that the giant was unobservant.

The door opened. I was startled to find Chrysothemis standing there. "You're here again, Hermione?" she asked. "And with your servant this time? I had no idea you and Electra had so much to talk about."

"I'd hoped to visit you as well, Chrysothemis," I said, improvising desperately. It seemed less and less likely that we would get through our scheme without being caught, but I pressed on. "My servant is feeling ill," I said, "and I must help her get down to the city, if you will kindly excuse us."

Chrysothemis frowned at Electra, bent over beside me in Ardeste's ill-fitting tunic, clutching her belly with one hand and drawing a shawl over her face with the other.

"There may have been something in the wine brought by Electra's servant that has had a bad effect on all of us," I said. My own "servant" groaned, and I put a helpful arm around her shoulders. "Please do excuse us, Chrysothemis," I repeated anxiously. Had she not noticed Pero slumbering soundly in the corner?

Chrysothemis continued to study the situation. When was she going to announce that her sister's disguise hadn't deceived her for a moment, and that she'd seen through our clumsy ruse? "Asius will bring a chariot to take you both down to wherever you're staying," she said.

"Oh, that won't be necessary!" I protested. "I'm sure we can do very well on our own."

But Chrysothemis insisted, and we were forced to wait for the gigantic guard to fetch the chariot. Still Chrysothemis lingered. A trickle of perspiration crept down my back, and I could feel Electra, hunched over beside me, trembling violently. Behind us, Ardeste, wearing Electra's peplos, was pretending to weave on Electra's loom, no doubt straining to hear every word.

Asius arrived and carried my ailing "servant" out of the palace, while I followed, and placed her in a chariot drawn by a pair of horses. Chrysothemis, apparently satisfied, went on her way. Electra looked up at me from under her shawl, eyes wide and frightened. I stepped aboard and had begun to breathe more easily when Asius suddenly bolted back into the palace.

"Where is he going?" Electra whispered.

"I don't know." I wondered if we had really succeeded in fooling huge Asius—or if he knew exactly what was happening and was on his way to alert Chrysothemis. "What should we do?" My voice was edged with panic.

"We'll take the chariot," she said. She stood up and grasped the reins. "I know how to drive it. I used to go hunting with Orestes, and he taught me."

"Wait!" I cried. "He's coming back, and he's got Ardeste!"

Asius galloped toward us with Ardeste, still dressed in Electra's peplos, slung over his shoulder. "I didn't have a chance to exchange clothes with the old woman," she whispered. She looked terrified. Asius dumped her unceremoniously next to Electra and me, vaulted into the driver's position, and snatched the reins from Electra's hands. We clung to the sides of the chariot, exhilarated and alarmed, as it careened down the steep road.

Asius slowed the horses when we'd reached the streets of Mycenae, and we moved at a stately pace through the city. Citizens stopped to stare at the chariot and its giant charioteer. Out of the crowd a musician playing a syrinx wandered into the street. I expected Asius to let the musician feel the sting of his whip, chasing him out of our way, as I'd seen other charioteers do, but the giant reined in the horses and stopped to listen to the music as though a spell had suddenly come over him.

"Take them to Nauplia," the musician told Asius, and our driver nodded courteously.

I didn't need to look for the wings on the musician's sandals. "My lord Hermes!" I called out. "We're going to Athens!"

"The road to Athens is too dangerous. A ship will take you there from Nauplia." The messenger god played a few melodious notes on his syrinx. "Don't worry—Zethus is waiting for you," he said, and disappeared.

Asius flicked his whip and resumed his reckless charge through the crowded streets of Mycenae, scattering merchants, women buying bread, shepherds and their sheep, children playing games. At a crossroads by the massive walls where the city ended and the countryside began, a familiar figure waited with a donkey laden with bundles. Asius reined in the horses. Ardeste jumped from the chariot and rushed into Zethus's arms.

What were we to think about Asius? We would surely attract attention all along the way to Nauplia. A chariot driven by a giant could scarcely be ignored. There would be no disguising either one. Yet Hermes had been clear in his instructions: *Take them to Nauplia.*

And so we turned off the road that led to Athens and went in the opposite direction.

WHAT AN ODD SIGHT we must have made—a giant and three women crowded into a chariot intended for two, with Zethus and the donkey plodding along behind. Sometimes Asius walked, carrying the donkey's load, to give Zethus and Onos a rest. Our progress was slow, but the farther we got from Mycenae, the less we feared pursuit and capture.

Asius tried to put our fears to rest. "Chrysothemis has few servants," he said, "and fewer friends. The people of Mycenae want a wise ruler, but they don't want Chrysothemis in that role."

We stopped in small villages and sent Zethus to inquire for lodgings. Once we spent a night in a sheepfold. Electra and I had put away our elegant gowns and dressed in plain tunics with knitted shawls and thick sandals. By ourselves, we blended easily into the crowd. But not Asius. Our unusual charioteer made us curiosities, and word of our impending arrival always reached the next village ahead of us.

At first this worried me, but Asius, in addition to his size and strength, turned out to be a fine storyteller and a great asset. Each evening the villagers gathered to see the giant for themselves and to listen to his stories.

"Yes, I am the son of a Cyclops," he told them. "My father was a Cyclops, from that race of men descended from Poseidon, brother of Zeus. My father's people were blacksmiths who worked the forge with Hephaestus to make Achilles' magnificent shield. And my father's family had the special calling of making Zeus's thunderbolts."

A little girl, who should have been asleep on her mother's lap, piped up, "If you're a Cyclops, where's the eye that's supposed to be in the middle of your forehead? You have two eyes like everybody else."

The giant smiled kindly. "For many generations the Cyclopes had only a single eye, as you've described. But when they married ordinary women, their children had two eyes, just like you."

"My mother says you eat little children," the girl said. The mother attempted to silence her, but the child tore loose and took a few bold steps toward the giant. "Are you going to eat me?"

Asius looked at her thoughtfully. "No," he said, "I'm not. Little girls who ask too many questions aren't particularly tasty."

The girl, wide-eyed, scrambled back to her mother, and that was the end of the questions.

When the crowd had dispersed, drifting back to their huts, I did have another question for Asius. "Why have you decided to come with us?" I asked. "It would have been easier for you simply to do as Chrysothemis ordered."

"I do it out of loyalty to Orestes," Asius explained. "I served as his charioteer at Troy after the first charioteer was killed. Orestes was a superb archer and a brave fighter. He doesn't deserve what's happened to him. And I know of the depth of his love for you, Princess Hermione. You were always in his thoughts. I want to help you find him and to bring him home."

29

Voyage

WE ARRIVED IN NAUPLIA on the coast of the Gulf of Argos with no idea of what to do next. There were five of us—Electra, Ardeste, Zethus, and me, plus the giant Asius—along with two large horses and a small donkey, all needing to be fed and sheltered. We also had a chariot, which would require us to find a ship large enough to transport it to Athens.

I walked along the water's edge, wondering why Hermes had sent us here, wondering how we would get to Athens, and wondering how I would then ever be united with Orestes. Fishing boats came and went. Merchant ships arrived from all parts of the Chief Sea, unloaded their cargo, stowed on board sacks of grain and amphoras filled with oil and wine, and sailed away again. Zethus tried every day, but no one was willing to take us to Athens.

The days passed. My spirits were low and sinking lower. Occasional storms swept in and drove us fleeing to shelter. But then, as the winter wore on, the first signs of spring began to appear. The days lengthened, and the air grew warmer. In the evenings people gathered to hear Asius's stories.

It was not enough. I often found myself weeping. "We've gone through so much," I complained to Zethus, "and now we seem to be stuck here!"

We considered retracing our steps to Mycenae, pushing on from there to Corinth, and joining the isthmus road that followed the coastline all the way to Athens.

"Hermes told us not to do it," Zethus said. "But what good is it to stay here?"

I agreed. "If Hermes had known this would happen, he wouldn't have sent us here."

"We should leave," Electra said. "What if Orestes and Pylades have already arrived in Athens and gone to Mycenae and we're not there?"

"Hermes would surely tell them we've come here."

"But suppose they've already gotten to Mycenae and they're on their way here and we suddenly find a boat to take us to Athens and we miss each other completely!"

We argued among ourselves, pulling first in one direction, then another. Only Asius seemed to have no opinion. He merely shrugged his great shoulders and agreed to do whatever we wanted. "Maybe we should divide," he suggested. "Half take the overland route, and half find a smaller boat and go by sea."

The mood grew tense. Zethus changed his mind and favored going by sea. Ardeste, who disliked traveling on a ship and had been so miserable on the journey from Krisa to Corinth, insisted that she would go only if we went by land. Soon she and Zethus were barely speaking.

Then one afternoon when sunlight glittered on the water like gold and the air was soft and sweet with the coming of spring, a small ship, larger than a fishing boat but not as large as a merchant vessel, sailed into the harbor. I was walking on the beach, gathering shells, and stopped to watch the bearded captain let down the anchor stone. He carried a little boy down the rope ladder, waded ashore, and set the child on the beach. The boy burst into tears when the man turned to leave, but the man stooped down and spoke to him, and left him with a kiss. Reassured, the boy squatted on the sand to wait. The captain went back to his ship and helped a young woman climb down the ladder. They waded ashore hand in hand, picked up the little boy, and began to walk up the beach.

As soon as I recognized them, I was running toward them, shouting. "Leucus! Astynome!"

Our problem was solved. I would ask Leucus to take us to Athens.

THAT EVENING WE CELEBRATED and stayed up late talking —we wanted to hear all that had happened since Leucus left us at Mycenae and began his long walk to Sparta.

"But why have you come to Nauplia?" Ardeste asked. "Where are you going?"

Leucus explained that they were on their way to the island

of Sminthos, where Astynome had been born, to introduce little Chryses to his grandfather. "And Astynome has agreed to marry me," Leucus added as the two gazed at each other.

Another pair in love! I was destined to be surrounded by lovers, while my own love was still far away. No doubt Electra felt much as I did, longing for Pylades as I longed for Orestes.

Astynome told us about the terrifying storms that plagued the journey from Troy and carried Menelaus and Helen to Egypt, followed by the long, meandering trip from Egypt back to Sparta and the news of the shocking murders at Mycenae that greeted them.

"The king and queen were kind enough to take me and my son with them after Agamemnon sailed for Greece without us. But Queen Helen does not much care for me." She glanced at me apologetically. "I don't wish to speak ill of your mother, Hermione. To King Menelaus she is still and always will be the most beautiful woman in the world, but her concern is mostly for herself."

Astynome was right. My mother was indeed a selfish woman, but despite her betrayal my father was still in love with her. I was her only living child, but I had heard nothing from her since I married Pyrrhus. I sometimes wondered if she ever thought of me, but I already knew the answer.

"Who can ever make sense of the way men and women treat each other?" I mused, but I knew the answer to that as well: *No one.*

"If Agamemnon had taken me with him as he'd promised," Astynome said, "I, too, would have been murdered. The gods were protecting me, but at the time I didn't understand that I was destined to find true happiness with my wonderful captain."

Leucus beamed, showing his gap-toothed grin.

"All is well and good that everyone is finding happiness," I said—sourly, I'm afraid—"but we must now devise a plan to reach Athens and find Orestes."

We sat talking on the beach long after a cloak of darkness had fallen softly around us. Clouds skittered across the night sky, veiling the moon and stars, then letting them shine again. Electra had traded a silver toe ring for fish and bread and jars of wine. We ate and drank and discussed how best to proceed.

"We brought four passengers with us from Gythion," Leucus said. "And there was plenty of room. But now you're speaking of adding a donkey, two horses, and a chariot."

"And a Cyclops," Asius added.

"The chariot and the animals could be sold," Zethus suggested, looking to Electra, to whom they belonged.

"Or we can buy a second boat. I have enough jewels to pay for it," Electra said.

I was relieved to hear that, for I had only a few gold beads left to trade.

The only one not in favor of this plan was Ardeste. She said nothing, but I could see her face in the firelight, and I knew she was unwilling. "You said you'd never go onboard a ship after our journey from Krisa to Corinth," I said, "but it's the best way. And then I promise, you won't have to do it again."

Ardeste excused herself and rushed off. "Even speaking of a sea voyage makes her ill!" Electra said, but I had guessed another cause. Ardeste was pregnant.

OVER THE NEXT FEW days, Zethus and Leucus prepared for the voyage to Athens, trading two of Electra's gold armlets and the last of my gold beads for a second boat, large enough to accommodate the chariot and horses and extra passengers. The two men hired rowers and brought aboard the necessary provisions. Leucus had decided to follow the shoreline, rather than making a straight line across the Saronic Gulf to Piraeus, the port of Athens. It would take longer, but it would avoid open sea and keep Ardeste happy—or at least less miserable.

Our two boats set out with good weather, steady winds, and a willing crew, with the exception of two rowers who arrived drunk and had to be sent away. For several days the boats stayed within sight of each other, letting down their anchor stones in the same coves at sunset and spending the night. One day as the sun burned directly overhead, Leucus led the way into the great port crowded with grain ships and merchant ships from countries surrounding the Chief Sea. For some of us, the journey was nearly over. Leucus and Astynome and little Chryses would continue on to Sminthos.

"We'll leave you here," Leucus explained, "but when the

moon has waxed and waned three times, we will come back to Athens and find you and serve you any way we can."

We embraced them and watched them sail away. Zethus hired porters to unload our boat in Piraeus and carry our goods inland to Athens, a half-day's journey. I made offerings to thank the gods for our safe arrival and prayed that I would find Orestes here.

Book V
Athens

Acropolis

THERE HAD ONCE BEEN a contest between Poseidon, god of the oceans, and Athena, goddess of wisdom. Both wanted to be the patron of the beautiful city ruled by King Cecrops, who had decreed that each must offer a single gift and let the citizens choose. Poseidon struck the ground with his trident, and a spring flowed forth, symbolizing the power of the sea. Athena planted an olive tree, a gift that would provide food, oil, and wood, symbolizing peace and prosperity. The people wisely chose the olive tree and named their city Athens in her honor.

I loved that story, told to me when I was a child at my father's knee. Now we arrived in the gleaming city that had previously existed only in my imagination. Athens lay in a fertile valley green with olive groves, vineyards, and fields of grain. Within its thick walls Athens appeared well kept and prosperous, unlike Mycenae, where a pall of death now lay over the city.

We were immediately caught up in a swirl of activity in the agora, the sprawling marketplace. Vendors stood by their small booths with folded arms and wide smiles, inviting prospective customers to purchase baskets of barley and jars of wine to offer the gods. When a grizzled old fellow approached us with cages made of twigs and filled with songbirds, I recognized Hermes.

"King Menestheus knows you're here," he said. "You'll receive a warm welcome from him." The messenger god/bird seller disappeared, leaving the twittering birds behind.

The Acropolis, a sheer-sided rock plateau, rose starkly above a sloping hillside. Carrying the bird cages and offerings of barley and wine, we climbed a steep path and long flights of stairs that brought us finally to an enormous double gate and guardhouse. At the shrine of Athena in a large open square Ardeste unlatched the cage doors, and the birds flew off in a flutter of wings and feathers. We tossed handfuls of grain into the air and tipped a few drops of wine on the ground, praying for the safe return of Orestes, Pylades, and Iphigenia.

The royal palace stood outlined against the startling blue of a cloudless sky. Heralds announced our arrival to King Menestheus, and a handsome man with a dark beard trimmed to a point came out to greet us. "Hermione of Sparta! Electra of Mycenae! It was my honor to call myself friend to both your fathers and to serve with them in Troy as commander of the

Athenian fleet. And I remain a great admirer of your mother," he added, embracing me warmly as though we were already well acquainted.

The king led us through the magnificent megaron painted with lively battle scenes and into a smaller room opening onto a broad terrace. Fruit trees displayed new blossoms. Thick carpets covered benches and chairs, and servants poured wine from golden ewers and offered platters of sweets. It had been a long time since I'd enjoyed such luxury. I felt embarrassed by the condition of my well-worn peplos.

The conversation proceeded pleasantly, avoiding all serious subjects, until Electra, her palms pressed together, bent toward King Menestheus and spoke earnestly for us both. "We've come to Athens with the hope of finding my brother, Orestes, and his friend, Pylades," she said. "They've been sent by Apollo to retrieve an image of Artemis from the shrine in Tauris where my sister Iphigenia has been kept for years by the Taurians. We pray that she'll be rescued and they'll bring her here. Have you had any word of them?"

The smiling Menestheus also turned serious, drumming his fingers on an ebony table. "I know about this. Orestes and Pylades stopped here on their way to Tauris." He looked at me, eyebrows raised in a question. "I take it you have more than just a cousinly interest in Orestes? I remember seeing the two of you often in each other's company in the encampment at Troy."

I felt myself blushing and lowered my gaze. "We planned to marry."

"But Menelaus had other plans for you, am I correct? And married you to Achilles' son, Pyrrhus?"

"He did, against my wishes. But Pyrrhus insulted the oracle at Delphi, and he was killed by one of Apollo's priests."

"I know about that, too. Sooner or later we learn about everything of importance that happens in Greece. But Orestes has been driven mad by the furies, his mind destroyed. He's become a different person from the young man I knew and admired at Troy."

"It's true," Electra said. "He might not even recognize Hermione."

"But I believe that once I see him, my love will restore him." I covered my eyes with my hands, unable to continue.

"So you believe in the curative powers of love!" Menestheus sighed. "I don't doubt that you can do that. But first he must return here to Athens with the sacred image, and—we hope—with Iphigenia as well."

"And Pylades," Electra murmured.

"Of course, with Pylades. A brave man. His mother was determined that he would not go to Troy and risk death. He walks with a stick, but that hasn't diminished his courage. I loaned them a ship and fifty oarsmen and sacrificed three fine oxen to Apollo for their expedition. And now all we can do is wait."

"You are most generous, my lord! But have you heard anything since they sailed from here? Any messages, or word of any kind?" I cried. "Because, as you said, sooner or later you learn everything that happens in Greece."

"Perhaps this is still 'sooner' and we must wait a while longer for 'later.'"

"Would it be possible to send another ship with a few men onboard," I asked desperately, "to offer help, if it's needed?"

"I can't risk any more men or ships against the Taurians, Hermione. They're a cruel people."

I heard the slight impatience in Menestheus's voice, but I could not give up, even at the risk of annoying him. "We came here in a small boat, not big enough to undertake such a long voyage. But if you would agree to lend me a larger ship and enough rowers, I'm sure my friend Leucus would serve as captain when he comes back from Sminthos. He was a captain in Pyrrhus's fleet, and he's been a great help to me. Zethus, too, would be willing to sail to Tauris, and Asius, who was once Orestes' charioteer. That would be enough, surely!"

It seemed so clear to me what should be done—why couldn't Menestheus see it as well? But his answer was no. I tried every way I knew, but I couldn't shake him from that decision.

He did, however, offer the hospitality of his palace. "It would be my pleasure for you and Electra and your friends to stay here as guests of my wife, Queen Clymene, and me for as long as you wish. And I promise to do everything I can to get news of Orestes and Pylades and Iphigenia."

My friends and I settled into a separate wing of the beautiful palace overlooking the city. Queen Clymene, a woman with a warm heart and a homely face, did everything to make us comfortable. I wondered at first how Menestheus could have married such a plain-looking woman—square jawed, her small eyes set too close together—when he'd once been in love with Helen of Sparta. But perhaps he'd been wise enough to recognize early that a warm heart is worth far more than all the world's beauty, and I admired him all the more for it.

Queen Clymene furnished us with looms and shuttles, and during the cool mornings her daughters and daughters-in-law joined us with their servants to spin wool while children raced in and out, shouting noisily, or played quietly beside us. In the afternoons Electra and I made the long walk from the Acropolis down to the agora. We wandered through the marketplace, examining scarabs from Egypt, wine jars from Canaan, tin ware and other goods brought by ship to the port of Piraeus. Sometimes we visited the Kerameikos, where the potters produced their excellent wares, and we always made offerings for the safe return of Orestes, Pylades, and Iphigenia at the shrines on the banks of the Eridanos.

In the evenings the king and queen entertained us at lavish banquets with spit-roasted meats, bread still warm from the ovens, and rich red wine from nearby vineyards. The king's four sons and their wives, and his four daughters and their husbands, along with numerous young children, all made us feel welcome. Musicians played, and poets recited stories about the lives of the gods, and afterward we retired to beds piled with soft fleeces.

I had fled from Pharsalos when the days were growing short and the nights long and bitterly cold. I had endured wintry days traveling on muddy roads and crossing wind-whipped seas and suffered through frigid nights trying to keep warm on musty fleeces. Now the days were mild, the air sweetly perfumed. Everything seemed fresh and new. I should have been content, but of course I was not. I was restless. If I were a man, I thought, I'd hire a ship and oarsmen and sail to Tauris myself. But a woman couldn't do such a thing.

"I must be lacking in courage," I grumbled to Electra, "or I'd smuggle myself aboard a ship as I did at Aulis when I sailed to Troy with the concubines."

"I hadn't heard about that!" Electra cried, and so I entertained the queen and her daughters and daughters-in-law with stories of my early adventures on the beach at Troy until they were weak with laughter.

Throughout the lengthening days of spring Electra and I wove glistening wool and soft linen for new gowns and tunics, and veils of rare wild silk, and we talked about the feasts we'd have when our lovers returned. But at night on our fleeces we wept in secret, not daring to mention our fear that we might never again lie in our lovers' arms or exchange caresses. That we might never even see them again.

Arrivals

THE FIRST SIGHTING OF the new moon after the summer solstice marked the start of the new year. Preparations for a celebration were going on throughout the city, and Electra and I went to the agora to watch. Ardeste didn't accompany us; her belly had grown large, and though the walk down was easy, the climb back up was not. After we'd bargained for a finely woven basket to buy for the baby Ardeste expected soon, we joined the crowd under the canopy waiting for the heralds. News from all over Greece traveled from runner to runner until it reached the agora and was announced to those who'd gathered to hear it. The noisy crowd quieted at once when the first of the heralds stepped onto a platform and raised a large cone to his mouth to make himself heard.

"Now hear this!" he cried. "The ship belonging to King Menestheus, graciously loaned to Prince Orestes of Mycenae and Prince Pylades of Krisa for the long and perilous journey to the land of the Taurians, has made landfall on the eastern coast of Attica. The sacred image having been left at the shrine of Artemis at Brauron, as the goddess decreed, the ship has again set sail and with favorable winds will arrive at Piraeus today or tomorrow."

The news created a stir of excitement. "They're coming!" Electra and I cried ecstatically and embraced with tears of joy in our eyes. "They're nearly here!"

We looked at each other. "We'll find Asius and ask him to take us down to the port," Electra said. "We can welcome them there."

Off we flew.

We'd waited for this day for months, dreamed of it, made and remade plans for it. We would bathe and smooth our skin with perfumed oils, clean our teeth, and put oil and honey on our faces, dress in our new gowns and whatever jewels we could find. Ardeste would arrange our hair and help us to extend our eyebrows and redden our lips with cosmetics made of beeswax.

But in our excitement we forgot all that. We also forgot that Helios's flaming chariot still rode high in the sky. There was no breeze to relieve the heat, not a single cloud, and we ran through the agora sweating like slaves and having no real idea of where we were going.

Where was Asius? Where did he keep the chariot and the

horses and the donkey? Neither Electra nor I was familiar with this part of the city. I thought I knew where the stables were, but now I couldn't remember how to find them.

"You've gotten us lost," Electra said, exasperated.

I admitted that I had. The sheer white cliffs of the Acropolis rose up from the center of the city, the only familiar landmark, and we hurried that way. Rather than searching for the broad path we always followed up to the citadel, we decided to take the first shortcut we found, a steep stairway cut into the limestone. We began climbing. Halfway up I stopped to look down. That was a mistake. I dropped the basket we'd bought for Ardeste's baby and watched it tumble down, down, down. Too frightened to do anything else, we forced ourselves to keep climbing.

"Never again those stairs," Electra vowed when we arrived, panting, at the palace. "There must be better ones."

Ardeste was waiting for us, pacing impatiently and wringing her hands. "I've been looking everywhere for you!" she said, breathless with excitement. "Have you heard? The king's ship has been sighted! Orestes and Pylades are coming! King Menestheus has already sent Zethus and Asius to Piraeus with chariots to bring them back."

Electra and I dropped wearily onto a bench, wiping our brows. "We know," Electra said. "We heard the news in the agora. We would have gone to greet them ourselves, but we got lost." She looked at me accusingly.

"I'm sorry to hear that," Ardeste said. "No one knew where you were. You could have gone to Piraeus with them."

"Well, then, there's time for us to bathe and make ourselves attractive!" I cried, trying to make the best of the situation. "We would not have wanted to greet them looking like this, would we?"

Servants hurried to carry up jars of water from the deep underground cistern. Oil scented with rose petals was rubbed on our skin, and we put on our new gowns. Ardeste, nearly as excited as we were, secured our hair with ivory combs.

Then we waited, trying to keep ourselves calm. I was so nervous that I kept dropping things. Electra hummed until I asked her to stop. When we thought we couldn't bear the suspense any longer, King Menestheus sent for us, and we hurried to the megaron. He and Queen Clymene, dressed in their splendid robes, sat on their ebony thrones. The royal sons and daughters and their families were gathered expectantly. We heard footsteps and hushed voices on the columned porch. Then the conch shell sounded, the double doors were thrown open, and the king's herald announced the arrival of the honored guests, one by one:

"Princess Iphigenia of Mycenae!"

Iphigenia entered, smiling, and greeted the king and queen. With a cry, Electra rushed to her sister for a tearful embrace. I hadn't seen Iphigenia since she lay on the sacrificial altar at Aulis. The sweet beauty of her youth had faded, her features had grown gaunt, yet she possessed great dignity and a regal grace. Iphigenia was a woman who would look as elegant in a peasant's tunic as she did in a fine peplos.

"Prince Pylades of Krisa!" cried the herald.

Pylades, Orestes' faithful friend and Electra's lover, limped into the great hall, leaning heavily on a carved stick. After acknowledging King Menestheus and Queen Clymene, he dropped his stick with a clatter and gathered a radiant Electra in his arms.

"Prince Orestes of Mycenae!"

I leaned forward, standing on tiptoe, straining for my first glimpse. I'd last seen him the night before he was to hide with the others inside the wooden horse for the invasion of Troy. That was the night he'd come to my tent with two halves of an intricately made golden goblet, and he'd filled the two halves with wine. That was the night we'd pledged our love, promising not to drink from the goblet again until the two halves were finally united on our wedding day. I wondered if, after all that had happened since that night on the beach, Orestes still had his half.

The young man who entered the megaron appeared just as I remembered him—a little thinner, maybe, but still handsome with the same splendid physique, the same dark curls falling across his broad brow. Orestes approached the king and queen and stood before them, silent and unsmiling. Menestheus studied his guest. The queen's sympathetic glance moved from

Orestes to me, and I saw her dismay. Electra detached herself from Pylades and went to embrace her brother, but Orestes' arms stayed rigidly at his sides.

"Look, Orestes, it's Hermione!" Electra urged, gesturing for me to join them. "Your own Hermione!"

Orestes regarded me without even a flicker of recognition in his eyes and greeted me as one greets a stranger in whom one has no interest at all.

"Orestes," I said softly, thinking the sound of my voice might stir his memory.

"Do I know you?" he asked.

"She's your cousin," Electra prompted. "Daughter of Mene-laus, our father's brother, and of Helen of Sparta, our mother's sister."

Orestes nodded. "I see," he said.

Iphigenia, who had been watching, stepped up and squeezed my hand. "We often played together as children," she explained to her brother. "Remember?"

"Ah, yes, I remember now," Orestes said, though it was obvious to all of us that he did not. In most ways his appearance hadn't changed. His front teeth still overlapped in the way that had always charmed me, but his eyes were no longer merry. The tiny golden fires that used to glow in them had gone out. This was not the same Orestes. This was not the young man I knew and loved.

I had to turn away.

Menestheus, witnessing this painful scene, looked distinctly uncomfortable. Queen Clymene cleared her throat. "Tonight we shall have a banquet in honor of our guests," she said. "But first they must have an opportunity to rest from their long and arduous journey." She signaled for servants to escort them to their quarters.

Iphigenia gave me a fleeting look as she led Orestes away. Electra hurried off to be with Pylades. I returned alone to my rooms and flung myself down on my bed. My heart was shattered, my pain too deep for tears. I felt as though my life with all my hopes and dreams had come to a sudden end.

Ardeste entered quietly and sat beside me, stroking my shoulder. I lay facing the wall, and I didn't turn to look at her.

"He doesn't remember me," I murmured.

"Not yet," Ardeste soothed. "But one day soon he will. Come, I'll help you prepare for the banquet."

"I can't bear to see him there. He doesn't know who I am, and he doesn't *want* to know." I rolled over and looked at her. "It's the work of the Furies, Ardeste. I didn't think he'd be like *this*."

"You've said all along that you believed you could heal him with your love. But you must have patience, Hermione. Healing doesn't take place overnight. Now if you will sit up, I can try to repair the damage you've done to your hair."

THE BANQUET GUESTS WERE eager to hear about Iphigenia's escape from the Taurians. Men were by tradition the storytellers, but instead of passing the myrtle branch to Pylades or to Orestes, King Menestheus passed it to Iphigenia. "She must tell the story herself," said the king.

Iphigenia accepted the branch. "When Artemis saved me from Agamemnon's knife, she wrapped me in a cloud and carried me to Tauris," she began. "She made me the chief priestess of her shrine, responsible for the sacred image. It was my duty to prepare for sacrifice any princely stranger who came to Tauris unaware. I always obeyed Artemis's wishes, though the idea of human sacrifice was repugnant to me.

"One day two strangers arrived at Tauris, left their oarsmen to guard the ship, and hid in a cave. But they were discovered by herdsmen, who delivered them to the temple to be sacrificed on a white marble altar stained red with human blood. I didn't recognize Orestes—my own brother!—until he spoke to me in our language, and I promised to help him and his friend. When the king of the Taurians demanded to know why I didn't immediately sacrifice these two, I explained that one was a matricide and the other his accomplice, unfit for sacrifice until they'd been purified. 'They have tainted the sacred image,' I told the king, and persuaded him that I must escort the prisoners down to the sea to cleanse them, and to carry the sacred image there as well. Then I instructed the king to remain inside with his head covered in order to keep from becoming tainted too."

"And the fool believed her!" Pylades cried.

Iphigenia's obvious trickery made us laugh, the king and

queen, having no love for the king of the Taurians, laughing hardest of all. For the first time, Orestes smiled faintly, but when I tried to catch his eye, he looked away.

Iphigenia went on, "It was very dark, a moonless night, and I called for torchbearers to light our way. This made us uneasy, but there was no way around it. We reached the sea and hurried aboard the ship, but the torchbearers sensed treachery and attacked us. In the struggle Pylades' injured leg was severely wounded again, but we escaped with our lives. Then a strong wind drove the ship back toward the rocks, and all would have been lost if the goddess Athena hadn't asked Poseidon to calm the wind and waves. We knew that Athena and Poseidon had been rivals for the honor of being chosen patron of this great city, and we were not sure Poseidon would do as she asked. But he relented.

"The storm drove us off course, but eventually we reached Brauron and left the sacred image at the shrine of Artemis, as she ordered. At long last the Furies abandoned their torment of Orestes."

"Ahhhhhh!" sighed the group, delighted by Iphigenia's story and its happy outcome.

"And now I have a surprise for you!" the king said, and signaled for the doors of the megaron to open.

A smiling Astynome stood waiting with gap-toothed Leucus. They'd arrived from Sminthos after visiting her father. After a flurry of greetings and welcomes, Astynome presented her little son, Chryses, and revealed to the king and his guests what some of us already knew: Agamemnon had been the father of her child; therefore, Chryses was the half brother of Orestes, Iphigenia, and Electra. Little Chryses gazed around him, wide-eyed, and ran to Leucus, who picked him up. The child shyly buried his face in Leucus's shoulder.

It was a joyous scene that couldn't fail to touch one's heart. I stole another look at Orestes, but his mind was far away.

32

The Man I Loved Before

NOW THAT EVERYONE HAD arrived safely, nearly all gave themselves to enjoying the hospitality of King Menestheus and Queen Clymene. Throughout the pleasant days of summer Menestheus arranged games and contests in his stadium. The young men wrestled and ran races and threw spears long distances. There were archery contests at which Orestes excelled. Asius challenged the men to wrestle, even offering to tie one hand behind his back, but no one wanted to accept his challenge. None could best him at throwing the discus. The giant was in a class by himself. There were boxing matches and sword fights that sometimes drew blood but never ended in serious injury or death.

The women were enthusiastic spectators at these games and contests, heaping praise on the winners and consolation on the losers, and after the contests they danced and sang.

There were nightly feasts, and bards plucked their lyres and recited poetry.

Through it all I remained sick at heart. I watched Orestes, convinced that, if I watched carefully enough, I could find a way to reach him and to bring back all he had lost. We would start over, as though we were meeting for the first time. I would strike up conversations with him and draw him out, little by little. We would become friends, as we had once been, long ago, before we became lovers.

I looked for opportunities to be near him, chances to exchange a few words. At first he was wary of me, skittish as a deer. No doubt he'd been told that we'd been lovers, that we'd promised to marry. I had to be careful not to move too quickly, to let him come to me naturally, on his own terms, as I had trained a bird to perch on my finger when I was a child.

Slowly he seemed to become more comfortable around me, smiling when he saw me, even calling me by my name. Sometimes he chose to sit beside me, and on two occasions he walked with me in the orchards near the palace.

Sometimes I stayed away from him for a day or two, to let him discover that he missed me.

Electra, now blissfully reunited with Pylades, encouraged me. "Orestes is making great progress," she told me. "He's much better now that the Furies have left him alone. He doesn't wake up screaming in a night terror, as he used to, and," she added mischievously, "I've even heard that he is growing quite fond of you. He calls you 'my friend Hermione.'"

But in a way, that was nearly as painful as his failure to recognize me had been. Orestes *liked* me, but he didn't *love* me.

After he'd grown to enjoy walking and talking with me, I began to speak about the days we'd spent in the encampments outside Troy. One day we were sitting under a shade tree on the banks of the Eridanos, a favorite spot to rest before we began the long climb back up to the Acropolis. "Do you remember Andromache?" I asked.

"Hector's wife. Yes, I remember her. Pyrrhus took her as his concubine after he killed her infant son. But before that there was the fuss with Astynome and Hippodameia, wasn't there? Achilles and Agamemnon, furious at each other, each refusing to give in, and Achilles refusing to fight unless he got the girl he wanted!"

"And do you remember when you and I had to persuade Achilles to give Hippodameia to Agamemnon, so that Agamemnon would agree to return Astynome to her father?"

"Did we do that? Tell me about it! I've forgotten."

Patiently, I described the scene. "Magnificent Apollo was furious, and our men were dying by the hundreds until Astynome was returned to Apollo's priest. I went with you to Achilles' camp, and we were both so nervous, wondering how Achilles would respond."

I remembered every detail, because that was the day I realized I loved Orestes and that I'd loved him for a very long time.

"And how *did* he respond?"

"Furiously!"

We both laughed, though at the time it hadn't been a laughing matter. Now we both fell silent, and I wondered—again—what Orestes was thinking. Did he remember nothing of what we once were to each other?

Suddenly Orestes leaned close and kissed me. "Hermione," he said, and lowered me carefully to the soft carpet of green beneath that tree. There were other people by the river —couples, mostly—but they were not interested in us. He kissed me again, more passionately, and I closed my eyes and returned his kisses, just as I used to. It was almost like it had once been, our bodies close, yearning to be even closer.

Except that it wasn't the same. This was a different Orestes. I knew I shouldn't weep, but I did.

Orestes pulled away. "I'm sorry, Hermione. I've offended you."

I protested, "No! No, you haven't offended me." To prove it, I moved closer to him and wove my fingers through his thick curls. "You've been away so long, and I've missed you so much, Orestes, and longed for you so many nights." Again I kissed his soft lips, even though it still wasn't the same.

Orestes must have felt that too. He rose and pulled me to my feet, and we began the long climb back up to the Acropolis, saying little, not touching.

NOW THAT ELECTRA WAS neglecting her loom in order to spend more time with Pylades, Astynome often came with little Chryses and sat with me as I wove. It had been hard to be back on the island of Sminthos, she told me; her father had grown old and feeble, and while she was there he had gone on to an afterlife in the Elysian Fields.

"Leucus and I married before my father died," she said, and I saw the special glow that told me she was probably expecting another child.

She didn't ask if Orestes and I planned to marry. I felt sure everyone was speculating, and just as sure they'd observed that something fundamental had changed between us.

I decided to bring up the subject myself. "I'm happy for you, Astynome," I said. "Leucus loves you, and he's a good man. I know you'll have a long and happy life together. But I don't know what the future holds for Orestes and me. He's rid of the Furies, but they took away his memory. He doesn't remember me as the girl he loved, and this Orestes, the one I see now, is not the man I loved before."

"But haven't you noticed, Hermione? *This* Orestes is falling in love with you! Doesn't this bring you happiness?"

I shook my head.

"Has it occurred to you," Astynome lectured, wagging a finger, "that you aren't the same Hermione he once loved? Since he last saw you, you've been forced into marriage to a man you despised, escaped from that brutal husband, and made a long and treacherous journey in search of the one you *do* love. You haven't been sitting with your spindle and your loom all this time! All of this has changed you. You're different too."

I knew she was right. But that didn't change how I felt.

Orestes and I continued to walk together, talk together, and sometimes simply sit quietly sharing the silence. I began to realize that I was not seeking him—he was seeking *me*. I think we were both aware that our friends were watching us, waiting to see what would happen.

And then one day something *did* happen that changed everything.

THE ACROPOLIS WAS ALWAYS a busy place, but on that day many were absent. The king and queen, along with Iphigenia, Electra, and Pylades, were attending a summer festival in the harbor at Piraeus. I had declined to join their party. Asius had driven them to the port in the royal chariot the day before, to meet the royal barge, on which Leucus now served as captain. They would return that day at sunset.

On that particular day, Orestes and Zethus were going over the plans for the construction of the queen's new megaron. Zethus had taken charge of the project and set up his workshop on the terrace, and slaves were carrying out their orders.

The main source of water for the Acropolis was a cistern, a deep pool collected from several underground springs. The cistern was at the bottom of a long shaft reached by five flights of slippery rock and wooden stairs leading down through the shaft to a platform built over a large catch basin. No daylight reached the bottom of the shaft, but torches burned near the platform, giving a dull, flickering light. Slave women descended the steps, lowered their empty amphoras into the basin, and then climbed up again with the full amphoras on their shoulders. They did this all day, every day.

I was at my loom with several other women when we heard screams coming from the shaft. We dropped our shuttles and rushed out to investigate. A slave ran shrieking across the terrace, and two more slaves emerged from the shaft, gesturing wildly, crying, "The boy! The boy!"

What boy did they mean? Where was Chryses? He and Astynome had been with us earlier, but she'd gone to see to Ardeste, who had been complaining of labor pains. Hadn't he gone with his mother? I remembered seeing him with his ball on the terrace. He'd taken to following Orestes around, which amused Orestes as much as it did Astynome.

None of us had noticed when Chryses' ball rolled away from him and into the shaft, bouncing down the steps. No one saw little Chryses go looking for his ball and venture into that ominous place.

I grabbed a slave running from the entrance. "What boy?" I demanded. "Who is it?"

"Astynome's!"

I ran for Orestes and Zethus, who were coming to see what had happened. "It's Chryses!" I shouted. "In the shaft!"

Orestes plunged down the steep, slippery steps, fighting to keep his footing, with Zethus close behind. Then Orestes made a desperate decision and dived into the unknowable darkness. Zethus leaped after him.

They found the boy beneath the surface and shouted for help, their voices echoing. They struggled to hold the boy's head above water, unable to tell if he was alive or dead, waiting for someone to bring a rope, something, anything!

Astynome reached the entrance to the shaft, Ardeste following slowly, clutching at her belly as a pain swept over her. We huddled at the top, frantic, urging the slaves to do what we could not—race down into the blackness. After a long, agonizing time, the limp body of little Chryses was carried up. Astynome screamed when she saw him. "He's dead! He's dead!" she wailed.

But the boy expelled water, opened his eyes, and looked around, frightened by the crowd surrounding him and his mother's screams, and he began to cry.

Next the men brought up Orestes and laid him down. I crouched over him as he hovered in that place between life and death. I lay down on top of him, my body over his body, my mouth against his mouth, and breathed for him, stopping now and then to speak his name. I don't know how long I did this. Even when I had lost hope I'd continued, until at last his eyelids fluttered and he coughed and gasped, and I wept with relief and gratitude.

It was much later when they brought up Zethus. Ardeste was on her knees, wailing, when they placed his inert body on the ground. She must have known at once that he was dead when she clumsily embraced his body, whispering into his deaf ears.

Orestes, sobbing, told us what had happened. "Zethus struck his head when he dived into the black pool. He was badly hurt, but still he struggled to keep the boy from going under. The men took Chryses, and I tried to keep Zethus up, but I couldn't support him, couldn't keep his head up—he was unconscious. He slipped away from me, beneath the surface of the dark water." Orestes shook his head, gasping. "I dove down, over and over, but I couldn't reach him. And then I went under too, and I remember thinking, *This is what it's like to drown; this is what dying is like.* They must have brought me up next, I don't remember, but they couldn't find Zethus. It was so dark! And then it was too late."

Orestes wept, and I did too. Zethus had once told me he would gladly give his life for mine, and I believed that was, in fact, what he had done.

Ardeste leaned heavily on me as I helped her back to her room, and I stayed with her through her labor and the delivery a short time later of a fine baby boy. She gave him his father's name.

Those who had been absent all day returned to find the palace in turmoil, a new baby born, and his father's body being prepared for a funeral. Little Chryses was robust as always, unaffected by his plunge into the black waters.

That evening Orestes and I sat together, side by side, silent, fingers interlaced. I noticed again that one of his fingers was missing—the one he'd bitten off to atone for his mother's murder. Zethus's death affected me like a missing finger. Our emotions overwhelmed us both. I knew that Orestes was in some way different, though I could not quite see just how. Into our silence came Pylades and Electra. Pylades had brought an object wrapped in a cloth that I remembered weaving long ago. He handed the object to Orestes, saying, "You once gave this to me for safekeeping, but the time has come to return it to you."

Orestes took the object with a puzzled expression and unwrapped it carefully. I drew a sharp breath. It was the other half of the golden wedding goblet.

I recognized it immediately, of course, but more important, so did Orestes. Holding the goblet, he gazed at me tenderly. "Hermione," he said. "You are my own Hermione, and I am your own Orestes."

Promise Fulfilled

WE MOURNED THE DEATH of our dear Zethus, we celebrated the birth of his son, and we planned two weddings—mine to Orestes, and Electra's to Pylades. It was also to have been Ardeste's wedding to Zethus, and that it was not continued to be a sorrow to us all. Ardeste bravely insisted that we must not postpone it on her account and that she would rejoice for our good fortune while she grieved for her own misfortune.

King Menestheus and Queen Clymene sent out messengers to every part of Greece, inviting them to the festivities to be held at the time of the harvest.

The preparations began. Electra and I wove wedding veils, and the king's daughters and daughters-in-law stitched and embroidered gowns of glistening linen. Sheep and cattle were fattened. Grapes were pressed, and the new wine collected in jars. Fruit was gathered and preserved in honey.

Guests arrived from every part of Greece. Menestheus kept us informed of whom he expected. "I wanted to invite Odysseus," he said, "but he's nowhere to be found. The oracle told him that he would not return to his home for ten years after the end of the war, and from what I hear, he has not yet reached Ithaca."

Chrysothemis had declined the king's invitation to the wedding. Orestes was relieved when he learned that his other sister would not make the journey from Mycenae. "The Furies were terrible, but I think my sister Chrysothemis was nearly as bad. She despises me. She was always closest to my mother." Electra was not only relieved but pleased. And when Asius heard, he said, "Chrysothemis would surely punish me severely for helping you both escape."

Iphigenia, though delighted that Orestes and I would marry, announced that she would soon leave Athens. "I'm returning to Brauron, to the shrine to Artemis," she explained. "I will spend the rest of my days there as her virginal priestess. I promised I'd dedicate my life to Artemis if she spared me for a second time. I owe her that much. I've persuaded our magnificent charioteer, Asius, to accompany me and to stay in Brauron and attend me, if our good king Menestheus will agree."

Menestheus nodded his assent.

"But I shall stay here for the weddings," Iphigenia said. "I don't want to miss any of it!"

ℓℓℓℓ

THE GREATEST SURPRISE WAS the arrival of my parents. Menelaus and Helen of Sparta would attend my wedding.

Heralds announced that the royal ship from Sparta had entered the port of Piraeus, and I asked Asius to take Orestes and me down to meet them. I was terribly anxious, but Orestes was completely calm. "If anyone should be uneasy, I should be," he said. "Menelaus tried to persuade the courts in Mycenae to sentence me to death."

Orestes and I had never talked about the murders. What was there to say? He had been severely punished for what most people thought was a justifiable killing. But I knew that my father felt Orestes had not been punished severely enough. Menelaus likely disapproved of my marrying a man who had committed matricide. I convinced myself that I didn't care if he disapproved—he had forced me to marry Pyrrhus, who was surely guilty of far worse crimes than Orestes could even think of.

I watched my father step from the ship into the small boat that brought them to shore. Menelaus's red hair was faded now and streaked with gray, but his strong body showed few signs of age. He walked a little stiffly, possibly from the wound he received at Troy, but that was all.

He turned to assist my mother. Boatmen on other ships in the port stopped what they were doing and stared at Helen. Nothing about her had changed. Her golden hair still shone like sunlight. Her flawless skin still glowed. Her gown clung to every curve of her lovely body. Her smile still dazzled. Only when she looked at me did a tiny frown appear between her eyes of hyacinth blue.

"Well, Hermione," my mother greeted me with her musical voice, the only quality I shared with her. "How nice that Orestes wants to marry you. But it seems you've been neglecting your appearance. Just look how dark your skin has become! All those freckles! Have you tried to bleach them? I'll send my maidservant to do something with that hair."

MY WEDDING DAY WAS both bitter and sweet. Like the scenes created by Hephaestus, the god of the forge, for Achilles' great shield, the celebration was filled with beauty and sadness. Zethus had been dead for a full waxing and waning of the moon. All of us mourned him. Ardeste suckled her baby and wept for the baby's father. I knew how deeply she must miss her Zethus. I missed him too. He had been an important part of my life since I was a young girl.

But still Ardeste wanted to celebrate my wedding to Orestes, and for that day she set aside her own pain to share in my joy. She had water brought from a sacred spring on a slope below the Acropolis and directed the servants to heat it for the baths that Electra and I enjoyed. Zethus's infant son kicked and gurgled in his basket nearby while Ardeste helped me dress in my new peplos, the color of pomegranates. She combed my hair into a smooth braid and arranged the lustrous veil glittering with gold and silver spangles. Queen Clymene made me a gift of a pair of jeweled armlets, and my servant tied on soft new sandals.

The day was cloudless and bright. It had been a fine harvest, and amphoras filled with wine lined the racks in every available storage room. The granaries were full to bursting with barley, dried lentils, and beans. Jars of oil, some scented with herbs, were bottled and stoppered and stored on shelves. Down in the agora the cooks had worked throughout the night, slaughtering sheep and cattle and roasting them on spits; ovens had been fired up to bake hundreds of loaves of bread; enormous platters were filled with juicy figs and pears soaked in honey and spices. The citizens of Athens had been invited by their king and queen to celebrate a bountiful harvest and the weddings of four royal visitors whom the gods had brought to their city.

We made a fine procession to the agora. King Menestheus escorted Electra, and my father escorted me. "A woman in love is always at her most beautiful," my father said as he walked with me to where Pylades and Orestes waited to greet their brides. "And I am well pleased by your choice of a husband." That was all he said about Orestes. It was all he needed to say, and all I wanted to hear. I cared for his approval more than I'd allowed myself to admit.

Musicians entertained the guests, and a bard plucked his lyre and recited wedding poetry. A pair of tumblers sprang and whirled through the crowd, leading the dancers; young girls held hands and swayed, and young men showed off their astounding leaps. A traveler in a broad-brimmed hat and winged sandals smiled and raised his hand. Above us Aphrodite, the goddess of love, spun in a cloud and blessed the marriages, and we felt her blessings fall upon our heads like warm sun and gentle rain. I hoped that dear Zethus was also rejoicing and sending his love to Ardeste, who stood quietly weeping, her baby in her arms.

The wedding party feasted and laughed and danced and sang until Helios drove his flaming chariot below the rim of the earth. Then we poured libations on the ground and drank wine blessed by the gods and began the long climb back up to the Acropolis as darkness wrapped itself around us and torches lighted the way.

Orestes brought his half of our golden wedding goblet to my quarters, and we joined the halves together and drank from the goblet and pledged our love anew, fulfilling our promise. We lay on fine new fleeces, making a gift of ourselves and our bodies until Dawn reached her rosy fingers into the great vault of the sky.

Epilogue

SOON AFTER OUR WEDDING, Orestes received an invitation from the people of Mycenae to return there and to become their king. His long exile was over. As a wedding gift King Menestheus gave Orestes a ship and fifty rowers. Electra and Pylades sailed with us, with Leucus and Astynome, little Chryses, and their newborn daughter. Ardeste, too, wished to come with us, and we welcomed her and baby Zethus into our household. The next summer my son Tisamenus was born.

Helen never lost her ethereal beauty, but she and my father grew aged. In time Helen and Menelaus departed this life for the Elysian Fields, and Orestes succeeded my father as king of Sparta. He ruled the two kingdoms fairly and well.

Notes from the Author

SCHOLARS HAVE LONG ARGUED about whether the Trojan War was an actual historical event and if Helen of Troy really existed. I have no idea if their story is "true," but I do know that the ancient myths have been told and retold in countless versions for thousands of years. Archaeologists have dug through several layers of ruins that once were Troy. Tourists clamber over the remains of Agamemnon's citadel at Mycenae. Thousands visit the Acropolis in Athens—although nothing remains there of the late Bronze Age, when most historians believe the Trojan War, or something like it, took place in what is now Turkey.

The most famous description of the Trojan War is the long epic poem that we know as *The Iliad*. The poet Homer lived in the eighth or ninth century B.C.—no one knows for certain—some four hundred years after the war supposedly took place; his poem is based on countless retellings by innumerable poets over four centuries, all passed on orally; nothing was written. Add to that the question of whether there was actually a single poet named Homer, or whether a number of "Homers" contributed their ideas. In any case, *The Iliad* covers only the final months of the ten-year war. The long and bloody story opens when Achilles, the Greeks' greatest warrior, gets extremely upset because Agamemnon has demanded the return of his girlfriend and refuses to fight unless he gets her back. (That raises another question: did it really last for ten years, or was that just another way of saying "a really long time"?)

The other great epic poem attributed to Homer, *The Odyssey*, covers another ten years (or another "really long time") after the war ends and centers on the adventures of another character, Odysseus, who takes his sweet time returning home to his patient wife, Penelope.

There are no written records of this period. The Greeks at this time, about 1200 B.C., had a writing system, but it all disappeared when their civilization fell apart soon after the end of what may have been a trade war with the Trojans. Nobody knows for sure. But that hasn't stopped historians from making educated guesses, and ancient Greeks and Romans and many others down to the present time from writing plays and poems and novels—and making films—about Helen, Orestes, Electra, Achilles, Iphigenia, and many other colorful and compelling characters who are the subject of myths.

You can add me to the long list of writers inspired by the

Greek myths. I've drawn most heavily from Homer's *Iliad* to imagine the story of Hermione, daughter of Helen of Troy, and the young man she loved, her cousin Orestes. Much has been written about Helen; painters and sculptors have tried to capture her beauty, but almost nothing has been written about Hermione. She can be found mentioned in various myths, but those brief references provided me with little material to write about her life—only that at one time she married the son of Achilles, a man named Neoptolemus in some sources and Pyrrhus in others, and that she eventually married her cousin Orestes. That gave me the idea for the basic and timeless plot of a novel that is almost wholly the product of my own imagination: Girl meets boy, girl loses boy, girl and boy find happiness at last.

Carolyn Meyer
Albuquerque, New Mexico

Main Characters

Greeks:

Hermione's family:

Menelaus, king of Sparta, Hermione's father

Helen, queen of Sparta, Hermione's mother

Pleisthenes, son of Menelaus and Helen

Agamemnon, brother of Menelaus; king of Mycenae

Clytemnestra, sister of Helen; queen of Mycenae

Orestes, son of Agamemnon and Clytemnestra

Iphigenia, daughter of Agamemnon and Clytemnestra

Electra, daughter of Agamemnon and Clytemnestra

Chrysothemis, daughter of Agamemnon and Clytemnestra

Warriors and Allies:

Achilles, the Greeks' greatest warrior

Pyrrhus, Achilles' son

Patroclus, Achilles' cousin and closest friend

Odysseus, close ally of Menelaus and Agamemnon

Hippodameia, girl captured by Achilles

Astynome, girl captured by Achilles

Menestheus, king of Athens

Clymene, queen of Athens

Trojans:

Priam, king of Troy

Hecabe, queen of Troy

Hector, eldest son of Priam; Troy's greatest warrior

Helenus, son of Priam

Deiphobus, son of Priam

Paris, son of Priam

Andromache, wife of Hector

Cassandra, daughter of Priam

Gods:

Zeus, greatest god

Hera, wife of Zeus

Apollo, Zeus's son, god of light and prophecy

Artemis, goddess of the hunt and of childbirth

Aphrodite, goddess of love, beauty, and desire

Athena, virgin goddess of wisdom and warfare

Hermes, messenger god

Poseidon, god of the sea and earthquakes

Aeolus, god of the four winds

Characters created by the author:

Pentheus, vizier at Sparta

Zethus, former servant of Paris, friend of Hermione

Ardeste, Hermione's servant and friend

Marpessa, old crone

Leucus, sympathetic seaman

Asius, giant guard and charioteer

(There are also dozens of other characters who make brief appearances.)

Bibliography

Homer. *The Iliad.* Translated by Robert Fagles. New York: Penguin, 1990.

Graves, Robert. *The Greek Myths.* Mount Kisco, N.Y.: Moyer Bell, 1988.

Vermeule, Emily. *Greece in the Bronze Age.* Chicago: University of Chicago Press, 1964.

Plus innumerable websites for information on Greek gods and the twelve Olympians; on characters of Greek mythology such as Helenus, Cassandra, Deiphobus, Philoctetes, Calchas; ancient sites in Greece and Troy such as Tenedos, Mycenae, Sparta, Gythion, Aulis, Dodona, Tiryns, Pharsalos, Iolkos, Delphi; and descriptions of clothing, food, and customs of Bronze Age Greece.

Carolyn Meyer is the award-winning author of more than fifty books for young people, including seven titles in the popular Young Royals series. She lives in Albuquerque, New Mexico. Visit her website at **www.readcarolyn.com.**